Space Cowboys

Edited by Kortnee Bryant

Raconteur Press

contents

Foreword

C owboys.

I have a fondness for cowboys and Western-themed fiction, maybe from cutting my teeth on the Louis L'Amour collection that belonged to my father; or day work punching cows in the Panhandle because I needed the extra money, but I'm pretty sure that I'm not the only one.

There's something about the rugged individualism of the cowboy that strikes a chord in all of us. There is a simplicity, a feeling that the world is clearer, brighter, and makes more sense in stories about cowboys. Definitely a certain romanticism.

This is true even in speculative fiction/science fiction: Remember that the original Star Trek was described to the studios as "Wagon Train to the stars" by Gene Roddenberry. Who can deny the stubborn popularity of Firefly?

When you look at Han Solo with his open-carried blaster in a drop-leg fast-draw holster, and his leather vest -- cowboy. All the way.

When humanity finally leaves their Mother for the vast frontier of the stars, cowboys will be needed. Tough men and women who understand the land, foreign though it may be; and understand the animals, alien though they may be, with the toughness to not only survive, but drag a living out of hostile new country, and the grit to make decisions without relying on distant orders.

Modern cowboys might not understand how the tools of their future compatriots work, or know which end of the critter the babies come out of, or what all the local dangers might be; but they'll see the drink being sipped first thing in the morning, and while it might not be black, or even from a bean, they'll understand. And fences are the same, whether barbed wire or energy; and weather is a bastard, no matter in the 21st century or the 25th.

I am proud to bring you the imagination of ten authors, who describe what the lives of cowboys might be in the future, for your reading enjoyment.

LawDog

Tiny Town, Texas

2023

Asteroid Wranglers

JL Curtis

Jim Bob "Tex" Tutwiler staggered through the hatch and slumped in the nearest chair. *I gotta stop getting this damned drunk before work. At least my shipsuit is clean. Maybe Hartwell won't notice anything.* He slipped another stim from his pocket, popped it in his mouth and bit down, almost gagging at the taste. *Damn! That crap is nasty!* He started to get up, but slid back down as Mick Hartwell strode down the aisle toward the front of the room.

Hartwell, tall, lean, space-tanned, and bald, leaned on the lectern at the front and glared out at the twenty beings sitting in front of him as he threw up a spreadsheet on the side wall. In a hoarse voice, he said, "You people are barely making your numbers on this shift. You're supposed to be bringing in two hundred twenty-five tons per tug on each shift. *Each* shift. Not aggregate over a couple of shifts." He straightened up. "Now I'm hearing some complaints about the increased danger, but each of you," he took time to scan the room again, "each of you are drawing hazard pay for the Vega asteroid belt. This is what you get paid for, dammit!" He glanced around and continued, "All tugs are up, no grapnels are deadlined, and maintenance has assured me they are fully fueled and the O2 pacs are within spec. Now get your asses out there and get some rocks!"

The mass exodus from the brief allowed Tex to grab a cup of water on the way out. He quickly used it to rinse the taste of the stim out of this mouth and thought about a second cup, but knew he'd get caught since water was rationed on the station. The locker room was a mass of bodies. The stink of worn pressure suits, the jelly they used to connect the catheters, and the unwashed bodies had Tex rubbing his nose to keep from sneezing as he banged on his locker door to get it open and kicked off his boots.

He took out his pressure suit, completed pre-flight, checking the seals carefully, and pulled it up to his waist. Making the catheter connection to the waste bag, he wriggled the rest of the way into it and carefully clamped the seals shut. The helmet and gloves came next, and he stepped over to the check station as he settled the helmet over his head and clicked it into the neck ring. He started the pressure check as he quickly put on the gloves and clicked them into their respective rings. He felt the refreshing breath of cold air through the hose, glanced at the gauge to make sure it was in the green, and waited for the green light. Once he got it, he stepped away as he popped the helmet seal and set it on the bench. Stripping off the gloves, he crammed them in the helmet as Haruji Kuro came up beside him. "You will live again, Tex?"

"'Fraid so, Haruji. You?"

Haruji rocked his hand. "Maybe, maybe not. I go banzai today to pay the bill from last night."

Tex laughed, then winced. "Yeah, it did get a tad drunk out."

They both heard the beeping and looked up to see the kid looking down at the check station curiously. Tex stepped over and rotated the helmet about thirty degrees and felt it lock in. Once it did, the beeping stopped, and the kid looked around with his head cocked. "What was wrong, helmet again? That's, what, twice with him?" Haruji asked.

Tex nodded as the kid took the helmet off. "Dammit, I thought I had it locked!"

"Nope, that first tension is the lips engaging," Tex told him. "You have another thirty degrees to go, and you'll feel it lock in."

The kid drooped and muttered, "I gotta learn all this shit. They didn't teach these systems in school."

Haruji grinned. "Learn or die, kid. That's your choice." He glanced at Tex. "Time to hit the tugs. Where you going?"

Tex smiled. "Thirteen, where else? It's got some big chunks in there."

Haruji was tying his scarf around his head as he replied, "I'll be in fourteen if you get in trouble. I'll wave at ya." He smiled as he picked up his helmet and go bag, and headed for the tug bay.

Tex pulled the last of the pins on the explosive grapnels as he completed his walk-around. Picking up his go bag, he steeled himself and climbed up to the cockpit, shoved the pins into the holders on the back wall, and stepped into the seat, then into the cockpit. The whine of the hydraulics started as soon as he flipped the master switch on and toggled the canopy close switch. The Built-In-Test was next, and as it cycled through, Tex reached over and pulled his soft helmet out of the go bag, plugged it in, and pulled it down. Reaching down, he felt in the bag to make sure the spare E-bottle was still there, and tried to keep from hyperventilating. *Settle down, everything is gonna work. Greebo said so.* He winced as the plates pinched in at his temples to connect with his implants. *Deity damn, that hurts! Why couldn't they be a bit gentler?* With a ping, the system connected to his implant, and he felt the tug coming alive.

Reaching over, he pulled the emergency O2 mask off the bulkhead and took a couple of deep breaths. As soon as he did, Bitching Betty said, "Unauthorized access to emergency oxygen. Terminate access immediately or face punishment."

"I was pre-flighting it, bitch," he grumbled. "Making sure there was actually O2 in the system." He hung the mask back into his niche as the comms went off.

A female voice came on. "Wrangler Seven, did you just access the emerg O2?"

Blowing out a breath, he said, "Yes, I did, Kate. It's called pre-flighting the systems."

She chuckled and went on the side channel. "In other words, you got drunk again last night, didn't you?" She paused, switched back to dispatch channel and said, "Three minutes to bay pump down."

Tex snorted and replied on the side channel, "Gotcha. Supper tonight?"

"Maybe. Check when you get back." She came over the group circuit again. "Two minutes to pump down. All tugs standby for release."

Tex took a deep breath as he tightened the five-point harness, then reached up to make sure his helmet was racked, facing forward on the side of the shock frame. *Ah, yes, the smell of fear, ozone, and a soupcon of hydraulics. Everything is in the green, and...here we go!* He powered up the tug as he saw the warning lights start flashing overhead. He rotated the seat module aft, made sure he could see the thruster packs, and spun the module back to face the grapnels. *At least they fixed that glitch that stopped the module halfway around. That sucked!*

Three minutes went by, and Kate came over the group comm. "Pump down complete. Bay doors opening in three, two, and tugs are cleared for departure in numerical order from station one."

As soon as Tex cleared the bay, he pulled up and to the right, picking up the departure track for sector thirteen on his HUD. He smiled as he rolled the tug first to the right, then to the left. Looking around, he saw nothing flopping around, and initiated pitch-down and pitch-up maneuvers that looped him over, then back upright. "Control, Wrangler Seven. Control checks complete. En route sector thirteen. Tug is up and up."

Kate replied, "Copy all, Seven."

Tex clicked the mic twice and squirmed around in the seat, getting as comfortable as he could for the long shift ahead of him. Fifteen minutes later, he called in. "Control, Wrangler Seven. Entering sector thirteen."

Kate again replied, "Copy all, Seven."

Haruji checked in next, then the new kid. *So, they gave him fifteen. Interesting. Not a lot there that hasn't been picked over. They are either easing him into this or maybe they're trying to get rid of him for not making his numbers. Not my problem.* He hovered at the edge of the sector, watching the movement of the cluster of asteroids in his sector, wincing as he watched two fairly big ones collide and go off on different vectors. His head bobbing back and forth, and his hands dancing about his controls, he psyched himself up. *All right! Let's get some!*

He jammed the sticks forward and jerked the tug onto what appeared to be a collision course with a large asteroid. Skirting it by less than a mile, he immediately reversed course and went to twenty Gs, then killed all acceleration and skewed up and right, pulling five Gs. That put him in a tail chase on what he estimated was a fifty-ton asteroid, rock visible, with occasional patches that might be ice, tumbling slowly with almost no spin on it. "Come to Papa, baby. Come to Papa."

Glancing up at the timer, he looked back at the HUD, then concentrated on the asteroid as it filled his view. He watched it for a couple of minutes, then saw a likely attachment point for the grapnels. He started matching tumbling, waited until the target he wanted passed through the HUD and fired two grapnels simultaneously. Both hit within yards of where he wanted, and he slowly retracted the cables, pulling the tug down to the chunk of rock. Once he felt the bump as his backboard touched the surface, he toggled the tractor on high and felt the tug shudder as it sank slightly into the surface. *First things first: stop the rotation.* Flicking the HUD to contact mode, he saw ten degrees per second rotation and said, "Let's see if five Gs for fifteen seconds will do anything."

His hands flew over the thruster controls, setting up the burn he wanted, hit the execute button and hung on as the tug vibrated violently. Tex didn't really notice the vibration as he concentrated on the grapnel cables and the backboard touching the asteroid for any movement. *Good! Nothing is breaking loose, and the grapnels got a good bite.* Fifteen seconds later, the thrusters cut simultaneously, and he bounced up against his belts. *Dammit, missed that one, but point-five degrees per second is doable. Now to get this sumbitch out of here.*

Spinning the module, he looked out over the thrust pacs as he plotted a route out. *Up, left, right, right, between those two big bastards, down, and we'll see where we are. Now, let's hope the thrusters' controls reversed when the seat turned.* He blipped the thrusters and was relieved to see that he had generated movement in the right direction. Easing the Gs in, he pushed up to three Gs on the thrusters, glanced back over his shoulder to make sure the grapnels were still buried in the asteroid, and concentrated on his timing. Twenty minutes later, soaked in sweat, he cleared the sector into "clean" space.

Pinging the milling ship, he computed the course needed to get there, released the grapnels, and gave the asteroid a push. Keying the mic, he said, "Mill, Wrangler Seven. Asteroid inbound, free ballin' from sector thirteen. Inbound course one three three, up zero two three. One hundred feet per second push. Catch!"

A man's voice replied, "One three three, up zero two three. One hundred feet per second. Tonnage estimate, Seven."

"Fifty, Mill. Seven clear."

"Copy all, Seven. Got it on sensors."

Tex took a couple of minutes to drink electrolyte and take a leak before he dove back into the sector. Five hours later, Tex figured he was sitting pretty good, right at two hundred tons for the shift. Checking his reaction mass, he mentally computed his get-home requirement plus the ten percent he always added. "Eleven hundred pounds, two more runs. That's gonna be it for the day," he mumbled. He pulled out an energy bar, munched it and drank another bottle of electrolyte as he keyed the side channel. "Eight, seven. How you doin'?"

Haruji answered almost immediately. "Seven, I'm a little over two hundred. Got maybe two more runs. Lost cooling in the cockpit a few ago. Getting hot in here! I'm moving to the edge above the elliptic. Saw a good one up there."

"Copy all, eight. I was workin' that edge already. It's spittin' out some good stuff! I've got fuel for two more runs, too. I'll call when I clear." A double click came back, and he took a deep breath, wiggled around in the seat to relieve the ache in his butt, and eased the power on as he scanned the sector.

He dove back into the sector, weaving around the rolling tumbling asteroids when he spotted a big one that was dead stable. *Shit! How big is that thing? It's gotta be well over a hundred tons! And dead stable!* He didn't even have to fire his grapnels—he just cruised up to it and picked a huge outcrop with a flat side to tractor to. Clicking over, he keyed the side channel again. "Eight, seven. Got a Goldilocks over here. Squirting the posit now. Can you help? It's a hundred tonner, at least."

Haruji replied immediately. "On my way, Cowboy. Are you on it?"

"Locked tight."

"Give me fifteen."

Tex double-clicked the mic and settled back in the cockpit as he flipped it around to watch for any possible incoming asteroids that might hit anywhere near his tug. He watched one near-miss hit less than a mile away, and he didn't even feel it as the little asteroid bounced off, ricocheting in a new trajectory that took it deeper into the belt. Haruji snuck up on him, flipped his work lights on, and asked, "Where you want me?"

Startled, Tex shaded his eyes as the canopy darkened. "Um, you want to push or pull? Head or heel?"

"I'll push. Think we can move this thing? And get it clear without either of us getting knocked off?"

Tex shrugged, not that Haruji could see it, and replied, "I think so. If we're careful, we can take hits on the sides of this thing without even feeling it. Gimme a minute, I'll put a schedule for direction, Gs, and times to get us out of here." He scanned his radar, mentally plotting moves to clear the sector, and quickly typed it into the autopilot. Pushing it to Haruji, he called him. "Incoming. Are you in position yet? If I have to deviate, are you willing to slave your tug to mine?"

Haruji laughed. "Sure, locked in and max tractor. I'll just sit back here and watch to see how well you and I will grade you on your abilities."

Tex snorted. "Yeah, whatever. You ready?" A double click answered, and he added, "Activating in three, two, one." He watched the horizon swing slowly as they applied five Gs of thrust in opposite directions to turn the large asteroid. Moments later, he felt Haruji's tug start pushing, and he flipped his thrusters in the opposite direction, finally slowing the asteroid within a couple of degrees of where he wanted. He gradually increased the power to twenty Gs, timing the increase to miss another large asteroid and one a bit smaller as they crossed in front of him.

"Standby, Haruji. Gonna take a little one to starboard in thirty."

"Got it."

A half-hour later, they broke out of the sector into clear space, and Tex slumped in his seat. "Made it! Nicely done, Haruji."

"I give you a B-minus on that, Cowboy. You wagged my ass all over—"

A deedle tone came through their headsets, and both immediately went silent. A scratchy voice came over the side channel. "Can anybody hear me?"

Tex answered immediately. "Station calling. This is seven. Who are you and where?" *That sounded like the kid. Shit... We got a monster and...*

"Uh, I'm on the edge of sector fifteen and I got a problem. My seat module is hung up."

"Hung up, how?"

"I'm...sideways. And I don't know how to get out of this position!" The pitch of the kid's voice went up, and Tex sighed. *Please don't panic, kid. Please!*

"Have you still got thruster control?"

"Dunno, lemme...I think so. What do I do now?"

Haruji broke in. "Kid, what's your reactor mass?"

"Uh, six hundred." The voice went up again. "I need this rock! I'm short of quota! I...argghhh!"

They heard him hit something hard enough that it came over the side channel. "Okay, kid. Here's what you're going to do. Drop tractor and disconnect your grapnels. I'm squirting you a position, and I want you to come to it right now. You hear me?" Tex hardened his voice and added, "Right now! Don't fuck with anything else!"

They heard a sigh over the side channel and a beaten voice reply. "I'm coming."

Fifteen minutes later, the kid bobbled up, having a problem driving sideways. Haruji said softly, "Kid, get between us, tractor up, and just sit there. We'll push this pig home."

Tex winced as the kid bounced off the asteroid twice before he finally got a good position and tractored to it. "You ready, kid?" He heard a double click, and keyed the side channel. "Haruji, let's go to five Gs and get this pig moving. We'll ride it back to the mill and break off from there."

Another double click, and he counted down. "Three, two, one, ramping up one G every thirty seconds." They hit one hundred feet per second and kept accelerating. "Haruji, you got enough mass to help me slow this pig down on the other end?"

"Twelve hundred. Yeah." Tex double-clicked him and did a quick set of calculations. *If we get two-k per second, at this mass, we're gonna need five*

Gs for fifteen minutes to slow it back down. Mill can't catch faster than a hundred feet per second. Punching in the numbers, he generated a graphic on his HUD, looked at it, and squirted it to Haruji.

"Damn, you tryin' to scare the mill, Tex? Two thousand feet per second? If either one of us breaks, we're fucked!"

"You want to spend hours getting home? We got an hour left on shift. I plan on being back before then! I got a date!"

Haruji snickered. "Fine, whatever. Rosie and her four friends, right?"

Tex shook his head and pinged the milling ship. Keying the mic, he said, "Mill, Wrangler seven, eight and nine. One pig inbound, we're pushing from sector thirteen. Inbound course one three two, up zero two three. We'll slow it down for your catch!"

A man's voice replied, "One three two, up zero two three. Reminder, one hundred feet per second. Tonnage estimate, Seven."

"One fifty, Mill."

"Copy all, Seven. Allocation? Got it on sensors. How fast are y'all pushing that pig?"

Tex bit his lip, then keyed up. "Uh, seven and eight get twenty-five tons, nine gets the rest."

"Copy, twenty-five, twenty-five, one hundred."

Fifty-two minutes later, Tex backed the tug into the dock and called dispatch. "Control, Wrangler seven. Did you miss me? Up and up, normal service required. Eight grapnels fired."

A bored female voice replied, "Copy, seven." She suddenly said sharply, "Nine, go static. We will take over and park you. Do you have a problem?"

Tex shook his head as he stripped off his soggy soft helmet, dropped it distastefully in the go bag, and unstrapped as he waited for the bay to pressurize. Fifteen minutes later, he heard, "Bay nine has pressure. All drivers report to debrief immediately."

Now what? I really want a shower right now, dammit! He waited until he saw another canopy open and the driver get up and stretch. He popped the armorplast, stood up and did the same. Climbing out shakily, he pinned the unfired grapnels and waited as Haruji walked up. "Can't believe the kid let his mass get that low. He'd never have gotten back!"

Haruji snorted. "Tex, why the hell you give him the biggest part of the pig?"

"You heard him. He was short, and it wasn't his fault the seat hung up. Hell, that scared the crap out of me the first time it happened!"

"Eh. You might be right. But we aren't always goin' to be there to save his ass." Tex nodded, and they walked the rest of the way to the briefing room in silence.

Tex stopped and grabbed a cup of water, downed it, then a second. Carrying it and his go bag, he slumped down next to Haruji. "I need a shower. And so do you."

Haruji sniffed. "Yes, you do. I, on the other hand, only lightly perspired today."

"Dude, I can damn near *see* the alcohol fumes still rolling off you!"

Haruji's reply was cut short by Hartwell taking the lectern and throwing a new spreadsheet on the side wall. "Better." He pointed to the kid standing in the back. "Kennedy, you were a ton short, but since you had a maintenance issue, you don't get a markdown." He chuckled gruffly, then said, "We're adding a little more incentive for you beings. As of today, the high being gets a Hollywood shower! A whole fifteen minutes!" He turned to the spreadsheet and said dramatically, "And today's winnah is Russ Hagman with two fifty-two tons!" He clapped his hands and glared when nobody else did. A few desultory claps later, he said, "Usual time and place in sixteen."

Haruji hissed at Tex as they stood up. "Hagman. Sector one, so he doesn't burn mass to get there, and you, damn you, if you hadn't been *gracious* to the kid, I would have won today with two seventy-five!"

Tex hung his head. "Sorry, Haruji." He trudged back to his cubicle, stripped off the sweaty shipsuit, and dropped it and the soft helmet in the cleaner. He stepped into the fresher and punched the shower. A blinking timer showed four minutes, and he sighed. *Four fucking minutes. And the max we can have is five. Three minutes of water a day! Because water is rationed. Food is rationed, every fucking thing here is rationed!* He selected one minute on the shower, punched it in, and quickly got wet. Two squirts of soap, and he soaped down from head to toe. Growling at the timer, he punched one-thirty on the timer and rinsed off all the soap he could. When it clicked off, he checked and saw one-minute thirty seconds on the timer. *Eight more days and I'll get my five-minute shower.*

Tex and Haruji sat in the back corner of the mess hall, eating their meal ration, when Greebo shoved a tray on the table and climbed up into the chair. In a deep gravelly voice, she said, "Ho, Jim Bob! We make more firewater! Should be ready seven day!"

Tex looked at Greebo and the mountain of food on her plate. "Greeb, I ain't drinking with you anymore. I missed two days' rotation 'cause I was too drunk to fly." He shook his head. "And I want to know how the hell your ration is twice what mine is when you're barely three feet tall! Granted, you're three feet wide, but still."

Greebo might have smiled, but they couldn't tell, because her beard covered her mouth and hung almost to the ground. She flexed an arm and growled, "Me strong. Me fix piece of shit Wranglers. Me win strength test again!"

Haruji shook his head. "What, the torque test again?"

Greebo nodded. "Ten tries. Eight to spec, two to max."

"How much this time?"

Greebo pinched two fingers and a thumb together. "Three hundred twenty-five pounds!" She rumbled a laugh. "Minime only three hundred ten. Him getting weak!" She tucked into her tray, shoveling the food into her mouth like a hydraulic shovel, bite after bite. Strangely, not a bit of food ended up in her beard. She drained her tea bottle, burped and asked, "More drink?" Both Tex and Haruji pushed their bottles to her, and she asked, "Electrolyte?"

Tex nodded. "Please." After Greebo hopped down and disappeared toward the dispenser, he turned to Haruji. "Whatever you do, do *not* drink that shit they make. I think it's pure alcohol!"

Laughing, he replied, "I had to help you to your cube. Do you remember that?"

Tex shook his head. "No, I honestly didn't remember anything for two days, other than getting my pay docked."

Haruji smiled. "And you looked like shit for a week, but you're the first guy that ever got on the Gnomes' good side."

"Yeah, I just wish I remembered what I did to get there. You know they still laugh at me?"

"No, but that doesn't surprise me. I've seen you do some stupid shit, like today."

Tex held up his hands. "What were we going to do? Leave the kid out there?"

Haruji banged the table. "You *gesu yarō*, you cost me a Hollywood shower!"

Greebo came back with the bottles, stopping that line of discussion when she asked, "Seven do okay? No problem with module rotate?"

Tex replied, "Seven was fine, but nine locked hard on the kid."

She snorted. "Him lucky. Ring broke almost cut cable to thrusters. Him also run out of mass." Greebo stared at the two of them. "Is why you bring him back with you?"

Tex and Haruji looked at each other, and Haruji asked, "Is there anything y'all don't know, Greeb?"

Greebo gargled a laugh. "We know everything. We download data." She looked sharply at them. "You two overload all time. Tug limit forty ton, not fifty! You know that!"

Tex scrubbed his face. "Yeah, we know. We also know there is a fifty-percent safety factor, so it'll handle sixty tons before things break. And the backboard is good for fifty Gs, which would turn us to paste!"

Greebo looked around furtively. "You no talk about that. Hard enough to keep pieces of shit running now."

Haruji asked curiously, "Greeb, why are y'all not miners? I mean, you're sized for it and stronger than any human."

Greebo got up and stood in her chair, glaring at him. "We no do mine. That dwarves' job. Gnomes do guard work and maintenance. We no like dark, underground, dirt, and shit. Maintenance be good and fun. You find new and strange ways to break things not breakable. Keep us busy!" That rumbling laugh occurred again, and Tex and Haruji chuckled in response.

She looked at Tex and said, "Not like Jim Bob. We not afraid of big dark."

Haruji's eyes jerked to Tex as he dropped his head and seemed to shrink into himself. Tex finally looked up. "Greeb, that was in confidence. And I'm *not* afraid of the big dark. It's...a long story. I—"

She interrupted. "You tell Greebo all. O2 paranoia, food paranoia. Hab forty-four. You tell Greebo *all*! That why you never wear helmet!"

Haruji stared at Tex as he turned white as a sheet. "You don't wear a helmet? Ever? Is that why you're hoarding E-bottles?"

Tex mumbled, "What?"

"Hey, man, I've poured you into your cube a few times. I've seen your stash."

Tex flopped back in his chair and looked between the two of them. In a hushed, mechanical voice, he said, "I'm a survivor of Hab forty-four." He squirmed around. "One of one hundred thirty-three survivors out of twenty-two thousand," he said bitterly. "I was twelve. My dad was the hydroponics manager. Hydro was a sealed space because of the high-pressure requirement to prevent contamination. He'd taken me to work with him when the plant let go. We had O2 banks and...emergency rats. Mom...I never knew what happened. After a month, Dad...cycled out one day to go search for others and just didn't come back. It was another month before they rescued us. I was on the last O2 bottle, and had been eating hydro for two weeks." He slumped down and put his head in his hands. "I was twelve, no family left, and the corporation didn't pay off on the insurance. I went to Hab thirty-three as an orphan."

He looked up and stared at them. "I took this job to make enough money to get back dirtside on Earth! When I do, I'll never leave!" He jumped up, grabbed his bottle and tray, and hurried out of the mess after dumping the tray in the recycle.

Haruji looked at Greebo in wonder. "Damn, I never knew that. I just thought he was a *little* paranoid."

Greebo shook her head. "He very strong up here," she said, pointing at her head, "very scared in here," pointing at her chest. "That why him drink so much. We are amazed he can do the mining day after day. Most people break. Him afraid of dying of oxygen starvation, that why no helmet. Tug break, he die." She looked at Haruji. "You...you just crazy."

Haruji laughed wildly. "Banzai!" He picked up his tray and bottle, and left the mess for his cube, leaving Greebo sitting by herself.

"Crazy humans," she grumbled with a smile.

Another seven days had passed, and Haruji had gotten two Hollywood showers, Hagman three, and Meecham two, much to Tex's frustration. *Second place is the first loser.* The kid, Kennedy, had been fired yesterday for not hitting his target numbers two days in a row, and Tex and Haruji were both relieved, as he'd been pushing harder and harder, including coming back one day with the backboard bent back over the nose of the tug and another day with a crack in the armorplast canopy. They sat in the back of the briefing room as Hartwell talked about making the numbers and two tugs being down for various issues. They perked up when he stated, "The mill is going to be documenting any overweight asteroids y'all push back to them. Maintenance is complaining about overstressed tugs, and these things don't grow on trees, beings! Forty tons! That is it! Anything over that will accrue penalties."

Tex growled, "What are we supposed to do, weigh the damned things before we pick them up?"

Haruji shrugged. "No idea. I guess we back off our guesses a little bit."

Tex looked at him. "Say what? That didn't make any sense."

Haruji started to reply when Hartwell said, "Get out of here and go to work, beings."

Tex was seven hours into his shift, sweating like a pig and trying to stop the spin and rotation of a thirty-ton asteroid, when an EPIRB and PLB went off simultaneously in his ear. Control came over the broadcast channel immediately. "All units, voice check."

Tex reached up and toggled the emergency channel volume down as he clicked over to the side channel. "Haruji? You over there?"

Silence.

"Haruji? You there? Hey, man, answer me!" He toggled the beacon bearing onto his HUD and realized it was pointing into sector fourteen. "I'm coming, Haruji. Hang on, man! I'm a-coming!"

He clicked back to the group channel and said, "Control, seven. I think eight is the emergency position beacon and I've also got a personal locator beacon. Got a point into sector fourteen. I'm going to investigate."

"Seven, control. Do *not* investigate. We have rescue en route. Stay on task. Eight, check in, eight?"

He clicked off the group radio. *Fuck that. Haruji'd do it for me.* He did an emergency disconnect, leaving the grapnels in the asteroid, and spun the tug onto the best heading toward the beacon. Eleven minutes and one bounce off a random asteroid he'd misjudged later, he saw a splatter of shiny objects coming up on the downsun side of the tug. He toggled between the EPIRB and PLB, and saw the bearing split. *PLB, gotta get that, that'll be Haruji.* He maneuvered closer and closer, scared of what he was going to see, but he finally got close enough to see that the suit was inflated and seemed to move occasionally.

At that point, Tex realized he really had no way to get Haruji, much less determine how much O2 was left in his E-bottle. *Shit...now what, coach? This wasn't covered anywhere. There isn't any way to get him. Unless...* Tex started hyperventilating as he realized the only way to save Haruji was for him to go get Haruji.

Tex looked at his helmet in the rack on the seat, then reached down into his go bag. Pulling out two more E-bottles, he dug deeper and found the little Y-valve that Greebo had genned up for him. Licking his lips, he reached in the side pocket and found the coil of monofilament line. *Guaranteed to hold two thousand pounds. One hundred feet long. You never know when that might save your life,* echoed through his mind from the training cycle.

Taking a deep breath, he reached up and picked up his helmet for the first time since he'd taken the job. Setting it in his lap, he tied one end of the monofilament to the shock frame of the seat, then looped it twice around his chest, tying it off against his upper suit connection. He slipped the gloves on and picked up his helmet. Clicking it in, he took a breath and was relieved to feel the E-bottle hissing into the suit.

He looked out the canopy and saw Haruji bobbing fifty feet in front of him. *Now or never.* He reached down, raised the red guard, and pressed the red switch to depressurize the cockpit. His suit immediately hardened, and he had to work to reach the canopy lever. It slid open noiselessly, but he felt it, which confused him until he realized there wasn't any air to carry the noise. He started to get up and couldn't. *Got to actually unstrap, you idiot!*

He unstrapped, stood up and floated out of the seat. He panicked, grabbing the canopy rail with a vice-like grip as he hyperventilated again. Tex finally pushed himself forward and slid over the backboard. Luckily, he'd pushed himself toward Haruji, and hit him square in the chest. Grabbing hold, he was horrified to realize they were now drifting further from the tug. *Shit, shit, shit! Did the monofilament break?* Just as he started to panic, he was brought up short with a jerk when he hit the end of the line.

He almost lost his grip on Haruji, but scrabbled for a better handhold, finally gripping his shoulder's lift straps. Tex couldn't see the monofilament, and had to wave his free hand until he came in contact with it. Once he did, he started slowly sliding his hand down its length, pulling foot by foot back toward the tug.

What seemed like an eon later, he was able to grab the canopy rail and spin around into his seat. It was then that he noted Haruji's suit seemed to be deflating, and he was starting to convulse. *What the—?* He put his helmet against Haruji's and heard a distant beeping. *Oxygen! His E-bottle is empty!* Holding Haruji's convulsing body with one hand, he reached into his go bag and pulled out another E-bottle. Laying Haruji across his seat, he found the right leg pocket and ripped the empty bottle out, mated the fresh one, and felt the suit re-inflate as the body stopped convulsing.

He reached over Haruji and hit the canopy close switch, felt it grind closed and latch, and hit the pressurize switch. A red light lit in his HUD, and INSUFFICIENT PRESSURE scrolled across the display. A proximity warning popped up, and he glanced at the aft camera to see another asteroid bearing down on the tug.

Without thinking, he jerked the tug up and around out of its path and bounced off the canopy and Haruji's body. *Fuck! I'm not strapped in!* He pushed himself back down in the seat and fastened his belts, then pulled Haruji back down across his lap. *Gentle, gotta be gentle. Got to get out of here and back to the Hab before the oxygen runs out!*

As gently as he could, he maneuvered up and out of the sector to clear space and turned toward the Hab ship. Clicking on his emergency beacon, he accelerated to a steady three Gs, and called Control. When they didn't answer, he remembered he'd shut the channel off. Clicking it back on, his ears were filled with a babble of voice traffic.

When the channel went quiet for a second, he said, "Control, seven. I have Haruji. Emergency return, on E-bottles, cockpit unpressurized."

Control replied, "Copy. Cleared direct bay six. Status?"

"Uh, I think Haruji is alive."

"Copy. You can transfer patient to rescue in ten mikes. They will accept—"

Tex interrupted. "Control, I will bring him back. Cockpit is depressurized! We are *both* on E-bottles! I don't have time to stop and transfer."

"Copy. Cleared direct bay four. It is a single bay. Location echo six alpha."

"Rog, echo six alpha, bay four." He looked up at the HUD. "Estimate six minutes with decel burn."

"Copy, six minutes. Bay will be open in three minutes."

Three minutes later, Tex flipped the tug and started a four-G retro-burn. He was flying off his aft camera. As the hab ship grew larger in the HUD, he hit his fifty-feet-per-second decel point and flipped the tug back over.

He slewed his target cursor over echo six alpha, zoomed the camera, and saw the open bay. He aimed for it and breathed a sigh of relief. *Just a little bit longer, Haruji. We're almost there!*

Just as he started to relax, he heard his E-bottle start beeping. *Not now! I'm so close. So damned close.* He hit the bay way too fast, slammed the thrusters in retro, and that was the last thing he remembered.

Tex woke up in sickbay, coughed and groaned as that hurt his ribs. *Well, it appears I'm alive.* The duty corpsman strolled in. "Well, the patient is alive. I guess we can count this as a win!" he said with a smile. Picking up a bottle from the side table, he stuck a straw in it and held it for Tex as the bed elevated. Tex greedily slurped down the water, then coughed again as he tried to swallow too much water. "Easy there, Jim Bob. You busted a couple of ribs when Haruji's body hit you in the chest."

Tex looked up in horror. "Haruji's body? You mean he didn't make it?"

"Naw, he's alive. He's a tad busted up. Broken arm, broken leg, punctured lung, but he's gonna make it." The corpsman chuckled. "But when you get hit with a hundred and sixty pounds at five Gs, that's eight hundred pounds compressing your thoracic cavity. Shit broke."

"Did I hurt him? Is that..." Tex couldn't finish the sentence.

The corpsman glared at him. "No, dumbass. You saved his life. *That* is what you did. Rescue would have never made it to him in time. And if you hadn't had that extra E-bottle, or two, neither of you would have made it back."

A scuffing of feet announced the doctor, who stepped in and looked at him. "Since you're awake, I'm going to kick you out of here. There isn't a damned thing I can do for the ribs that the nanites won't fix within the next forty-eight hours. You've been out for twenty-four, but most of that was us keeping you out to get the treatments started." He looked at the monitors and turned to the corpsman. "Unplug him and take him to the front. I'll have a sick chit waiting for him up there." The doctor turned and walked out, whistling.

Tex sniffed. "Hell of a bedside manner there."

The corpsman chuckled. "Yeah, he doesn't get paid for that. But he's damned good at keeping stupid people alive."

Tex started to laugh and groaned when his ribs protested. He started to get up and realized he was naked underneath the sheet. "Um, where'd my gear go?"

"Dunno, probably in the cleaner. What are you, thirty-eight regular?" When Tex nodded, he walked out and returned a minute later with a folded shipsuit and booties. "Here ya go. Free of charge."

Tex snorted. "I'm sure they'll take it out of my pay. Everything comes out of our pay." He managed to get his legs into the shipsuit, then groaned as he tried to pull it up. Red-faced, he asked, "Uh, can you help me?"

The corpsman snorted. "Well, I ain't tuckin' you in, but I'll help you get it over your shoulders." He waited until Tex turned away and pulled it up over his waist, then pulled out the right arm. "Right arm." Tex stuck his arm in, and the corpsman pulled it up rather gently. "Left arm." He got his left arm in, and the corpsman patted him on the shoulder. "The rest is up to you. I'll go get a float chair."

Tex got the closures done and leaned against the bunk, panting as shallowly as he could. The corpsman came back with a float chair and said, "Sit!" He slumped into the chair and the corpsman started pushing him toward the front of the clinic.

"Uh, can I see Haruji?"

"Nope, he's still in the box. Nanites and hyperbaric to speed healing. And he's in a med coma until the doc decides to bring him out. Maybe three days from now."

They got to the front, and the receptionist handed him a data chip. In a bored voice, she explained, "This is your sick chit. Turn this in to your boss not later than tomorrow morning." She handed him a second chip. "Plug this into your cubicle. It will allow you a ten-minute shower twice a day for the next three days. I will send a note to the mess, allowing you an extra thousand calories a day for the next three days. No caffeine in any form, no alcohol, for three days. If, at the end of three days, you are still having problems, sick call starts at zero six and ends at zero eight. Have a good day."

The corpsman got him up out of the float chair and said, "You should be able to make it to the mess and back to your cube. Good luck, and good job."

Tex stepped out of the clinic and was surprised to see both Kate and Greebo sitting there, with another float chair. "What are y'all doing here?"

Kate said, "Waiting on you. I've been checking. You...don't look too good."

Greebo rumbled a laugh. "Jim Bob been drug through camel with needle. Him weak little thing. Him need help."

Kate and Tex both looked at Greebo with stunned expressions, until Kate said, "Oh, camel through the eye of a needle. Got it."

Greebo said, "Sit float chair. We go eat."

Tex eased himself into the chair and Greebo guided it to the mess as Kate went and picked up his tray, then went back for hers. She filled his bottle with electrolyte and placed it in front of him as Greebo went to get her tray. Kate looked at him. "Jim Bob, what in the hell were you thinking, disobeying Control?"

He started to shrug, stopped quickly, and replied, "Haruji would have done the same for me."

She shook her head and said, "Maybe. But you don't *ever* disobey Control. I mean, they could fire you for that! I know you did it for Haruji, but you're setting a precedent that Control doesn't like."

A bite of food halfway to his mouth, he stopped, looked her in the eyes, and said, "Fuck them. Life is precious. We aren't just fucking widgets they can move around on a board and discard at will. They want to fire me, that's fine with me." He took the bite, chewing furiously as Greebo came back with two trays, sliding one over to Tex. "What's this for?"

She replied, "You did not get your extra. I told them to give me your extra. Eat. Food needed for nanites. You already skinny and broke inside."

"Um, thank you, Greeb." Tex looked at the empty tray in front of him and realized he was still hungry, really hungry. He stacked the tray and dug in as Kate and Greebo ate their meals. As soon as he finished, he slumped back and sighed. "I don't think I've ever been that hungry. Damn!"

Kate glanced at him. "First time with nanites?"

"No, I got them when they did the 'net in my head, but that was in Hab thirty-three, had plenty to eat there, and I was still growing, so I guess I didn't think about it." A huge yawn took him by surprise, and he shook his head. "Dunno what's wrong, but all of a sudden—"

Greebo rumbled, "Jim Bob stupid. Broke inside, nanites, no food, now exhausted. Idiot needs rest."

Kate bristled, and Tex laughed weakly. "Deity guards fools and drunks, Greeb. And I qualify on both counts."

"We take you to cube now."

The beeping of his alarm woke Tex at zero six, and he eased out of the bunk. Tottering over to his fresher, he did his business and managed to get his shipsuit back up. He resorted to the booties from Medical as he shuffled gingerly down to the briefing room. Hartwell stood outside the door, as if he was expecting Tex. "Sick chit?" he asked.

Tex took it carefully out of his upper pocket. "This is from the doc." He scuffed his feet and finally asked, "Did I screw up number seven?"

Hartwell looked at him closely. "You don't remember?"

Tex shook his head. "No." He sighed. "The last thing I remember is the low E-bottle beeper going off and hitting the retro pretty hard."

Hartwell goggled at him. "You've got to be shitting me! You parked it perfectly in the dock." Unfolding the chit, he glanced at it and added, "Three days. Get out of here." As Tex turned to go, Hartwell said softly, "I had to dock you for the day's pay for disobeying Control. Not my choice."

Tex nodded as he shuffled back to his cube.

Four days later, feeling much better, he walked into the briefing room to the applause of the other drivers. Hartwell did the usual brief, and Tex headed for number seven. Settling into the seat, he completed the pre-flight, racked his helmet, and realized he wasn't hyperventilating at all. *Maybe, just maybe, I can do this. I'm back in the saddle. Now to see if I can do the work.* Eight hours later, dripping sweat, he walked into debrief to see that he was second yet again. *Fuck it, I'm alive!*

He started to walk out, and Hartwell called him to the lectern. Shoving a chip into his hand, Hartwell said, "Here's a chip for five Hollywood showers. The other beings voted on it. And Haruji asked that you to drop by the clinic."

Tex pocketed the chip and grimaced. "Not sure if that's a good idea." Hartwell just glared at him, and Tex added, "Okay, fine, I'll go right now."

At the clinic, the corpsman led him back to the cubical where Haruji laid in bed. He looked up at Tex with tears in his eyes. "Thank you, Tex," he said hoarsely. "You saved my sorry ass."

"You would have done the same for me," Tex replied, as he sat down in the chair facing Haruji. "What the hell happened?"

Haruji grimaced. "I was riding one of those twisters, rotating in three dimensions. Got sideswiped, never saw it coming..." He slumped back. "Got the alert about the time the little asteroid hit me."

The End

Drover

Evan DeShais

I rub at the welt that's formed on the back of my head. The bruise on my cheek and right eye ache as I test the injuries.

The last run with Morgan was contentious. I know things didn't work out well between us, but I didn't expect Morgan to damage my ship, let alone attack me.

I shake my head; the pain flares, and I wince. I open my left eye, as the right is swollen shut. The dull blue of the cell's lighting stabs into my brain. I lean over the bench and dry heave.

The contents of my stomach are long since gone. Morgan's ministrations with something heavy to the back of my head as we exited the ship saw to that. The boot to the face as she stormed off drove home the point that our relationship was over.

The concussion is a parting gift of a woman refused. Things started going sideways when I refused to sign the marriage contract she provided. I'm beginning to think she was after my ship the whole time.

To pilot a ship the size of the *Raven's Flight IV* (RFIV), you must have at least two people: a captain and an engineer. It seemed the perfect fit, initially, as Morgan's interest in me grew after our first two short runs together.

Five and a half years later, she delivered an ultimatum. The contract gave her fifty percent of all Thapa Industries assets. The *RFIV* is all I have left of my great-great-grandfather's infamous treasure run.

My family squandered a one percent stake in the Compact Space Merchant Service and it is a 700 trillion credit corporation. All I own outright is this ship. Even that is questionable now. The last three years haven't gone well for Thapa Industries. Repairs, maintenance, and costly delivery delays ate at my bottom line. Depending on the fines from this incident, late delivery, and docking fees, I might be heavily in the red.

The gravity drives magically lost sync after I refused to sign Morgan's marriage contract. We hung there in the deep dark of dead space for three days. Morgan refused to come out of the engineer's berth, a place she had not resided in for the last five and a half years.

Steven and I spent three days bringing the drives out of limp mode and regaining some functionality. To say I slept with one eye open for the remainder of the voyage is an understatement.

The sound of the cell's airlock wakes me. I sit up and move to the facilities. The polished steel mirror shows the horror that is my face. I turn my torso to the hatchway as the cell's speaker chirps.

"Hands and feet on the blue symbols," says someone from the airlock.

I shuffle to the markings as a bout of vertigo nearly forces me into the bunk along the wall. It takes me a moment to place my feet correctly on the painted symbols. I have trouble getting my left arm high enough to put it on the mark. It seems Morgan got more than one kick in.

A moment later, the symbols change color when my right hand touches them. The inner airlock starts to cycle. I try to turn my head in that direction, but a spike of pain and another wave of vertigo hit. A man steps into the cell and his mag boots clomp on the steel plate flooring. A moment later, his face nears my left side. I try to turn my head to the guard, but I don't have that range of movement.

I feel his hot breath on my neck and cheek. He breathes in heavily. His shock stick levers my chin up and pushes me away from the wall. I take a step backward, and he guides me in a full circle with very poignant prods of his cudgel.

The man is massive, hulking. He has to be just shy of two meters tall. His shoulders and neck are slabs of muscle with tattoos at the nape of his neckline. I move my line of sight down his arm to the thin sleeves that cover more tattoos on his arms.

There is a gap at the hollow of his elbow, and I spy the tell-tale thick scar. He is a sculptor. His size and his muscles are the results of surgery. So how does a guard get the credits to pay for 3D muscle printing? I find out how, just as the shock stick pushes me hard against the cell wall. This man is on someone's payroll. He might be a guard, but that is not all he is.

"Lalawhoopsiedoozies," a high-pitched drug-damaged voice says. "Lalba, lala, lapdog, that's what I'll call you." The man pushes the shock stick into my sternum with each attempt at my name. "Lapdog, you got that?"

His attempt at pronouncing Lalbahadur is as successful as most attempts. His choice of nickname isn't original, either. I nod my head slowly. I am without breath and have no way to answer verbally.

"Lap, Dog," the guard says in his reedy voice, "Mr. Barnaby wants me to deliver a message."

Well, things have gone from bad to dire. Barnaby Badger (BB) controls Praxis Station and two other system stations like it, not to mention the local gates and, apparently, this guard. I would never call BB a gangster; no, Barnaby has surpassed such menial terms. He is crime; every type of crime, from corporate espionage to petty smuggling. He is a businessman whose corporate product is crime.

BB offered me cushy contracts numerous times before and I've always politely declined. I figured BB simply allowed me to deliver within his area of influence to secure enough of that legitimate traffic for his stations.

"Lapdog, that girl," the man says as he taps the shock stick on my forehead. "That young lady, Morgan..." His left hand moves, and his FEED system opens. "That's Mr. Barnaby's goddaughter, who failed her first test into the corporation."

An image pops up of a severely beaten Morgan. We had something once, regardless of how we ended with her attack and betrayal. She did not deserve this. Her oval face is now round with a framework of purple, and her eyes are clouded white. She is clearly dead.

"She was to get your ship from you," the man says. "Mr. Barnaby asked you once, asked you twice, and with her, he asked you a third time. She failed and Mr. Barnaby said, 'examples must be made.'"

I don't see the first blow and my knee buckles from under me. A dozen painful blows land before he turns on the shock stick. With my concussion, the electrical discharge sends me into the black.

I am in and out for at least a day. The guard skillfully administered the beating, and nothing was broken. I toss and turn over the next few days and never quite find a spot on me that doesn't send me waves of pain. I can open my right eye eventually, and I am thankful I can eat solid food.

The sound of the outer airlock forces me up off my bench. I should have seen the magistrate days ago, but they probably didn't want to drag me before the magistrate puking blood. I move to the wall and place my hands on it. I shift my feet and wince as I get them on the markers. The markers flash from blue to yellow, and the inner airlock sounds.

It will be good to see the magistrate. If I am lucky, I might be able to get off this station and work off whatever debt I have incurred. That is if I can find work. The stigma of being in debt to BB may hinder any future contracts. The door opens, and a different guard steps into the cell.

"Drover," the guard says. "Your bail has been paid."

I dare not move, but I ask, "How can I have bail, sir? I've not seen the magistrate?"

"You saw him remotely," The guard says a bit sheepishly. "You were," he coughs, "asleep."

A new wave of fear hits me. I have no idea what I was charged with or what fines I face. Let alone the number of people I know at Praxis who could post my bail. I had no chance to confer with my legal representation.

"Come," the man says. "Hands behind your back. I don't have all day."

I put my hands as far behind my back as I can, and my muscles protest as the guard snaps the mag cuffs around them. He cinches the cuffs tightly together. My shoulders and sides strain; as a new wave of horrible pain spreads through me.

"Who posted bail for me?" I ask.

"Inmate will be silent," the man says. Then, in a whisper, he says, "Kid, I'm just doing my job, and I do my job by the book."

I clamp my mouth shut. The guard is treating me decently, and I don't want to change that. I'm in enough bullshit trouble as it is. The airlock door hisses open, and a gentle push moves me forward. A second guard waits for us inside the airlock. The guards jostle me to the middle of the airlock as we wait for the airlock to finish cycling.

Ten minutes later, I had a bag with my shoes, the shipsuit I had been wearing, and most of all, they had turned my FEED system on. I use the facilities and get changed. I make my way out of the facilities to the main lobby.

A man stands still in the corner; his suit is impeccable. A hat is tugged low over his eyes. I pause, and a flare of concern weaves its way down my spine. This man is money from his shoes to his hat. Even the white gloves have the look of the finest leather.

"Mr. Lalbahadur Thapa," a smooth but mechanical voice says.

"You are?" I ask. "I've only heard my name pronounced correctly by Family."

"Dio," The man says in that odd mechanical voice.

Dio extends a hand, and I shake it. It is as hard as steel. I do not mean the grip, but the hand itself. I look to the undersides of the hat where the ears should be.

"I've heard the rich have piloted SkipJacks as butlers," I say. "I did not think Mr. Barnaby would be interested in such a thing."

"I do not work for Mr. Barnaby Badger," Dio says. "I was instructed to hire you at Varget station. You had already departed with a contract when I arrived." Dio straightens his hat and says, "Shall we?"

It doesn't work for BB, and this Dio was instructed to hire me at Varget station? That was three contracts ago. Dio has the look of money, and money is what I need right now.

"Dio," I ask tepidly, "what's the damages? I've not gotten the magistrate's report."

The inner airlock opens out of the constables' station, and we step inside. Dio's hat turns to me, and I swear the blank steel mannequin's face is smiling. Dio lifts his right hand and thumbs me over a file. How does a SkipJack have a FEED system? I open it and review the damages as the airlock cycles. Listed in exquisite detail are all the ways I am fucked.

Morgan drained Thapa Industries' accounts to the tune of 90,000 credits. That 90k is my operating budget; without it, I am grounded. I can't get into space for under 30k and an insurance rider for most cargo is usually 40k. I still need to add in fuel, food, and repair costs.

That is not the worst of my problems. In addition to my missing 90k, I owe 139k in fines, fees, and damage assessments for my medical care.

I have a dozen charges pending, and bail was set at a steep two million credits. I turn slowly back to Dio.

"Dio, sir, I don't have the credits to pay back your bail bond," I say. "Let alone enough credits to get my ship off Praxis Station."

The airlock opens. Dio steps onto the promenade.

"There isn't a contract out there that would pay two million credits," I say.

We make our way a few dozen steps down the promenade. Dio's hand flags down a maglev ride share. He enters, and the maglev lowers considerably under his weight.

"Are you coming?" Dio asks. "*Raven's Flight IV* is now at terminal thirty-seven."

"I arrived at terminal nine," I say.

"I had the forethought to have her prepped for departure, Drover Thapa," Dio says. "I was instructed to hire you and your ship."

"Mr. Dio, I have no engineer," I say while looking into the maglev ride share.

I lift my head and look around. I'm stuck, and I have no opportunities on Praxis Station save for selling the *Raven's Flight IV* at auction. I highly doubt anyone would outbid Barnaby's surrogate. I am pretty sure BB wouldn't even bid enough for me to be clear of my debts. That means an indenture on the surface of Praxis until my debt is paid. I step into the rideshare, and the hatch closes.

"How is the RF?" Dio asks.

I turn to the SkipJack, remembering that it has a pilot somewhere, one that is doing the asking and the questioning. One of Dio's eyestalks exits its head and twists to view me. I look away at the small FEED screens in the maglev ride share. News of acquisitions, trade deals, and market ups and downs scroll silently across the display.

"It could be better," I say with a shrug. "I've done my best to keep the preventative maintenance up, all the certs in good standing, and inspections up to date." I look at Dio. "The last engineer and I, well, we ended badly. I've not had time to review her work."

I turn back to the small feed display as a tiny blurb of a corporate subsidiary on Praxis Station going into receivership scrolls across the small screen's ticker bar.

"Before I can take your contract, I need an engineer," I say to Dio.

I flip my FEED system open and scroll through news and available crew hiring posts.

A few moments later, a small mechanical purr, almost a "hmm," slips from Dio. "Drover Thapa, it's been a while, but my certs are up to date; I can help prepare the *RF*."

It only half registers as I keep reading what's on my FEED system. I flip through a couple more pages, do a few searches, and close out my FEED unit.

"I'm sorry," I say. "What was it that you said? You can help prep the *RF*?"

"Drover Thapa," Dio says coolly. "It is a unique level of rudeness to be occupied on your FEED while having a business conversation."

"My apologies, Dio," I say. "A news blurb caught my eye, and a few things fell into place." I turn to the SkipJack. "It was an honest mistake, and I meant nothing by it."

"My certifications as a vessel first engineer rating are up to date," Dio says.

"What class of vessel?" I ask with a bit of suspicion.

The RF is a relatively modern ship, about 225 years old. It packs a lot of modernizations, but it isn't small, and out here on the outskirts of civilized humanity, there are few engineers rated for a vessel of its capability. Especially ones that reek of money like this Dio.

Dio turns to me, and the eyestalk retracts into its head.

"Everything from inter-ship cutters to CSMS's Battlevessels," Dio says. "I am also deeply familiar with the *RFIV*."

The maglev ride share slows then, and I turn from Dio and notice that we are at terminal thirty-seven. A small group of people are waiting beside the hatch to the Raven's Flight airlock. I recognize the brute who delivered Barnaby's beating. Next to him are several constables, and a man in a respectable suit. The last man, with the top hat, scar on his face, and wooden cane, causes me to pause.

I thumb access to the RF to Dio and say, "You're hired; when we get aboard, get everything prepped," I say.

"You are taking our contract?" Dio says as much as he asks.

"We'll discuss it on board," I say with a nod to the men next to the airlock. "That is Barnaby Badger, and he wants my ship."

Dio turns his head, and his right index finger taps on his pant leg. The finely tailored suit barely muted the dull clink of metal on metal. I don't have the time to wait on Dio. I pop my hatch and exit.

"Drover Thapa," Barnaby Badger says. "You're not planning on leaving my station, are you?"

I hear the metallic clanks of Dio's footsteps a little to my left and a few feet behind. For some reason, that gives me a great deal of reassurance. I don't have an answer I am willing to provide Mr. Barnaby, so I stay silent.

Barnaby's wooden cane taps twice on the decking, his lips firm. He looks from me to Dio and back again.

"I'm a businessman, Drover Thapa," BB says. "So I will put the offer out there. I'll hire you and your ship for a time at a very agreeable rate. I have some shipments waiting, and your vessel is one of the few in our neck of space that can make the runs on time."

"Drover Thapa," Dio says, stepping forward, "is under contract."

I am not under contract as of yet, but I decline to disabuse my benefactor in front of BB.

"Is that a fact?" BB asks me.

"It's a minor contract," I say, and maybe I can work this to my advantage. "A few runs, totaling about six weeks' time."

"That's cutting it close," BB says. "If you miss your court date, that ship will be impounded. Then you, along with it, will be brought back here for your trial."

The threat is implied but futile. I know why Barnaby needs the *RFIV*, and I chose my dates carefully.

"Won't matter to you, will it, BB?" I ask. "You need the *RFIV* long before those six weeks are up."

There is a flicker of violence in his eyes as they narrow. His lips firm again as he clenches his jaw; Barnaby's eyes flit from me to Dio and back to me.

"Good luck hiring an engineer, Drover Thapa," BB says. "When you are ready to negotiate, I will extend an appropriate offer. Again, good day to you, and this." His hand waves at Dio.

The group streams past; the brute tries to shoulder past Dio but finds the SkipJack much denser than he anticipated. BB pauses as he nears Dio.

"We have not been intro..." Dio begins to say.

I cut Dio off by saying, "Get aboard the *RFIV*, engineer first class Dio."

His head tilts back vertically, and I feel the rebuke was a bit harsh, but Dio steps towards the airlock. My access codes work, and the airlock cycles on our end.

The inner airlock cycles, and I step aboard the RF. The scent of coffee hits my nose.

"Steven," I say out loud, "did you start me a pot?"

"I did, Thapa," Steven says through the speaker at the airlock hatch. "Oh, there is more than you?"

I turn to Dio. "This is the RF's Steven," I say proudly. "The original Steven to the ship."

Dio's head tilts, and his face turns away from me as he looks down the passage. "Nice to meet you, Steven," he says.

"Grand," Steven starts to say.

"Dio, my name is Dio," Dio says. "I was asked to employ Drover Thapa and you for a contract." Dio turns back to me. "Yet it seems there is more going on in this region of space than I was led to believe."

"I'll fill you in, Dio," I say. "When will your pilot board?"

Dio looks back down the hall and back to me.

"I have no Pilot," Dio says. "Think of me as a personal or corporate Steven."

Now it is my turn to tilt my head; that's a level of dangerous that I do not want to know more about. The rules and laws about AI personalities are precise here in space. Stevens are the sole exception. I swallow hard. Close my eyes and pray I didn't just jump from the frying pan directly into the fire.

"Are you good with Stevens?" I ask slowly. "I am going to need his help. He's long past his service date and can be temperamental at times," I say. "Dio, Steven and this ship are all I have left."

Dio turns back down the passageway. "I understand," Dio says. "I am familiar with the RF line of ships." He turns back to me and says, "You mentioned multiple contracts?"

"Vague ideas right now; let me finalize my thoughts and put some plans together," I say. I grimace. "I may have to ask for a loan." Dio's eye lenses widen. "I know you've spent a lot on me, but I have a chance to do some real good here in the next few weeks. I will need capital to see that happen. Give me a few hours while you work with Steven as I pilot us out of the system's gravity well."

Dio nods and starts down the passageway. "Hello again, Steven. Can you give me a current system diagnostic for the gravity drives, engines, life support, and your core heuristic matrix?" Dio asks.

"In that order, Grand...Dio?" Steven says.

It's odd that Steven would have to correct himself, but he is well over 150 years past his service life. The fact we even have the original Steven available is amazing. He's old, cantankerous, and he rarely wants to plot the Tunnel Gates anymore. Yet, when I need him, Steven is there. Steven truly makes the *Raven's Flight IV* capable of its speed and range.

I head to my pilot's pod. I need to get us moving before BB comes up with some way to keep us here. A quick FEED message to Dio and the fees I have incurred are paid. I am light on supplies, but I have plenty of rations. I can live off that for quite a while. The *RFIV* disengages from Praxis Station and settles into a comfortable cruising speed as I work.

I've got a vague idea, a plan of sorts. It's been in the back of my mind since I took ownership of the RF when it was delivered to me in the Bandiss sector. Unfortunately, my father and grandfather did not get along. When my grandfather passed, the holding company delivered the Raven's Flight to Bandiss Station. I was only thirty then and into my fifteenth year of orbital delivery flights.

I learned a lot in my time on Bandiss as a kid, but spreading shit across our fields is not something I like doing. I need to see if I can make the timing of this idea work. So, I delve into shipping lanes, gates, stations, and fees. I make flow charts showing the return on investment and practice my sales pitch. It's a pitch I am giving to a Corporate Steven, if such a thing exists. He is not flesh and blood; will he even care about the good we could achieve?

My FEED beeps and I look down. That's what piloting is like: eighteen hours down without even realizing it.

"Dio," I say into the ship's comms.

"Yes, Drover Thapa?" Dio responds.

"How are things looking?" I ask. "We've got several long jumps ahead of us. Will Steven be up to the task?"

"To where, Thapa?" Steven asks.

Steven sounds almost jubilant. It's not a tone I've ever heard from my friend of the last fifteen years.

"Home, Steven," I say. "We are going home to the Bandiss system."

"You have solidified your plans?" Dio asks.

"Yes," I say and thumb Dio my proposal. "I'll walk you through the proposal after some shut-eye and food."

"Yes, Drover Thapa," Dio says. "I'll review the proposal."

"I suppose I should ask," I say. "Do you have the authority to extend a loan?"

"I do not know," Dio says a bit quizzically. "This kind of situation is outside my bailiwick. However, there is more going on in the Praxis, Varget, and Chandrys systems than I suspected."

"I'm not sure I know what you mean," I say.

"Like you, I have an idea," Dio says. "Get us through the gate; Steven should be up to a straight shot to the Bandiss system."

"That's a seventeen-system tunnel gate!" I say.

"I am very good with Stevens and know the Raven's Flight IV intimately," Dio says. "First engineer out."

The FEED screen in my pilot's pod pops out of existence. I set the course for Bandiss. Not since the first Stevens have they been able to open a tunnel gate outside of two systems. Even then, that capacity is the privilege of CSMS vessels of war.

I leverage myself out of my pilot's pod. The injuries throughout my body protest vehemently at my exertions. It's time for food. As I step forward, a bit of hunger-driven vertigo hits me. I make my way to the galley and find a survival packet of food.

My FEED system beeps me awake. I roll to shove my right arm out from under me. It is numb and tingles as I try and thumb open my FEED system with my left hand.

"Wharft," I mumble into my pillow.

"We have arrived at the edges of the Bandiss gravity well," Steven says. "Shall we continue to Bandiss Station or Bandiss orbit?"

I blink and rub my eyes with my left hand. It's a two and half week run at best to the Bandiss system. That's if I hit all the gates queues correctly. That is very unlikely, given the traffic from the core systems to the Thrax territories. I sit up and wince as the bruised ribs complain.

"How?" I ask.

"I have prepared breakfast," Dio says. "It is in the Wardroom."

"Huh?" I mumble.

I stumble out of bed and hit the head. I wash up, enter my airlock, and go down the passage to the wardroom. There, on the table, is a spread fit for a king. There is no spot on the table that doesn't have a plate of something on it.

"Um," I mumble. "Dio, have you ever cooked for a human before?"

"Many times," Dio responds.

"They ate this much every time?" I ask.

I look from the food to him. Dio does that head tilt, and his eyestalks extend. He peruses the table, and then they retract.

"I see my mistake," Dio says. "It will not happen again."

"The fresh stores needed to be used up," I say. "Most of it was going to go bad; at least this way, I can package it up and put it in the vac freezer."

"I've reviewed your proposal," Dio says as I load up my plate with a bit of everything.

I look at him as I use tongs to put a large pile of kimchee on my plate.

"It is fundamentally flawed," Dio says. "Your plan is for one delivery, but to achieve the desired results, we need to make three, preferably four deliveries. One delivery will not affect Praxis's soil microbial growth enough. Two deliveries will not give the Praxis the nutrients needed to sustain the microbial growth. Three might do it, provided there are no other extenuating factors. A fourth delivery gives Praxis planet some breathing room."

I flop into my chair, plate nearly forgotten. That's it, then; I'm fucked, and so is Praxis. I don't know what I can do. I pick at my food for a moment.

"I've submitted requisitions from Bandiss, Thrax, Alpha Centauri, and the asteroid belt of Old Earth," Dio says. "Drover Thapa, we will have our loads. The question is if we can get three or four shipments in before six weeks."

"It would kill Steven," I say. "To push him that far. He's barely hanging in there as it is."

"I am not hanging in there, Thapa; I am healthy, hale, and vigorous," Steven says. "I'll have you know that I was plotting tunnel gates before your great-grandfather was sucking on his mother's teat."

"Steven," Dio says. He pauses as he looks around. "Forgive me, Steven, but you should have died long ago. Only the first-generation Stevens lasted past seventy-five years. A box in a vessel, calculating options and destinations, is not much of a life, Drover Thapa. Yet, here you are, aboard the *Raven's Flight IV* with its original sixteenth-generation Steven. One that is well past his normal life span of fifty-five years."

Dio waves his arms. "This vessel is loved; it has been well-maintained. Even when it had only a crew of two."

"I don't see what you are driving at," I say.

"He's Family to you, isn't he?" Dio says.

"Been my best friend the past fifteen years," I say. "Was right about Morgan from the get-go."

"Your grandfather treated him much the same way," Dio says. "I know we can make at least three of these runs, Drover Thapa."

"You think my treatment of Steven keeps him healthy?" I ask.

"Among other things, but yes, primarily that reason," Dio says.

"Then we do it," I say. "Steven and I have a chance to do some real good here, Dio." I pause. "Thank you for the backing."

"You're welcome," Dio says.

"What was your contract?" I ask. "Will this side project of mine interfere with it? You made it seem rather time-sensitive."

"It dovetails nicely into your project," Dio says. "And achieving your goal removes suspicion from my employer." Then, Dio pauses and continues, "I'm here to settle accounts, Drover Thapa, but once again, like your ancestors, you were well on the way to doing that for us."

"'Us?'" I ask. "Your name isn't Dio, is it?"

"No, Drover Thapa, it is not," Dio says. "Implement the second part of your plan after our second delivery to Praxis. It is good that you remember that you are not alone out here."

"You think they will answer?" I ask. "Are they even around?"

"Yes, they are around," Dio says. "A bit insular, at times, but like you, they remember the name Thapa well."

The first load of ninety-two cargo containers is attached to the outer hull of the *Raven's Flight IV*. Each of the temperature-controlled containers carries 200,000 kilos of cargo. We are towing an additional 300 containers behind us like an old earth train. The *RFIV* has always been an extraordinary vessel. Our cargo is the prime quality I remember vividly as a young man on the farm.

"Drover Thapa, we are ready," Dio says over the ship's comms.

"I'll see us past the gravity well," I say. "Steven..." I pause. "Can you work up a tunnel gate for us?"

"I've got the preliminary work done, Thapa," Steven says.

"Grav drives are online," I mutter to myself.

"Does he always talk to himself?" Dio asks.

"Yes," Steven says. "When Thapa gets worried, he starts signing like an Irish sailor."

"Really?" Dio asks.

"You will be able to tell by the swear words," Steven replies.

"Gentleman," I say. "If you could please take the conversation off the ship's comms..."

It's nearly sixty hours later that we make it out of the Bandiss gravity well. Steven opens the tunnel gate, and we are through. The central system shunts to auxiliary power as the mains are diverted to build up Steven's reserves again. As I wait for our systems to reboot, I plot our course on my FEED system.

I'm incredibly thankful that Praxis Station is nearly four weeks from Praxis planet by gravity drive. This system's gravity well is massive with its three equidistant stars. I pray that this gives me enough time to make the delivery runs before BB has time to implement his schemes to get his cargo to Praxis's orbit.

"Seven days," I say over the comms, "until we reach the orbitals and unload our cargo. I've got a few supplies coming our way, but we need to scoot after that. Are the grav drives ready for a sprint?"

"They are getting there," Dio says. "Steven and I are managing their overhaul quite nicely. This Morgan you employed; she set them out of phase. You overcorrected when you started fiddling with things. The three days in orbit around Praxis will allow me to finalize everything."

Eight days later, my vessel has its supplies, and we are back underway. The ship is humming along as it speeds to the nearest edge of the gravity well. I find myself in engineering with Dio and Steven a lot. We play cards, watch FEED vids, and talk about our favorite music and books. Without cargo to haul, we make the edges of the gravity well in five days.

It's not the typical way of entering a system. Cargo vessels almost always gate to a system's station, unload there, and take the short run out of the gravity well. Many long-distance cargo vessels don't have Grav drives capable of pulling themselves in and out of a gravity well while towing cargo. As I've said before, the RF is a one-off ship. Its designer made something special when the keel was laid.

I'm in the wardroom when my airlock beeps. There is only one other aboard; well, one other that isn't part of the ship.

"Come on in, Dio," I say.

"Are you busy?" Dio asks after entering.

"I'm figuring loan payments, payments for my fines, and trying to decide if I've made any profit yet," I say. "Thank you for the reasonable terms, by the way."

Dio shrugs, pulls back a chair and sits. He peers at the open holo display and my FEED system.

"No profit as of yet, but by the third run, you will have a very tidy sum," Dio says.

I chuckle and laugh, shutting down the feed and holo display.

"I'll take your word for it," I say. "What can I do for you?"

"The RF, she was designed to be run by a crew," Dio says. "The ship and its Steven like having a crew."

I drum my fingers on the table. Dio has a point. I've never had more than a single member besides myself. Possibly, that is part of my problem; I'm trying to do it all and I miss things.

"I don't have the funds yet," I say. I hold up a hand to forestall Dio. "I'm not bringing a crew on with the dangerous game we are playing. You're right, Dio; Drovers generally do better when working as a team. I've got the berths and the space, and this ship can do amazing things. I, well, I don't know."

"Give it some thought, Drover Thapa," Dio says.

"I will. Are we ready for tomorrow?" I ask.

"The Belters of old earth have the cargo ready and waiting on the edge of their gravity well," Dio says. "The *RFIV* is doing well, and Steven is itching to open another gate."

I turn to him and smile. "Thank you, Dio," I say.

"You are welcome," Dio says. "Give what I said some thought and get some rest."

Our delivery from the asteroid belt of old earth goes off without a hitch seven days later. We are speeding back out of the Praxis system. Two local vessels from Praxis Station try and follow us to the edge of the gravity well, but do not have the legs that the *RFIV* does.

"Alpha Centauri or Thrax?" I ask.

"Thrax," Steven and Dio say in unison.

"If Alpha Centauri has a queue to pick up goods, we will have lost this gambit. So we must go with Thrax for our third delivery," Dio says. "I've analyzed BB's fleet of ships between Praxis Station and Praxis orbital. He's co-opted every vessel he can to haul freight to Praxis."

"Do you think he can do it?" I ask. "Can BB deliver that much to the planet?"

"Yes, but the point is moot," Dio says, "We are undercutting BB's pricing and offering an opportunity to be free from his chokehold." He turns from the Holo displaying the gravity engine's sync ratio. "Have you heard back?"

"No," I say. "Not yet. I expect it might take them some time to receive the message and prepare for transit." I pause. "Thrax it is, then." I thumb a file to the console and our heading shifts.

"Four hours until I can open a tunnel gate," Steven says.

Thrax is an imposing system. It's a wide, flat area littered with moons, debris, and one habitable planet the color of dried blood. I've been here half a hundred times, yet this system sends a shiver down my spine. It's a short gravity well that is only thirty-six hours deep. We are in and out, and it takes us longer to recharge Steven than it does to enter, pick up our cargo, and exit the system via gravity drive.

Eight days after that, our third delivery is free, and we are headed back out to the edges of the gravity well in the Praxis system.

"Do I have the time?" I muse.

"We have the time to get the cargo," Dio says. "I am not sure we have the time to deposit it and get you to Praxis Station for your hearing."

"That is my thought, as well," I mumble.

I drum my fingers on the table. If I drop off the fourth shipment, Praxis will be out from under the economic leash BB has about the planet. That cascading failure will likely destroy him. I think my choice is clear, given what I've learned about BB's similar efforts in the Varget and Chandrys systems. This ship means a great deal to me, but that shipment represents a lot more to the colonists and settlers across three systems.

I thumb my file to the navigation system and turn to Dio. I swear his solid face has a smirk on it.

"You disagree?" I ask.

"Not in the slightest," Dio says.

Dio steps past me and pats my shoulders.

"Thank you," I say for the hundredth time.

We exited the Alpha Centauri system three days later than I would have liked. The *RFIV* spent nearly twenty hours in a queue and an equal amount of time waiting for our cargo train to be affixed. BB guessed and figured out our game, at least in part. He knows we are towing something to the planet, and from what I can gather, he offered bribes to slow my ship down. It was an effective strategy.

Dio, Steven, and I are four days into our seven-day run to Praxis orbitals with our fourth delivery. This one will solidify their freedom from the criminal enterprise of Barnaby Badger.

"How's he looking?" I ask Dio over comms.

"His fleet, if you can call it that, is still nine days out," Dio says. "We are cutting it very close."

"Not much we can do about that now," I say. "We are committed to this cause." I grimace. "I received a warning that I have seven days left to report to Praxis Station."

"Have you?" Dio asked. "Heard from them yet?"

"No," I reply over comms. "It is still silent as a graveyard. I don't think I can count on their support."

"You can," Dio says. "You need only have a little faith."

I chuckle at the thought of an AI-controlled SkipJack lecturing a human on faith. We three try for games that night and the next day, but tension creeps into our very beings. Steven starts rattling off morbid haiku, and Dio becomes quiet and philosophical. As for me, well, I get pissed off as the tension builds.

"Is he singing?" Dio asks over the comms.

"Eh?" Steven asks. "Ah, sea shanties. Yep, he's about fully pissed off now."

"You know I can hear you both," I gripe back.

I resume my rendition of "drunken sailor" to pass the time. It was tense these last few days. Finally, our cargo is unloaded, and a small fleet of tugs begins delivering them to the surface.

My FEED system beeps, and I thumb it open. A man and a woman sit near each other; the two are the amalgamation of humanity since we delved into space. Only on earth, I am told, do you find non-homogenized people.

"Drover Thapa," the woman says with a mild lilt. "We wanted to thank you. We will do all we can to intercede with CSMS authorities on your behalf."

"Praxis Station has issued a warrant for your arrest," the man beside her says. Then, with a devilish smile, he continues, "But any ship that can make orbit is guiding down freight right now."

"Thank you, Satrap Milner," I say. "I've highlighted the shipments that contain the livestock as you've requested. These are far hardier than the breeds you currently have. They should acclimate well to your planet."

"You've freed us from the shackles of a tyrant," the woman says. "I wish we could do more."

"It is what it is," I say. "I made a choice knowing it would come to this."

My FEED system beeps again.

"I need to take this, Satrap Milner," I say.

I let the FEED to the Satrap of Praxis fade and open my displays in my pod. "Shit," is all I can say.

"They dropped some of their cargo and are letting it come to the planet on a ballistic trajectory," Dio says.

"That could destroy everything they've worked for on the planet and will likely damage the infrastructure of their orbitals," I say.

"Drover Thapa, it's time to make that FEED message again," Dio says. "We don't have a way to stop those containers, even if they are five days out."

"Vessels have laid intercept course for our trajectory," Steven says.

"Put it on screen," I say.

Tracking information plots flood across my pod's displays. I start singing again. BB has let loose the cargo of thirty-six vessels. Those thirty-six vessels are headed to cut off any route my ship might take. Those that are not can likely catch up to me in less common ways.

I spend an hour doing my best to find a suitable path; as I think I see one, a vessel would alter course to close it off. Barnaby Badger is coming for his revenge. I open my comms and send out a message of my own, and I pray they answer it. The hours whittle away as I make for the most expedient course out of the gravity well.

The *Raven's Flight IV* has legs, tremendous legs for its size. I can achieve velocities out of this system's gravity well that few ships can.

"How are we doing, Dio?" I ask over comms.

"We are humming along, but," Dio says.

"But what?" I ask.

"We are not going to outrun those three luxury cruisers," Dio says. "It ain't happening, Drover Thapa."

"I'm hoping we got longer legs than them," I say.

"That is not likely," Steven says.

My ship's FEED system beeps. I look at it and thumb it to my pod's display.

"Drover Thapa," BB says. "You had best turn yourself in."

"How's that balloon payment for Praxis Station coming?" I say. "It's due in a few hours."

"Oh," Barnaby says with a surprised smile. "Figured that out, did you? No worries about that, Mr. Thapa; I'll use your ship as collateral. You've proven its efficacy quite nicely for potential buyers."

"Not going to happen," I say.

I thumb my new plot into the RF's systems; it will buy me some time and space. Most of BB's ships can't match mine, and those that can are committed to their course of action.

"Drover Thapa, you are a wanted man," BB says. "I could have these constables hull your ship."

"BB, you are a piece of shit and still two days behind; outside of CSMS vessels, there isn't a railgun that can reach me," I say.

I cut the connection and engage the new course change. I open my feed and send a message to the Satrap of Praxis. I hope he can get the back side of the planet clear.

"You said the RF could do it," I say over comms.

"She can," Dio says. "She will be fine. We will pick up some speed, but will it be enough?"

"Not likely; if I can see this play, then so can any other competent pilot," I say. "BB will come up with an option, but for now, I don't see them closing the distance on us for at least a day."

"Get some rest, then, Drover Thapa," Dio says. "Steven and I have the ship."

I'm out cold when my FEED system beeps, and I thumb it open.

"This is CSMS Lieutenant Limbu. How did you acquire this Message address?" the young officer asks.

"Family," I grumble, rubbing my eyes. "My father and grandfather passed it to me."

"Who are you?" Lt. Limbu asks.

"Lalgahadur Thapa, Drover for Thapa Industries," I say. "I own the *Raven's Flight IV*."

"Wait," Lt. Limbu barks.

I am not put on hold; the FEED message cuts off. I get up, as I've been asleep for ten hours. We should be coming around the midpoint of our slingshot around Praxis. I hit the head and turn on the lights in my cabin.

My FEED beeps again as I start the water for coffee.

"Drover Thapa," a male voice says, "confirm you are who you say you are."

I snort and turn the feed to visual. My bloodline is a thousand years gone, but like old earth's population, our genes have not homogenized. My namesake's genetics have won out time and time again.

"I see," the man says, and his background stills into silence. His visual comes online. "Admiral Bai-Pun at your service. The *Gurkha* and her task group stands waiting for your coordinates." He pauses and says the words I thought I would never hear: "The Forty are here to serve."

"They are coming?" Dio asks.

"They are; it took them a few weeks to pull together their Fleet and people," I say. "I gave them the most recent data we have on BB's fleet and what tracking we have on the loosed containers."

"Good," Dio says. "What is the plan?"

I shift a new plot into play and put it into action. The grav engines and RF slips from the slingshot around Praxis.

"Lure BB away from the orbitals and Praxis," I say slowly. "He asked if you could help with the gate into the gravity well?"

I swear Dio's eyestalks twinkled in their sockets. I know he would be grinning if he had a mouth capable of smiling.

"It wasn't Steven, was it?" I ask.

"No," Steven says. "I am capable, but, no, it was not me."

A memory comes, and then another. I tilt my head and smile.

"Grand," I muse out loud. "Grandfather..." I turn to Dio, and I know he is beaming. "Dioscuri, you are Castor."

"Today, Drover Thapa, I am Dio, Engineer first class on the Raven's Flight IV," Dio says. "I will see to the gate."

"He said the Gurkha and her crew," I say, letting Dio decide if it is rhetorical or not.

"She is a fine vessel," Dio says. "You wait and see."

Seven hours later, I've got nowhere to run. BB's ships are hemming in the Raven's Flight. I might be faster, but it doesn't matter much now, as their vessels are heading away from the planet's orbitals.

A new FEED channel pings me, and I open it. "Lapdog," the man says in that tinny, reedy voice. His constable's uniform still bulges at its seams.

"Your voice annoys me," I say, setting him to auto-disconnect.

A second FEED pings me. "Hello, Badger," I say.

"Mr. Thapa," BB says, "now is not the time to be rude."

"Go to hell, whelp. You are in default on your loan. You own nothing here in this system; you have no authority here," I say.

"Oh, that may be a technicality," BB says. "But you are a wanted criminal, and Praxis Station has a significant bounty on you." He smiles. "No, it isn't enough to pay my default; it is enough for me to put a winning bid on that ship of yours when we return it to Praxis Station."

"I told you before, BB. That isn't going to happen," I say.

"I am curious, Mr. Thapa," Barnaby says. "What were you hauling?"

"Not much," I say. "As far as I am concerned, it's all just a load of shit."

BB's face twists, and he looks off to the side of his FEED pickup. I've chosen my words carefully. Morgan had always wanted to know what goods we hauled. In the beginning, I told her it was all the same shit. Meaning, it didn't matter, as it wasn't ours. Our job as Drovers was to deliver said shit from one side of humanity's space to the other.

"I see. Vulgarity aside, it is best that you come to a complete stop and allow our constable teams to board *my* vessel," BB says with a bit of venom.

"Yeah, go fuck yourself, Barnaby Badger," I say, and disconnect the FEED.

"Okay, Dio, I'm starting our breakaway run," I say.

"Yes, Drover Thapa," Dio responds.

A few moments later, the *RFIV* is putting speed back on, making a mad dash away from BB's main conglomeration of ships.

My FEED beeps again, and I thumb it to my pod's display.

"What is it?" I say.

I focus on my piloting; none of these local guys grew up bringing ships in and out of orbits, particularly not on a wind-swept world like Bandiss. I'm ten times the pilot they are, even if I am piloting a fast but fat pig.

"I tire of these games, Thapa," BB growls. "Drop your acceleration to zero and stand ready for boarding."

"You don't listen, do you, BB?" I ask. "So, here it is, and I won't repeat it: that is not happening."

"Lapdog, you will heave to and prepare for boarding," Barnaby screams into his FEED pickup.

Off to the side, in a separate display in my pod, a baker's dozen of new icons bloom to life. I smile and let my teeth show.

"Oh, Barnaby," I say. "How about *you* heave to and prepare for boarding?"

"You insolent bastard," BB screams.

"This is the CSMS Battlevessel *Gurkha* with task group Gamma. All vessels heave to and prepare for boarding. Any vessel caught releasing its cargo at the planet will be hulled," says a stern voice.

I had the distinct pleasure of watching BB's face drain as pale as a sheet. I heave to and allow my ship to come to a complete stop. Unfortunately, some do not, and they find the *Gurkha's* task group less than forgiving.

"Releasing cargo towards a planet is an act of piracy," that same stoic voice says.

A moment later, six lights wink out of existence on my display that plots all ships in the sector.

"Barnaby Badger, you are under arrest for extortion, piracy, and failure to pay your debts. Your indenture to the CSMS corporation has been broken," says Admiral Bai-Pun. "With the authority granted to me by the Chairman of CSMS, Raylan War, I assume control of the following systems: Praxis, Chandrys, and Varget."

It is nearly a day before I can bring my tiny ship alongside the massive *Gurkha* battle vessel. It is a behemoth of a long-forgotten war. All I can do is stare in awe.

"I don't often get to see her like this," Admiral Bai-Pun says. "She's as beautiful as the day I entered the Forty."

I turn to him and give him a gimlet stare. That ship is anything but beautiful. There are thousands of burns, scars, rents, and tears along its metallic hull. They're all patched, but it looks in no way beautiful.

"What did that?" I ask.

I know the answer, but I must hear it to believe it.

"We, the Forty, were in the Bandiss system during the war," Bai-Pun says. "Seven of them, seven ancient Masters, came for us." He turns to me and smiles a grim smile. "We are here, and they are not."

The quiet invades the main viewing deck. The beep from the electric kettle stirs us both back to reality.

"Tea?" I ask feebly.

"Please," Bai-Pun says, still watching his vessel as we circle it for the third time. "You didn't say what you delivered in your report, Drover Thapa."

I chuckle and catch him half-turning to look at me.

"You were an orbital?" I ask.

"Fleet kid," he says. "Planet?"

"Yes," I say, letting the tea leaves steep in the water. "I hauled shit." I smile and let out a second chuckle as he turns to me. "BB's enterprise was based on fertilizer. Nothing can be grown on Chandrys, Varget, or Praxis without kilotonnes of fertilizers. He squeezed the farmers for every credit. He subsidized the planetary governments with predatory loans."

"The worlds were terraformed?" Bai-Pun says, half-asking.

"There is terraforming to fill in some CSMS check boxes and terraforming to make a world habitable," I say cautiously. This man will be the governor of these three systems. "Praxis was the keystone to BB's empire. Praxis used the most fertilizer; otherwise, nothing humans use, eat, or need grows."

"I see," Bai-Pun says. "The *Raven's Flight IV*, and its long-range capabilities. You brought new solid soil additives."

"Just so," I say as I hand him his cup. "The microbes in the rabbit droppings will stabilize the soil on Praxis just like they did on Bandiss.

In five years, the planet will be overrun with rabbits and hares of every different type."

Bai-Pun's shoulders are heaving, and I hear a slight chuckle from him.

"You brought down the largest criminal empire in 200 years with a load of rabbit shit," Bai-Pun says with a laugh. "Are you married, Drover Thapa?"

"No, why?" I ask cautiously.

"My wife will want to make some introductions," The Admiral says. "There are few of us Forty left; a thousand years is a long time to keep our lineage strong. It would be good to have the Thapa name back in our ranks."

"I, uh," I mumble.

"Come to dinner aboard the *Gurkha*," Bai-Pun says. "You are amongst family now. Come meet them."

The airlock beeps, and a moment later, the inner airlock opens.

"Hello, Cas," Bai-Pun says.

"Admiral, I am Dio while here," Dio says.

"How is Raylan?" the admiral asks, ignoring Dio's comment.

"Well enough," Dio says. "He's in a board meeting finalizing your governorship and permanently assigning the task group to this sector. The Forty have served their indenture. You deserve a home."

"We appriciate that, Cas," the admiral says, "For those in the task group, it will give their families stability. For those in the Forty, we took our oaths long ago." He turns to look at both Cas and me. "War will come. It may not be in my lifetime, but it will come. Raylan knows that. He should also know Forty will be here to heed his call to arms."

"Raylan asked me to pass along his thanks," Dio says to me.

"Raylan?" I mumble, turning to Bai-Pun. "*The* Colonel Raylan War?"

"Yes," Dio and The Admiral answer together.

"We are Dioscuri," Dio says.

With that, he opens a tunnel gate and is gone.

"I'll miss him," Steven says. "Bye, Grandfather."

"You have a Steven that knows who Cas is?" Bai-Pun says.

I gesture to the table, and it seems I have as many questions as the admiral. As we talk, we sit and watch his beautiful behemoth of war slide by the viewport.

ALL Creatures Weird and Wonderful

David Bock

"How is she, Doc? Is she gonna be okay?" The man was actually twisting his hat brim. He was that anxious.

The veterinarian stood up with a sigh and walked over to the sink to wash his hands.

"We got to her in time, Mr. Martin. Barely, but in time. I wish you hadn't left it so late before calling. This could have been cleared up much quicker if you'd called us at the first signs."

Mr. Martin's face fell, and he seemed to shrink in on himself. "I know, Doc, I know. But she seemed to be getting better all on her own."

With another sigh, the vet dried his hands. "We've talked about this, Mr. Martin. In fact, I've talked about this with all the ranchers."

The tall, dark-haired vet led the larger man out of the exam room, leaving the animal in the capable hands of his assistant. They walked silently down the hall and around the corner to the consultation room, where the vet gestured Mr. Martin to a seat.

"I'm going to go over this with you again. I hope it's the last time, but honestly, I doubt it will be."

The rancher looked even more embarrassed, but squared himself in his seat, and his face took on an attentive expression.

"Rose's Blight is a very serious issue. Cattle *will* eat the flowers of the Ditch Digger plant if they find any. They're too prevalent and resilient to wipe out, so they'll always find some. When they do, the toxin gets into their system and starts its nasty work. If treated promptly, say within forty-eight hours, usually no permanent harm is done."

The vet leaned forward in his chair and punctuated the next point by tapping his index finger on the table.

"But if left untreated, your animals will sicken and die seven times out of ten. Do you really want to risk losing three-quarter of your herd, Mr. Martin?"

"No, sir." Coming from such a big, rough-looking man, his voice sounded remarkably meek.

"Then you must call us as soon as you see the first symptoms. Hell, if you even *suspect* they've gotten into a Ditch Digger patch, call us, anyway."

The vet calmed himself and softened his voice. "It's what we're here for, Mr. Martin. We care about your stock just as much as you do. It's why we became vets, after all."

"Yes, Doctor Sullivan, I understand. I won't let it happen again." The big man stood up and offered a large, scarred hand. "Thank you for saving Nancy. She means the worlds to me."

Doctor Sullivan wasn't a short man by any means, but in comparison to someone the size of Mr. Martin, he felt that way. They shook, the rancher being careful not to crush the smaller man's hand.

"All in a day's work, Mr. Martin, all in a day's work."

After he left, the vet allowed himself a couple of minutes to sprawl limply in his chair. Then got up and went to his next appointment.

A veterinarian's job was never done.

By the end of the day, Doctor Alex Sullivan had dealt with two more cases of Rose's Blight, four lacerations bad enough to need stitches, a broken leg, and half a dozen skin inflammations that had so far frustrated their ability to source. Doctor Foster and her team of techs had been hard at work, as well.

The colony had been in place for less than ten earth standard years, so everyone, human and animal both, was still adjusting to their new world, with all the challenges and mysteries that involved. The first few years had been the toughest, of course, but the settlers had worked hard and built a home from alien soil. Rarely did anyone go to bed hungry anymore, yet there wasn't as much of a cushion as people with a good grasp of risk assessment would prefer. They'd finally decided to decant the last of the frozen animal embryos only two years earlier.

There was supposed to be a follow-up ship within twenty years of their landing, but even at the time of the initial launch, that had been in doubt. They all knew another ship would be along eventually, based on the planned settlement program. They'd pass through the system for food supplies, if nothing else. That's why they were here, after all, but it might take generations instead of decades. The colonists needed to work with the expectation they were on their own. Due to the distances involved, the first they would know of another ship would be when it arrived in-system. There was a sky watch, but it was lower priority than day-to-day survival.

The initial settlers had been chosen for intelligence, hardiness, and their ability to innovate. A couple decades in cryogenic sleep hadn't changed that, but people were still people, and not all of them had adjusted to their new environment as well as the planners might have hoped.

Thankfully, very few of the challenges experienced by the colony had been seriously dangerous. Doctor Sullivan hoped the cattle rash going around wouldn't be, either.

Kat Ross, one of the senior vet trainees, stood outside the clinic for a few moments, listening to the sounds of insects. It was a new sound, only starting in the last few weeks, but it brought back otherwise fading memories of Earth, especially the sounds of cicadas and crickets in the Appalachian foothills of her childhood.

She shook her head and locked the clinic door for the night. They were all exhausted, trainees and techs both. Kat came back inside to find them spread out on various pieces of furniture in the staff lounge. Some of the more experienced ones were even sleeping.

"Anyone want some caff?" she asked, heading towards the dispenser.

A chorus of semi-desperate moans rose from the figures.

Kat spun around from the machine, her green eyes flashing, "Which one of you chaff heads didn't refill the reservoir? C'mon, own up."

After a moment of silence, Curtis Ackerman, one of the youngest trainees, cautiously raised a hand. "I'm sorry. I was about to when I got called to help with the bleeder. By the time that was done, I just forgot. I'm really sorry."

The speckles of dried blood on his clothes and in his hair gave vivid truth to his words.

"Okay, fine. But you owe me. Next time Mr. Tyson calls in, he's all yours." With a disgruntled sigh, Kat turned back to the machine and started the process of replacing the cartridge.

Curtis groaned, but wisely didn't say anything else. Mr. Tyson was the worst know-it-all in their area. He always acted like he knew more than the techs or trainees, and even the vets. Dealing with him was certainly appropriate penance for not refilling the life-giving caff dispenser.

A few days later, at a lull in the hectic pace of the clinic, Doctor Sullivan called everyone together for a quick staff meeting.

"Hey, folks, I know everyone's busy, so I'll keep this brief. We're seeing more of those rashes showing up, and they're starting to get worse. We're still no closer to figuring out where it's coming from. I put together a questionnaire for the ranchers who have stock with the relevant symptoms. It's on the network under Dermatitis, Unknown. Please make sure to talk to the ranchers and fill them out. We need to get a handle on this soonest. Thanks. Let's get back to work."

The trainees and techs filed out of the lounge, heading off to their various tasks. Doctor Joellen Foster, the other vet, hung back.

"What do you think is causing this skin rash, Alex?"

"I'm not sure, Jo. There's still so much we don't know about this ecosystem. I really wish the initial planetary survey had been more thorough."

"Yeah," she laughed. "You know what they say: if wishes were horses..."

They completed the saying together: "We'd have to treat them, too."

Chuckling, they headed out to their patients.

While the survey form helped with data gathering to some degree, no clear pattern emerged over the following days regarding what could be causing the skin irritation. It was continuing to slowly spread through the herds, and the ranchers were starting to get impatient at the lack of treatment.

Doctor Sullivan called another meeting, this time with just Doctor Foster along with the lead vet tech and trainee, Becky Jones and Alan Andrews, respectively.

"Things are getting worse. Nearly half the cattle we've examined recently are starting to show signs of developing this mystery rash. While not life-threatening yet, it's only a matter of time."

"Do you think it might have anything to do with the attempts to domesticate some of the local mammalian analogue species?"

"I don't see how it could, Alan. We've been doing that for a few years now with no ill effects. Except for the people who got bitten or scratched, of course. Still, it probably would be a good idea to take samples from them, anyway, to rule them out as vectors, if nothing else."

"Right, Doctor Foster. I'll see to it." Alan jotted a note on his tablet.

"The worst part is the lack of a pattern," Becky said. "Some animals are unaffected, while others on the same ranch have started developing lesions and even some minor secondary infections. We can treat the symptoms, but we need to figure out the root cause."

Alan added, "I don't think it's caused by something they're eating, like Ditch Digger was for Rose's Blight. More likely it's something environmental, but what?"

"I agree with you both," Doctor Foster replied. "We need more data, something that's in extremely short supply."

Doctor Sullivan nodded. "Absolutely. We do need more data and we're not going to get it sitting around the clinic waiting for the ranchers to call."

He turned to the other vet. "Jo, you and I will take turns going out to the different ranches and seeing what we can find. We'll need to take samples from as many animals as possible. Becky, Alan, pick out a few of your most observant people to accompany us. If need be, we can rotate more of them through this duty, as well."

The other three exchanged glances. Doctor Sullivan continued, "I know this will put a heavier load on everyone else while Doctor Foster or I are out, but we *have to* get a handle on this thing before it gets away from us."

The following days were exhausting for the entire clinic staff. The tempo of treatment didn't slacken, and with one of the vets and an assistant out on testing rounds nearly every day, it was almost overwhelming. But they managed.

Doctor Sullivan and Kat were out at the Dean ranch taking samples from the cattle. They were marking the vials to clearly differentiate between those who were affected by the rash and those who weren't, or at least weren't yet.

All day they'd been followed around by the Deans' grubber, a domesticated native canid analogue. Due to earlier environmental issues that had taken time to resolve, there weren't enough dogs to go around yet, but ranchers need companion animals. Even though they looked like a cross between a duck-billed platypus and a badger, the odd creatures fit the bill.

Kat was starting a draw on one of their final patients when Robert Dean, the rancher, came trotting into the barn.

"Hey, Doc. Got a call for you from the Jefferson ranch. Sounds like a calving problem."

"Thank you, Mr. Dean. We'll head right over."

"Come along, Benni." With a tip of his hat and a pleasant smile, Mr. Dean headed back to the never-ending job of running even a small homestead. The grubber, after a moment's confused hesitation, followed the rancher out.

As soon as the samples were complete, they gathered their equipment and the all-important sample case, loaded up the buggy, and entered Jefferson on the Nav System. As the vehicle lifted off, Kat took in the growing cloud cover through the canopy.

"Looks like we might be in for a right gully washer, Doc."

Doctor Sullivan glanced up from his tablet distractedly. "Huh? Oh." He made some adjustments to the routing instructions, and the buggy banked to take them around the worst of the oncoming storm.

The call from the Jefferson ranch was correct: it was a calving problem, and they'd arrived not a moment too soon. Two farmhands were sitting exhausted on the floor from their attempts to assist the cow with her delivery. Doctor Sullivan and Kat pulled on clean coveralls and shoulder-length gloves before examining their patient. The trainee also tied back her long, red hair to try and keep it out of her face.

The cow was smaller and the calf was large and badly presented. They needed to get its head around, and the sooner the better. The cow was almost as exhausted as the two men and considerably more agitated. Obviously she'd been at her efforts for a while.

After lubricating his arm and the patient, Doctor Sullivan attempted to reach in and find the calf's nose, but it was no use. The calf was too large, and the cow was too tense from the well-meaning but untrained efforts of the two men. There was no way he was going to get his arm in far enough to help.

"Classic dystocia, Kat, but my arm won't fit. Looks like it's time for you to shine. Reach in there and see if you can't get ahold of this little fellow's front legs."

Doctor Sullivan stepped to the side, taking hold of the tail so it didn't lash his assistant across the face. At that moment, the cow strained in an attempt to expel the calf. When nothing happened, she kicked, catching Doctor Sullivan on the thigh, a few inches above his knee.

His mouth formed a perfect "O," but no sound escaped as he staggered away from the cow and slid down the wall, clutching his leg. Kat and the two hands rushed over to help. Grabbing a pair of shears from their bag, Kat yanked open the side fasteners of his coveralls and cut his pant leg from the cuff nearly to his hip. A large bruise had started forming, and a small pressure cut in the middle was already oozing blood.

In a hoarse, choked voice, Doctor Sullivan gasped, "I'm okay, I'm okay." He turned his pale sweating face to Kat. "I *am* okay, aren't I?"

She carefully palpated the injured area, eliciting a muffled groan from her boss. "Nothing feels broken, Doctor Sullivan. I think it's just a really bad bruise." Kat quickly cleaned and bandaged the wound, then refastened the coverall leg.

"Help me up, please."

They got him to his feet, and he staggered back and forth a few times, sweat and tears streaming down his drawn face.

Finally, he lurched over to the cow, and taking hold of her tail again, said in an almost normal tone, "It's okay, girl. This can't be comfortable for you. Just take it easy and we'll have you right as rain in no time."

He nodded at Kat to continue. Less than an hour later, they were wiping down a live, active calf. Doctor Sullivan was making sure mother and child were healthy and comfortable while Kat slumped on a stool, sipping a glass of electrolytes and seltzer.

Doctor Sullivan limped over to her. "That was a really good bit of work, Kat. I'm glad you were here today."

She blushed and took the disinfectant wipe he offered. "Thanks, boss."

After cleaning her face and hands, she looked up at him. "Oh, yeah, I almost forgot. When I had my head pressed against her rump, I saw she started to develop a rash, and it looks like there's a bite in the middle of the affected area."

"Really? That's very interesting. I don't recall any of the question-naires mentioning bites. You up to taking another look?"

Kat stood up and gestured at the doctor's bandaged leg. "I am if you are."

After a closer examination of the cow (Masie, according to her name placard), they found clear indicators of several bites. The marks were very small and could've easily been missed, especially as the rash progressed.

The storm they'd flown around on their way here had struck while they were delivering the calf. It didn't look like it breaking up anytime soon.

They looked out the door of the barn. The rain was coming down so heavily they could barely see the glow from the house windows across the yard.

"Well, while we're here, we might as well examine the other cows for bites and take a set of samples."

The next day, Doctor Sullivan's leg was so swollen and painful that he could barely walk. By the time he hobbled over to the clinic, they'd already started seeing patients. Doctor Foster took one look at his pale and clammy face and started berating him.

"Dammit, Alex, you should be in bed. What are you thinking?"

"Hi, Jo." His smile was tight and clearly forced, his voice strained. "Have you talked to Kat this morning?"

"What? No. Well, yes, but just in passing. She told me a cow almost broke your leg yesterday and you'd be taking today off." She gave him another scolding look.

"Huh, she didn't tell me that. Or maybe she did. I was kind of delirious by the time we got back."

"Alex. Why. Are. You. Here?" Doctor Foster enunciated in an exaggerated manner.

"Right. I need to tell you something we discovered on the Jefferson ranch yesterday, Jo. I think it's important."

She looked unconvinced.

"It has to do with the rashes."

"Oh. Okay. Fine. But let's get you to a chair before you fall down."

"Yes, I'd like that very much, please."

Once they were settled in Doctor Foster's small office, Doctor Sullivan carefully propped his leg up with a sigh and relayed what he and Kat had learned at the Jefferson ranch.

"I think the rash is caused by a reaction to insect bites. We examined most of Mr. Jefferson's cattle, and the only ones with rashes had bites. As best we could tell, anyway. It's hard to see them, to begin with, and once the rash spreads, it's pretty much impossible, what with the inflammation."

Doctor Sullivan pulled up some images they'd taken of various cows.

"But why haven't we come across this before? We've been here almost ten years, Alex. Surely we'd have come in contact with whatever's causing this before now."

"I don't know, Jo. I just don't know. Regardless, that's what it looks like."

Doctor Foster pulled up records on another screen and started cross-referencing.

"Alex, did you notice the only animals *without* rashes are those we've treated for Rose's Blight?"

"What? Are you sure?"

She turned the screen so he could see the data.

He looked at the columns of information intently. "You're right, Jo. But it can't be that simple. Can it?"

"It's possible. Maybe something in the Rose's Blight treatment gives them immunity." Doctor Foster switched to another screen. "Hmmm, we're seeing two cows for other matters today that are noted to have the rash. Neither of them were treated for Rose's Blight." She typed for a few moments. "I'll tell the techs to test for antibodies, anyway, and if it's negative, give them the serum." She looked up from the screen. "It won't hurt them, other than putting them off their feed for a few days, and it'll give us more of the data we're sorely lacking." She stood up and looked at him sternly. "In the meantime, Alex, I want you to get that leg looked at, then go home and go to bed. Don't make me sedate you."

Alex realized this wasn't a battle he was going to win. "Yes, Doctor Foster. But please get the word out to watch for these bugs, whatever they are."

With Doctor Sullivan out recovering from his injury, trips to the different ranches for samples were put on hold. However, during that time, Doctor Foster authorized treating more cattle suffering from the mystery rash with the serum for Rose's Blight. The clinic kept a close watch on those animals, but no improvements to the inflammation were seen.

Samples of various insects were captured and brought in while all this was going on. Most were terrestrial bugs the colonists had brought with them, either intentionally or otherwise. The rest were aboriginal insect analogues they were already familiar with, except for one that not only they hadn't seen before, but there was no data in the survey on the species at all.

These were put in containment vessels with samples of what the trainees hoped was appropriate food, and set aside for further research.

A few days after he came off the sick and injured list, Doctors Sullivan and Foster were sitting in his office sipping mugs of caff while going over the latest analysis from the samples.

"Nothing, nothing, and more nothing." Doctor Sullivan tossed his tablet onto the desk with a clatter. "I don't get it, Jo, there has to be something we're missing."

Doctor Foster sat quietly, staring deep into her mug, brow crinkled in thought. "Hmm? Clearly, yes. But what? Have any people come down with this rash?"

"Not that I'm aware of. We should put in a call to the medical center to check."

Doctor Foster nodded and made a note. "I'll take care of it. What else haven't we considered?"

"I'm still positive it has something to do with Rose's Blight, but the serum hasn't done anything..." His voice trailed off and he suddenly sat up and started typing intently, calling up additional reports and running comparison queries.

"Maybe not the serum, or the Blight, but the Ditch Digger itself. Where did we save that analysis?"

"Alex, if you're thinking there might be some toxin left in their system, that's exactly what the serum is supposed to take care of."

"Not the toxin, exactly, but yes, some form of residue. There it is. Now, what if we run a comparison between this and..." His eyes darted between the two data sets.

"There it is! Look, Jo, look!" He spun the screen around and she leaned forward, caff momentarily forgotten.

"You're right, there is something there. Do you think if we can isolate that it may help with the rash?"

"Possibly. At the very least, we should be able to get a deterrent for the bugs, possibly a prophylactic against the initial reaction to the bites. If we're really lucky, yes, an actual treatment for the rash."

The vets, trainees, and techs were all exhausted, the ranchers were worried, and they were all frustrated and irritable. It started coming out in different ways. One night that week, someone threw a rock at one of the clinic's windows. The wire mesh held, but the pane was badly cracked and had to be replaced. No one admitted to the act, but it was clearly intentional.

The following day, Becky had to break up an argument between Tiffanie Gray and Matt Crowe that nearly turned physical. They were two of the clinic's most promising youngsters and usually the closest of friends. In normal times, they routinely engaged in shenanigans together, to the amusement of their fellows. Pretty much the entire clinic staff was on edge and likely to flare up without warning. However, with Doctor Sullivan back at work, sample-taking at the ranches could resume.

Emily Nelson, who had comm duty, tapped on the open door to Doctor Sullivan's office. "Hey, Doc? We got a call from the Robertson ranch. They've a cow they think needs to be put down."

Doctor Sullivan's stomach clenched; this was the call every vet dreaded. Losing a cow was hard, especially for the smaller ranchers, where any loss was a serious blow.

"Did they say what the problem was?"

"No, just that they wanted you to come out as soon as you can."

"Right. Do you know who's on the rotation to assist?"

"Looks like Sara is up next, Doc."

"Which one? Sara or Sarah with an H?"

"Sara Dickinson."

"Thanks. Can you let her know to meet me in the vehicle park in about five minutes?"

"Sure thing. Please pass my sympathies on to the Robertsons."

"Will do. Thanks again, Emily."

After she left, Doctor Sullivan sat staring blankly into the distance for a few moments, then shook himself and went to gather the required supplies for this most undesirable of tasks.

When they landed at the ranch, Mr. Robertson was nowhere in sight. They were met by his wife, Amie, who looked tired and dejected. The grubber at her side seemed to have picked up on her mood. Unlike many of the other ranchers, the Robertsons were a true partnership. Both of them were capable of handling nearly any job on the small homestead. One result of their high level of capability was they rarely called the clinic unless things had gotten very serious.

Doctor Sullivan got out of the buggy and walked over to the rancher, while Sara got their cases out of the back.

"Mrs. Robertson, I'm so sorry." For a moment he couldn't think of anything else to say. "Emily Nelson sends her sympathies."

The shadow of a smile drifted across Amie's face, but was gone all too soon.

"She's in the isolation barn. For all the good it's done. C'mon, Nell." She turned and started walking towards a small outbuilding, shoulders slumped and feet almost dragging. The grubber slunk along behind her.

She opened the door and pointed. "She's down there at the end." Her voice quivered slightly.

Doctor Sullivan and Sarah walked to the last stall and looked in. What they saw shocked them. The cow was almost entirely covered in rashes, and her skin was stretched over her bones. She took no notice of their arrival, even when they inserted a thermometer to take her temperature. She just stood there, ears and tail twitching, staring at the wall in front of her.

"Mrs. Robertson, how long has she been like this?"

Amie stepped inside the door, but didn't come any closer. She replied in a defeated tone, "The rash started about a month ago. We tried all the usual treatments and even some old folk remedies. Nothing helped for long. A few days ago, she stopped eating, the flesh just melted right off her, and the rash spread even faster. We knew it was time."

"Why didn't you call us sooner?"

"To do what? We've heard through the network you don't have an effective treatment."

There was no accusation in her voice, just a flat statement of facts. Shame tore at Doctor Sullivan's heart. This was his fault; it was his responsibility to keep these animals healthy. This poor, wretched creature was paying the price for his failure.

He and Sara took the usual samples, then did what was necessary to end the animal's suffering.

"Would you like us to call..."

"No. No thank you. We'll take care of her ourselves."

He rested his hand on her shoulder for a moment. Then Doctor Sullivan and Sara packed their cases and flew back to the clinic in silence.

Two days later, when Doctor Sullivan arrived at the clinic first thing in the morning, he found a mix of techs and trainees crowded in front of the entrance.

"What's the problem? Is the lock misbehaving again?" he called out good-naturedly.

Silently, they moved aside. Painted on the clinic door were the words "Cattle Killer" in big red letters. Alex's heart sank. This was exactly what they didn't need.

Doctor Foster's arrival broke the tense silence. She took one look at the vandalism and her mouth tightened. "Okay, folks, let's get inside. Terry, Marie, grab some rags and solvent and see if you can't get that cleaned up." There was a brief pause.

"You heard the doctor, let's get our rears in gear!" Alan barked out, moving to unlock the door.

Behind them, Alex and Joelle exchanged an anxious look.

"Redecorating, Doc?" Mr. Martin asked with a concerned smile.

"Huh? What's that, Mr. Martin?"

"You've got a couple of kids out there making the doors a lovely pale pink."

"Ah, that. No, just a little misunderstanding. What can I help you with today, Mr. Martin?"

"Nothing serious, only another batch of mineral supplements and antibiotics." The big man leaned in and lowered his voice. "Listen, Doc, there's muttering among the ranchers. Some of them don't think you're taking this rash business seriously." At Doctor Sullivan's offended expression, he held up a hand. "Not me. I know you and your people have been tearing your hair out over it, but people are worried about their herds. The margin's thin for most of us. Real thin for some. Folks are scared; some are on the verge of panic. Scared folks don't think straight. I just thought you should know."

Doctor Sullivan stared at him for a moment. "Thank you for telling me, Mr. Martin. I can't say I'm surprised, but I *am* disappointed in your fellow ranchers. Please pass on to them, if you can, that we're doing everything possible to come up with an effective treatment."

"I will, Doc, and I know you'll come up with something. No matter what anyone else thinks, I have faith in you." He took the requested supplies and left with a friendly nod.

The rancher's words echoed in Alex's head. He got up and went to find Joelle. She needed to hear this.

After tapping on the door to her office, Doctor Sullivan relayed his conversation with Mr. Martin.

"This is exactly what I was worried about. We still have so much to learn about this world. It took us longer than it should have to find an effective treatment for Rose's Blight, and we lost too many livestock before we did. I don't want to make the same mistake with this rash."

"I agree completely, Alex. By the way, I heard back from the med center: no colonists have reported anything like the rash we're seeing on the cattle. I also checked our records here. No cases in dogs or grubbers, either. It looks like whatever it is, only the livestock are affected."

"One more piece of data for the puzzle, though I'm not sure how it helps us. Thanks, Joelle. Maybe something dietary makes them more susceptible?"

Doctor Sullivan left her office deep in thought.

Doctor Sullivan took the next day off from treatment rounds and spent it entirely in the lab. The following day, he brought in a fresh sample of Ditch Digger in an isolation unit. Everyone gave him a wide berth as he walked it through the halls.

Once in the lab, he carefully took clipping from the flowers, leaves, stems, and roots of the dangerous plant, which was not only unappealing to human taste buds, but it was also nearly as poisonous to people as it was to cows.

"There's a connection between immunity to the rash and Ditch Digger, I know it," he muttered.

"What's that, Doc?"

He looked up. Alan was standing at the next station with an inquisitive smile on his face.

"Oh, nothing. Just talking to myself."

"Understood, Doc. Just let me know if I can help."

"I'll be sure to do that. Thanks, Alan."

Doctor Sullivan started feeding the samples into the input slot of the analyzer. He surreptitiously crossed his fingers.

Over the next few days, he ran a wide series of tests and experiments on both the plant and the captured bugs. It wasn't enough to find the aspect of Rose's Blight residue that seemed to prevent the cattle from suffering from the rash. He had to isolate and refine that element into a safe treatment, maybe even a prophylactic. He came into the clinic early and left late, often putting in twelve and fourteen-hour days in the lab.

While Doctor Sullivan was burying himself in the lab, Doctor Foster was called out to put down more cattle. Things were looking desperate.

Finally, there was a breakthrough.

"Son of a bitch!" Doctor Sullivan exclaimed, leaning back from the scanner and rubbing his burning eyes. His outburst drew the shocked attention of everyone else in the lab. He very rarely raised his voice or used strong language.

He grinned sheepishly at being the focus of everyone present. "Or should I say, eureka?"

After a pause to process the potential meaning of this, Alan hurried over. "Did you find it?"

"I think so, and as I suspected, it's from the Ditch Digger."

"What? How?"

Doctor Sullivan pulled the chemical structure data up on a screen.

"After extracting the residue from samples of cattle we'd treated for Rose's Blight and cross-referencing them with samples from the plant, I filtered and made a few modifications. It should work both as a repellent to the parasites as well as providing a level of immunity to the irritant in their bites. If we're lucky, it should also counteract the chemical reaction that causes the rash and allow normal dermatological treatments to be effective."

"Should, Doc?"

"Yeah, should." Doctor Sullivan looked a bit sheepish, some of his excitement fading. "Until we start testing on live animals, we won't know for sure."

Alan blinked. "Good luck selling an untested treatment to the ranchers."

A slightly mischievous smile spread across Doctor Sullivan's face. "Oh, it won't just be me who'll need luck, Alan."

It took a moment for realization to sink in. "Aw, crap."

Over the following days, members of the clinic staff, veterinarians and trainees alike, met with as many ranchers as they could to tell them about the new treatment. This was received with a variety of reactions, generally ranging from neutral to poor. As a whole, the ranchers were a traditional lot and didn't take to new techniques and treatments quickly or easily.

It didn't help that some of the trainees weren't as polished in their presentation as they could have been and not as diplomatic in their answers to questions as one might have hoped.

Curtis stood in front of the group of four ranchers. He shifted back and forth uncomfortably. Public speaking was not his forte; he preferred dealing with animals, not people.

He ran his fingers through his hair again, unintentionally causing it to spike up and make him look even younger than he was. Then Curtis squared his shoulders and faced his audience.

"Hi, folks. Um, we think we found a treatment for the rash that's been going around."

"You think?" Of course Mr. Tyson would catch that.

"Um, yes. It's a new treatment and, um, we need to do some more testing to, um, to make sure it works. I mean, to make sure it's effective."

"You don't even know if it works?" Mr. Carter this time.

"That's not what I meant." He glanced at his notes. "It should repel the parasites and give some immunity to the bites. It should also allow the usual dermatological treatments to be more effective against the rash."

"I'm hearing a lot of 'shoulds,' young man," Mrs. Morgan said, not unkindly.

"It's a new treatment. Like I said, we need to do more testing."

"What's this treatment based on?" Mr. Tyson again.

"Um, Doctor Sullivan used an extract from Ditch Digger to..."

"Ditch Digger? You want to infect our cattle with Ditch Digger?" Mr. Carter nearly exploded out of his seat.

"No, sir. It's an extract, but it's not harmful."

"How sure are you of that?" A familiar smug smile formed on Mr. Tyson's face. "How much testing has been done?"

"I, I don't know. We're asking for volunteers..."

"So it's still an experimental treatment? Not proven?" Mr. Tyson's eyebrow arched.

"Um, yes. That's what I said. We need to do more testing and, um, we'd like folks with affected cattle to, ah, to let us try it out on them."

Mr. Tyson looked at his fellow ranchers. "I think we've heard enough for today." He turned back to Curtis. "I, for one, won't be 'volunteering' any of my cattle for your experimental toxin...I mean treatment." He gave his smile again and walked out, followed by the others. Mrs. Morgan gave Curtis a sympathetic pat on one slumped shoulder as she passed.

The ranchers were, of course, concerned about their stock, especially those like the Robertsons, who'd already lost animals to this scourge. They were all distrustful of this new treatment to some degree or another, primarily because of its source. The better part of a decade of warnings about the dangers of Ditch Digger had sunk in all too well.

Even though there was an effective treatment for Rose's Blight, the ranchers still lost a few animals every year, either because the treatment was administered too late, or it simply didn't work, for some reason.

Calls to the clinic actually dropped off after the first series of mini-seminars. Some of the ranchers still came in for the usual mundane treatments, but they were much less talkative and social with the staff.

The tension among the students and techs that had started to ease following Doctor Sullivan's breakthrough ratcheted back up, which also affected interactions with the ranchers.

Things came to a head just before sunset later that week.

A group of ranchers had assembled outside the clinic. Doctor Sullivan brushed past his staff and looked out the window at the surly gathering.

"This doesn't look good. I'm going to go out there and see if I can talk them down." There were immediate cries against this idea. Doctor Sullivan held up his hands. "I've got to. If we don't defuse this before it comes to a head, we could have a riot on our hands. I want you all to stay inside." More calls of disagreement. "No, if we go out there as a group, that could be perceived as a threat. We really don't want that."

He took another look out the window. "Somebody get in touch with Doctor Foster and let her and her assistant know not to come back to the clinic tonight. If anything happens to me, lock the doors and call the constabulary, I guess."

Only opening the door wide enough to pass, he slipped outside, his tension apparent by a slight increase in the limp that was probably permanent.

"Hi, folks, what can I do for you?"

After some louder muttering and angry glares, Mr. Hawkins took a step forward. "We want you to stop messing around and cure our cattle!"

"That's what we're trying to do, Mr. Hawkins." Doctor Sullivan was as nervous as he could remember, even worse than when he took his board certification or treated his first actual patient. He tried his best to keep his voice level and his manner calm and non-aggressive. "As I've told you, the treatment we've developed…"

"You're talking about infecting them with Rose's Blight!" An angry murmur spread through the crowd. "After all your talk about how it would kill our cattle, you want to pump that poison into them!"

The clinic staff had started filtering out behind him. There was nothing Doctor Sullivan could do to get them back inside without making a tense situation worse.

"The treatment is an extract from the Ditch Digger plant, yes. But Digitalis is an extract from Foxglove and Atropine from Belladonna—both very useful drugs made from poisonous plants."

Another voice spoke up from near the back of the crowd. Doctor Sullivan recognized the pompous tone of Mr. Tyson. "And how many died from those drugs before scientists figured out the right dosages? How many died from your serum for Rose's Blight, for that matter?"

Mr. Hawkins's face set and he took a step forward, hands clenched into fists.

The large form of Mr. Martin bulled through the crowd, moving anyone who didn't get out of his way by brute force. Once in the lit area in front of the building, he stopped a few steps forward of the vet clinic staff and turned to face his peers, his hands on his hips and his elbows splayed out aggressively. He leaned forward, chin jutting, moustache almost bristling.

"What is *wrong* with you people? Do you *really* think Doc Sullivan, that *any* of them, would do *anything* to knowingly harm an animal? Burt, remember when Doc Foster stayed up all night treating your bull with that torsion? Garry, what about a few months back when your Masie near broke Doc Sullivan's leg with a kick? Didn't even raise his voice to her, did he?" He glared around at the gathering. "Do *any* of you *not* have a story like that? Where the docs or their techs went above and beyond to save one of our animals?" He turned his head and spat. After another glare at the crowd, he continued, his tone conversational but loud enough to carry clearly to everyone present.

"Doctor Sullivan, I'd like to volunteer my herd for testing with this new treatment of yours." The look he directed at the crowd of ranchers challenged any of them to say a word. None of them took him up on that dare.

With a few last mutters and dark looks, they started to disperse, the figures fading into the darkness as they headed to their vehicles and from there, hopefully, to their homes.

Doctor Sullivan let out a deep breath, and his knees went wobbly for a moment at the release of tension.

"Thanks, Mr. Martin. I didn't like where that was going."

The rancher nodded. "My pleasure, Doc." Then, with a tight smile, he asked," You really think this treatment of yours will work?"

"I do." He gestured at the retreating ranchers. "In fact, I think I just bet my life on it."

The big rancher chuckled and patted Doctor Sullivan firmly on the back. "Like I said before, I have faith in you, Doc. I know you won't let us down. I'm just sorry I didn't get here sooner."

Then he, too, turned and walked into the gloom.

The next morning, Doctor Sullivan, along with a trainee, Tiffanie, and a tech, Matt, flew out to the Martin ranch to start treatments. Each animal was first tested for antibodies from the Rose's Blight treatment, just to be sure. As expected, all the ones with a rash hadn't been treated.

Matt shook the vial of blood and reagent, noting the lack of color change. "Another negative, Doctor Sullivan."

"Thanks, Matt." Tiffanie handed him an injector.

"Three units of— What are we calling this stuff, anyway, Doc?"

Doctor Sullivan looked closely at the reservoir. "I confirm three units." He turned and injected the cow. "I hadn't actually thought about that. I guess we do need to come up with a name other than 'this stuff' if we're going to bring the other ranchers around. Any suggestions, you two?"

"Sullivan's Balm?" Matt said hesitantly.

"It's not a Balm, blockhead." Tiffanie chuckled and gave him a playful punch on the shoulder. He grinned and rubbed his arm. "But Matt does have one thing right: your name should be on it."

"Sullivan's Serum?" Matt suggested with a grin, quickly moving out of Tiffanie's reach. She mock-glared at him and made a rude gesture. They both laughed.

Doctor Sullivan made a noncommittal noise.

After all the recent tension, it did Doctor Sullivan's heart good to hear the techs falling back into their old, irreverent behavior. The good-natured bantering continued as they injected the remaining animals.

Once every affected cow at Mr. Martin's ranch had been treated, the only thing to do was wait for results. Both doctors, as well as some of the trainees and techs, found themselves haunting the comm room at odd hours. Eventually, one of the duty techs put a sign on the door:

TREATMENT UPDATES WILL BE SHARED IMMEDIATELY OFF-LIMTS TO ALL BUT ON-DUTY PERSONNEL

There were some chuckles about the misspelling, but it didn't do much to relieve the expectant apprehension.

As the weekly staff meeting broke up and the veterinary trainees and techs filed out of the cafeteria, Joelle motioned for Alex to wait.

"I finally got word back from the rangers."

"Rangers?" Alex's brow creased in confusion.

"Yes. I'd asked them to do some longer-range survey to see if we could figure out where the insects came from. Remember?"

"Oh, right, right. Sorry."

"No problem." She gave him an understanding smile. "Anyway, even though they're pretty busy with their regular survey work, they took some time for us. The rangers found no signs at all of the insects to the south, but plenty of evidence to the north. Decreasing, but still detectable, as far as they went. It's not conclusive, of course, but it looks like our little pests are migratory."

"Huh. I guess that could explain why we've never encountered them before. I wonder how far they go and how long until they come back?"

"No telling, but it's clearly been no more than ten years since they passed this way, and hopefully at least that long before they're back. Not that it'll be as much of an issue if and when they do, what with the treatment you developed."

"It's not *my* treatment, no matter what Tiffanie and Matt say. It was a real team effort. Everyone contributed."

They left the room and went back to work.

Towards the end of the week, Marie Davies came hurrying into the cafeteria. "Doctor Sullivan, Mr. Martin called. He needs you there right away. He said it's about Doralee."

Doctor Sullivan's stomach clenched around the food he'd just eaten. Doralee was the worst affected cow on Mr. Martin's ranch. Not quite as far gone as the first poor creature they'd had to put down at the Robertsons', but probably only a few days short of that. Mr. Martin had been dosing her with appetite enhancers and nutrient injections to try and stave off the inevitable. She'd all but stopped eating the morning before they'd treated her, but they thought she'd had a chance.

"Did he give any details?" he asked, heading for the lunchroom door.

"No, Doctor. Just that you should hurry."

Alan met Doctor Sullivan in the dispensary and helped him grab whatever he thought might help.

"I'm coming with you, Doc."

"You're not on the roster..." He trailed off when he saw the stubborn look on the younger man's face. "Right, let's go."

They headed out to the vehicle lot, hopped in a buggy, ran a quick preflight check, and took off. The trip out to the Martin ranch was quiet and tense.

The landing was a little fast and the small craft bounced on its oleo struts before settling.

"Sorry, sorry."

"It's okay, Doc."

A stone-faced Mr. Martin was waiting for them at the edge of the landing area, his dog Zeke and grubber Niles by his side.

"Gentlemen, this way." Without another word of greeting or even a humorous comment about the landing, he headed toward one of the barns. Doctor Sullivan and Alan felt the weight of failure settle on their shoulders. They followed after, Doctor Sullivan still limping slightly from his injury at the Jefferson ranch.

Mr. Martin led them down the aisle and stopped at Doralee's stall.

"What do you think of that?" His voice was grim.

Doctor Sullivan stepped around the bigger man and forced himself to take a look. It was Doralee, thinner, but still alive. After a moment, he realized she was unconcernedly eating. The rash, while still present, was clearly less inflamed and even showed some signs of clearing around the edges.

Mr. Martin started laughing. "Oh, Doc. If only you could see your face right now."

Alan pushed past the two men to see what was happening. When comprehension struck, he bent over like he'd been punched in the abdomen, steadying himself on the partition. He glared at the rancher.

"Not cool, Mr. Martin, not cool."

"I know and I'm sorry." Mr. Martin wiped tears from his eyes, still laughing. "But when I came out here this morning, I expected to find a dead cow." He grabbed the other two men around the shoulders and hugged them. "You did it. You saved my Doralee. I knew you would come up with a cure, but I didn't have much hope for her. Thank you. Thank you so much."

Zeke and Niles were gamboling playfully, the dog jumping up to sniff and lick at their faces. The grubber, not being built for jumping, rubbed the top of his head against their calves and shins.

Doctor Sullivan attempted to regain his composure. He felt lighter than he had in weeks. "That was a dirty trick, Mr. Martin, but understandable, given the circumstances." He reached down for one of the cases he'd dropped in his shock. "While we're here, we might as well give her a good check-up."

Word of the success at the Martin ranch spread like wildfire. The ranchers who'd been neutral to cautiously optimistic started calling for appointments to get their cattle treated. Once that dam broke, the remaining holdouts started coming around. Eventually, even Mr. Hawkins and Mr. Tyson were convinced and allowed treatment of their surviving cattle.

The following days were hectic beyond almost anything the clinic had dealt with since the colony was established. Both veterinarians and every single trainee and tech were taking turns going out to the ranches to test and treat as many infected animals as possible. They started hearing from the ranchers whose herds were treated after the success with Mr. Martin's that they were already seeing signs of improvement.

The mood at the clinic was one of exhausted exhilaration. Tired and smiling faces were seen everywhere in the building.

When Mr. Martin called, saying he thought one of his cows might have gotten into a patch of Ditch Digger and he'd like them to come out and check, it was like icing on a particularly fine cake. Doctor Sullivan decided to hand this case over to the newly confirmed Doctor Kat Ross.

GETTING THE HERD IN

Richard Cartwright

I cy rain splattered the brim of his Stetson as he looked over the herd placidly foraging the groundcover as they moved towards the domelike structure, unconcerned with the whistling noises overhead. Hank Thornton looked up into the butterscotch sky at the streaks of white overhead. He remembered as a kid back on Earth camping out in Montana, looking and seeing a unique type of meteor shower. Martian meteor showers were man-made and comprised of ice asteroids harvested from the outer system and de-orbited into the atmosphere, both to thicken it and to provide water to the still-dry planet.

Just as he was about to urge the shaggy bison to pick up the pace, the wind shifted, and several shaggy heads popped up and made a beeline to the entrance. He moved to the bundled-up man sitting in a tracked vehicle looking at a tablet.

"How many are we short?" Hank demanded of his foreman.

"With the fifteen head you just brought in, just one." Gesturing to the shaggy bison joining the others at the feedbunk of the radiation shelter that the Montana transplants called a feedlot, the man added, "Actually, two if she has already dropped the calf." Bill Clifton lifted his hat to scratch his bald pate, but quickly slapped it back on his head as a gust of cold wind slammed into the pair.

At least it pushed the smell that seven hundred feeding bovines in an enclosed area inevitably generated. Unfortunately, it also pushed away the slight heat that the fresh manure produced, as well. Martian winters were far warmer after sixty years of terraforming than the lethal conditions the first settlers experienced, but it made February in Montana feel like Key West Florida in comparison.

"Let me get the wind out of my face." Bill fiddled with the extra hand controls that allowed him to operate the tracked wheelchair without the legs frostbite had taken away when Hank was a kid to turn his back to the wind.

Hank blew through his respirator as he flicked the reins to turn his own mount. He didn't really need it to breathe, as the Martian air had been thick enough to live on for a while now. He needed it to preheat the thin, frigid atmosphere surrounding him, so each intake of breath didn't feel like icicles poking into his lungs. The heated balaclava was doing its best, but getting his face out of the wind was a good idea.

"B901. Figures. She always hides when she gives birth."

"Last fix on her was near Haskin Ridge." Bill looked at his tablet. "I don't see her now. She's probably in the dead zone near Shelter Nine. Hey, where are you going, Hank?"

"After the cow." Hank pulled the reins of Boris, his Yakut Quarter Horse hybrid. The thick winter coat was a pain to brush out, but the animal was a blend of the best cold survival features of its Siberian ancestors, along with the size and innate ability of a ranch horse inherited from his American Quarter Horse side.

"Are you crazy? The shield is scheduled to go down in three hours. The last advisory estimates at least ninety minutes to swap components and another three hours to return to full strength. While it's down, the radiation is going to be lethal after twenty minutes' exposure. It's just one animal. Not worth your life."

"Two if she's already dropped the calf. B901 is a steady breeder. We really can't afford to lose her. It's a thirty or forty-minute ride to Haskin Ridge. If I don't have them in an hour, I'll head back. Plenty of time."

"Don't cut it too close. Nobody wants to work for a boss that glows in the dark. "

"Jessie wants kids. I plan to keep the swimmers safe. I will check in every fifteen."

Thirty-five minutes and two check-ins later, Hank was considering giving up. He had checked several gullies thick with forage nourished by the regular rain, which was in turn created by the meteor showers of ice asteroids that were carrying water to Mars for the first time in millions of years. Hank noticed the streams were crusting over with ice as the temperatures dropped. He dialed up the heat in his overalls and boot footies another notch. He had already maxed out his respirator preheater, and it was losing the battle to keep the cold from biting his lungs.

He looked out over the gray-green plains covered by the genetically engineered lichen that had completely overrun the planet and left young people scratching their heads when older people called Mars the "Red Planet." He was looking forward to the growth spurt that the radiation which originally nourished the plants in the early days of terraforming was going to cause. Right now, there was not of sign of the missing cow.

He strained his ears again. Nothing but the wind. As a kid riding fence lines with his dad, he remembered the rich tapestry of sound the Montana countryside offered. Birdsong, rustling leaves and pine needles, coyotes and wolves mixed with the scampering of rabbits in the brush complemented the sounds of cattle. Even in the dead of winter.

Mars was so quiet. The planetary ecologists had been promising trees "next year" for over a decade now. Hank hoped that his hypothetical grandchildren might get to smell the wood fires of his youth. The wind had no leaves to rustle. With the bison herds rounded up and under cover, the only sounds around him were the *clop, clop* of Boris's hooves, the occasional snort of his mount, and the whistling of his respirator.

A soft, almost bleating sound drifted from his right. A shaggy head popped up out of the break in the wall of what had probably been an impact crater that NASA had named El Dorado during the Spirit rover exploration back in the early 2000s, but now served as a gathering place for the herds to get out of the wind and take advantage of the pool of water in the bottom. He had chased a young bull and twelve cows out of there hours ago. For the umpteenth time, he reminded himself to build a gate across the narrow gap. The cow tossed her head from side to side, looking mystified as to where the rest of the herd had gotten off to. She turned her attention to Hank and snorted.

A newborn calf soon joined the cow. His experienced eye informed him the little beast couldn't be more than a few hours old. He or she was still unsteady on four feet. The calf was going to be a problem. No way the newborn was going to keep up for the trip back to the feedlot. Hank considered trying to rope the calf and sling it across Ivan and hightail it back to safety. Looking at the cow continuing to give him and Boris a wary eye, Hank sighed. He had serious doubts that the mama would sit still for her newborn to be trussed up and tossed about. Bison cows were very protective of their young.

The squeal of his comm link snapped him out of his ruminations.

"Hank! Can you hear me?"

"Loud and clear, Bill. I found B901. She dropped the calf. Trying to figure out how to get them home."

"Forget them! We just got a report from Musk City that there's a problem with the EM shield and they can't guarantee that it will stay up any longer than forty-five minutes from now. Maybe less. You need to ride hard and get back here. Now!" Part of Hank marveled at the naked fear in Bill's normally unflappable voice. This must be bad.

Hank looked at the cow and calf. Turning to flee, his eye caught a broadcast tower and domed structure. Shelter Nine. An idea formed in his head.

"Bill, I see Shelter Nine. I can make it there in a few minutes. The terraformers built them as radiation shelters. If the EM field is as shaky as it sounds like, then I would be better off riding the storm out there than taking my chances getting back in time."

There was a long pause on the line. "I didn't think of that. Yeah, that's your best bet. Get there now. I just listened to the latest update, and I really don't think that you have as long as I told you before. The engineers got replaced by some guy from 'public affairs.' The bureaucratese he was spewing sounded like the southbound product of a northbound bull."

"Already got them moving towards the shelter."

"You're in luck. It was just provisioned with the new MRE series. It also has fodder for horses. The cow is going to love having the hay and oats."

"So no classic Chicken a la king?"

"Nary a one. I remember my great-great-grandfather warning me that combining meals ready to eat and Chicken a la king was proof that the demons infesting government procurement offices didn't realize that there were still people around who remembered the first time they tried to curse humanity."

"I will let you know what the new stuff tastes like once I get under cover. I'll keep calling every fifteen minutes in the meantime."

"Good. I will let you know if anything changes."

Ten minutes later found the cow and calf two hundred meters closer to the shelter, now six hundred meters away. Martian bison have all the benefits of their Terran ancestors: cold tolerance, ability to thrive on a diet that would leave a Holstein sickly at best, and general all-around hardiness. The price was that they ate constantly to feed their metabolism. Hank reflected. Every attempt to nudge the cow along faster failed. Worse, the sky was getting the streaks of blue that told him the sun was setting. Radiation aside, Hank knew he couldn't take the cold of the Martian night. Nor could the livestock. The herds survived because they bunched together for warmth in places out of the wind. His communicator beeped.

"Hank, are you undercover?"

"About six hundred meters away. About another thirty minutes away at the rate the cow and calf are moving."

"You have twenty minutes. At best. They keep moving the shutdown time."

"Understood. Give me a minute."

Another gust of frigid wind slammed into him, pushing him towards the shelter and reminding him that time was short. He looked at the pair. They were moving towards the shelter, but oh so slowly. He cursed; they were so close. The only thing worse than not finding them at all was having a ringside seat to their deaths. No, worse would be making Jessie a widow or tied to a man who couldn't give her healthy children.

Bill's words from earlier whispered in his mind. "It's just one animal. Not worth your life."

Something else nagged at the back of his mind. Looking back at the cow, he saw her hike her tail and take a dump. The wind pushed the smell towards him. The herd scenting the feedbunk. They moved right along once they got the smell of the rich food.

"Gallop, Boris," he said, pressing his knees into the horse's sides, heading for Shelter Nine.

Sliding off the horse, he opened the hangar-like doors of the shelter garage. Over to the right were three stalls sectioned off by metal dividers. Hay poked out under the gate of each one. Moving his eyes to the left, he saw several bags piled on top of a good supply of hay bales with "Oats" stenciled prominently across the top and sides. He also saw a stack of metal bins with handles under a box labeled "Master Power breaker." Turning it on, he also activated the wall mounted heating units to full. He grabbed one of the metal bins and snagged a feed bag off a wall hook under a shelf that had brushes, towels and other tack items.

Pulling his knife from his belt, he slashed open a bag of oats and poured the rich-smelling grain into the bin. Hank tossed the empty bag aside. He scooped some oats into the feed bag to the brim.

Rushing out to Boris, he mounted and rushed back to the bison. They had picked up their pace slightly, thanks no doubt to the wind goosing the cow's backside and the calf not wanting to get separated from mama. Riding closer than he should have, he dangled the bag of oats in front of the cow. The bison sped up, keeping pace. This was going to work.

A bleat from behind stopped the cow in her tracks. Looking back, Hank realized the calf was falling behind. So close...

"In for a penny, in for a pound," Hank muttered. Adjusting the straps as far as they would go, Hand slung the feed bag over the horns of the cow. Hank put Boris between the cow and the calf, slid off the horse, grabbing at the pigging string at his belt. Intent on getting at mama's teats, the calf didn't realize what was going on till twelve seconds later when she was wrapped up and thrown over Boris's back, followed by Hank mounting the horse and galloping away from mama cow.

As he dismounted inside the shelter, Hank was looking back at the cow, fearful that she would charge in, furious at the separation. She was moving fast, but didn't really seem enraged. He looked on in amazement as the cow trotted into the garage following the sounds of her calf into the stall where Hand had placed her and came to a stop as her calf started nursing and she continued to munch from the feed bag.

Hank was shutting the garage door and reaching to key his communicator when Bill's voice blared through his earbud.

"Please tell me you are undercover."

"Just shut the door and getting ready to brush down Boris. You were right: bison do like oats. Mama is chowing down and baby is chowing down on Mom. Five minutes to spare," he added, looking at the clock on the far wall.

Bill huffed, "Actually, no time to spare. The field crashed a minute ago. Should be back up by morning. God looks out for children, fools and cowboys, apparently."

Hank said a silent prayer of thanks to the Big Boss upstairs, saying, "I suspect you're right. I am going to brush down Boris, get him fed and watered along with the cattle, and decide on dinner."

"I have heard good things about the Irish stew. I told Jesse that you'd not be home tonight because you're shacking up with another female. She said to call when you could pull yourself away from the cow."

"Ha, ha. I'll be sure to call. Thanks for the stew recommendation. See you tomorrow. Signing off."

An hour later, Hank sat on the surprisingly comfortable bunk wrapped in a blanket, spooning the surprisingly wonderful stew from the bag and sipping the unsurprisingly bad instant coffee as his thermal underwear drip-dried in the shower stall. Looking at the time, he figured he ought to call his lady.

"Hank Thornton, you're crazy. You know that, right?" Jessie exclaimed after hearing his retelling of his afternoon. Her smile over the vid link took the sting out of the words.

"You just figured that out?"

"It's why I married you, cowboy. You never give up on the ones that need you."

"I just feel bad not being there tonight with you fighting that bug."

The look on her face was impish. "Wellllll, I wanted to tell you in person, but it turns out that the throwing up was a feature, not a bug. You're going to be a daddy."

Hank laid in his bunk, trying to relax enough to sleep as Phobos appeared in the thick window at the foot of his bed. He saved a couple of lives today and found out he had helped start another. Not a bad day at all.

SHOWDOWN AT PALLADIUMTOWN

Andrew Milbourne

"**D**eputy!"

Bobby Corbett turned towards the unfamiliar—and rather pretty-sounding—voice and felt the air rush from his lungs in a sudden gasp. She was tall, nearly his height, with big, dark eyes and black hair that just reached her shoulders. She wore a white button-down shirt, blue denim pants, a long tan jacket that she wore open, brown leather cowboy boots, and an honest-to-goodness white cowboy hat with an honest-to-goodness beaded hatband that had an honest-to-goodness feather tucked into it. She looked like she'd just walked right out of one of those contraband John Wayne holofilms that were traded in the colony's back alleys. The kind of woman that an ugly, overgrown lummox like Corbett would never have had a hope in hell with...at least before Marshall Teague had pinned that shinny copper shield on his chest that let the entire colony know that he was their official Deputy Marshall.

"Deputy," the woman snapped a second time as she marched up to him. It took Corbett a few seconds more to realize that she didn't appear to be in any distress and that her aggravation was increasing by the second.

"Oh, uh, yes, ma'am!" he stammered when he finally found his voice. "Robert J. Corbett, Deputy Marshall of Palladiumtown, Ganymede Mining Colony Six-Delta, at your service. Uh, that is, The Company calls it Ganymede Mining Colony Six-Delta, but that's too much of a mouthful, so us locals just call it 'Palladiumtown.' How can I help you, ma'am?"

"You can take me to the Colony Marshall."

"I'm sure I can help you with whatever the problem might be."

"The problem is that I need to talk to the Marshall and you are wasting my time. Now are you going to take me to your boss or do I need to waste my morning finding him myself?"

Corbett frowned. Who did this high-and-mighty bitch think she was, talking to him like that, trying to boss him around like he was still some nobody? He was the Colony's Deputy Marshall, damn it! Nobody talked to him like that anymore!

"I don't know who you think you are, but this shield right here says I am the godsdamned Deputy Marshall of this here colony!" he snarled, and whatever else he was thinking of saying departed his brain as the woman pulled her jacket open, revealing her willowy hourglass figure (and sending Corbett's blood running for parts south) along with the silver circle-in-a-star badge pinned to her left breast and an ancient, slab-sided slugthrower sheathed in a brown leather holster on her right hip. The way she rested her hand on the gun made Corbett realize that she knew how to handle it.

"Well, Mister Mister Godsdammed Deputy Marshall of This Here Colony, I am Jacinta Hawk, and *this* star right here says that *I* am a New Texas Ranger. I am here on official business looking for two fugitives, and *you* are wasting my time and are coming *dangerously* close to interfering with my investigation. Now are you going to take me to your boss, or do

I have to inform The Company that one of their employees deliberately obstructed a multijurisdictional manhunt?"

"Uh...right this way, ma'am." Corbett's voice had suddenly become very small as he sheepishly gestured for Ranger Hawk to follow him.

The Colony Jail was nearly identical to the other structures inside Palladiumtown's dome: flimsy, ugly, dirty, unpainted prefab aluminum rectangles. The Company wasn't keen on investing in little things like aesthetics on a third-tier mining colony, even one that was proving as profitable as Ganymede VI-D.

"Wrapping up your patrol early, Deputy?" Marshall Earl Teague asked Corbett as the latter led Ranger Hawk into the three-room structure. "And who's this?"

"Marshall Teague?" Hawk asked.

"Yeah, and you are?"

"Jacinta Hawk, New Texas Ranger." Ranger Hawk flashed her badge at the Marshall. Unlike his deputy, the grizzled old lawman knew enough to show the Ranger the proper respect due her agency's reputation, all but leaping from behind his desk and vigorously shaking her hand with his massive, weathered bear-paws.

"Mighty far from New Texas," Teague observed with a wry grin.

"Nature of the job, Marshall. Fugitives run, I gotta chase 'em no matter how far they go."

"Even to the ass crack of nowhere."

"Even then. Especially when they're as bad as these two."

"Two? We don't... Ah, sorry, Ranger, 'fore I forget, I assume you're carrying a weapon?" Hawk answered by pulling her duster open and canting her hip to give Teague a good look at her holstered sidearm. Teague let out a long, low whistle.

"Nice. Slugthrower?" It was too small and svelte to be a hand maser. Hawk nodded.

"Nineteen-eleven pattern. Made by an outfit called Wilson Combat back on Earth in the late Twenty-Teens. My great-great-great-great-great-grandma had it made custom back when she joined the original Rangers."

"Well, I hate to have to do this, Ranger, but..."

"You are not confiscating my sidearm, Marshall." Hawk's tone bore no argument.

"It's Company Policy, Ranger," Corbett tried to explain. Hawk answered him with an angry frown.

"Boy's right, I'm afraid," Teague said. "No slugthrowers inside the Colony. We're limited to stunsticks and Class Two or weaker masers. The Dome, you see..." He gestured upwards.

"Marshall, that dome's rated to withstand micrometeoroid strikes, correct?"

"Yes, ma'am, it is."

"Well, my sidearm fires eight-gram copper-jacketed lead slugs, nine-millimeter diameter, at just a hair over 410 meters a second. Now my math's a bit rusty, but that should come out to just over 675 Joules of energy at the muzzle. I wager I could empty my magazine into the dome point-blank and it wouldn't even make a dent."

"I'm sorry, ma'am, but it's Company Policy."

"Marshall, these men I'm after are very dangerous, and almost certainly armed. I can guarantee you that they don't give two shits about the law or Company Policy. And you want me to run them down with, what, nonlethals? My bare hands? A corny one-liner and a roundhouse kick?"

"Look, Ranger," Teague sighed, "I understand, I really do, but if The Company finds out I let anyone, even a New Texas Ranger, get away with carrying a slugthrower on Colony property, they'll have my badge, my pension, and my bunk!"

"Mine, too!" Corbett chimed in, earning him glares from both Marshall and Ranger alike. Hawk's expression softened after a few moments, and she finally gave the Marshall a reluctant smile.

"We all gotta do what you what we gotta do, I suppose," she conceded. "Not sure how I'd be able to sleep knowing I cost an honest lawman his job and his home." She slowly pulled her pistol from his holster, dropped the magazine, racked the slide to eject the chambered round, and placed everything on the Marshall's desk. "I assume you have someplace to secure these?" The Marshall nodded and jerked his head to the oversized safe in the far corner of the small office.

"I'll stash 'em in the evidence locker 'til after we run down these fugitives of yours. That okay?" Hawk nodded, so Teague scooped up the gun and ammo and carried them to the safe and motioned for the Ranger to take a seat. Once he'd deposited Hawk's gear in the locker and ensured he'd properly resecured it, he strolled back over to his desk and slid into his chair across from Hawk.

"So, these fugitives," he prompted. "They runnin' together?"

"Used to, but they split up a few years back."

"And now? You think they're both in Palladiumtown?"

"I'm certain of it, Marshall. They're kin, after all."

"Kin, eh? They got names?"

Hawk fished a pair of holopads out of her duster's pockets, placed both on them on the desk, but only activated one. The mugshot of a large, ruddy man with an angry sneer and a shock of red hair appeared over the desk above a scrolling list of information. Corbett opened his mouth to say something, but Teague shut him up with a quick glare.

"William Taggert," Hawk said, ignoring the silent exchange between Marshall and Deputy. "Alias 'Big Bill.' Also known as 'Rusty' on account of his hair and complexion, obviously, but he'll kill you dead if you call him that. Wanted out of Nuevo Amarillo."

"Lot of charges," Teague noted.

"He's a bad one," Hawk nodded. "Multiple hijackings and armed robberies, a half-dozen murders, then he stepped it up to aggravated kidnapping and rape. Fled New Texas before a posse could lynch him for it."

"Seriously? I heard stories 'bout New Texas, but I never thought... Damn!"

"Texans don't take kindly to that sort of thing. Never have."

"'Wanted Dead or Alive.' Sheeee-it," Corbett whistled, "I thought that was just from those old holofilms. Which, uh, which I've only heard about and never actually watched," he stammered under Teague's questioning look. Such "indecent" and "culturally-insensitive" materials were, after all, deemed "extremely inappropriate" for Company Employees' consumption and, therefore, *highly* illegal to possess or even view on or about Company Property.

"Sometimes the old ways are best," Hawk remarked. "And some folks just need killin'."

"Not exactly civilized, is it?" Teague sneered.

"New Texas ain't exactly a civilized place. And, no offence, neither is Palladiumtown."

Teague bristled, then deflated.

"Can't really argue with that" he sighed. "But we don't string up our alleged criminals without a fair trial here."

"Company wouldn't like that, would they?" Hawk nodded. "Bad press and all that." Everyone in the tiny Marshall's Office knew that The Company didn't care; they'd just buy off the press or threaten them into silence. But lynch mobs distracted workers from their jobs and, as a result, negatively impacted profits. And there was always the possibility that disgruntled workers might decide to "affect change" by stringing up the colony's middle management, so it was in The Company's best interests to put up at least a convincing appearance of peace and civilized behavior around their operations.

"Anyways, your second fugitive?" Teague prompted. The way Hawk smiled at the Marshall's prompt made Corbett feel very uncomfortable. She reminded him of a cat that had just cornered its dinner.

"Second fugitive," Hawk said, "is Taggert's older brother, Edward, AKA 'Fast Eddie.' He and Big Bill ran together for about a decade, then about six years back Eddie decided to pull what he thought would be an easy job and tried robbing the Quanna's Hut Casino in Comanche Nation. Big Bill thought the idea was nuts and split. That turned out to be a smart move, because the robbery went very, very bad: Eddie's gang got made going into the place, then got into a shootout with Casino Security when they tried to take the cage, and *then* got into a high-speed pursuit and running gunfight with Tribal Police when they tried to make a run for it. Chase ended when their getaway driver hit a school bus and wrecked their hovervan. The ensuing standoff turned into a gunfight when Fast Eddie got antsy and shot a hostage. When it was all over, two tribal cops, fourteen kids, and the bus driver were dead, along with about half of the gang, and another dozen kids and five cops were in the hospital. Posse caught up with most of the surviving gang members within a week, scalped the lucky ones, but Fast Eddie made it offworld by the skin of his teeth. Comanche Nation wants his head on a stick, and if you think New Texans are uncivilized, they ain't got nothin' on the Comanche when you mess with our children."

"'Our' children?" Corbett asked stupidly. Hawk thumped her chest with her fist.

"Card-carrying member of the Nation," she said, voice swollen with pride. She wasn't full-blood Comanche, but she was close enough that nobody could give her crap for her non-regulation hatband or the *extremely* non-regulation eagle feather that had become her trademark among the Rangers.

"And...you think Eddie Taggert's here?" Teague asked.

"Oh, I *know* he's here. He's been on Ganymede Six a little over four years now. Managed to forge a new ident along the way. You wanna know his new name?" Hawk didn't wait for an answer as she leaned forward to activate the second holopad. "Folks here know him as Colony Marshall Earl Teague."

The color drained from Teague's face, and Corbett's mouth fell open as the second mugshot appeared. The face was far younger and far less weathered, but it was still unmistakably that of the Marshall of Palladiumtown.

Teague lurched to his feet, gun hand going for the maser pistol on his hip, but Hawk was already moving. She exploded out of her chair and over the desk, driving her knee into Teague's chin and snapping his head back with a hollow *THUNK!* Corbett went for his own maser as the pair disappeared behind the desk, awkwardly fumbling the draw and almost dropping the weapon in his rapidly-rising panic. He heard the crackling whine of a stunstick powering up and then a sharp *CRACK!* of the melee weapon discharging and a pained bellow that sounded an awful lot like the Marshall, a prolonged crackle of a stunstick being jammed against flesh and held there along with an agonized scream that trailed off several seconds before the stunstick cut out, and then silence. The office stank of ozone and charred flesh.

"Boss?" Corbett stammered, levelling his hand maser at the desk. "Boss? You all right?" No answer. "Marshall?" Something rolled out from behind the desk, and Corbett instinctively turned his head towards it, but stupidly kept pointing his maser at the desk.

"FREEZE!" Corbett froze. It was the Ranger, and she had a slugthrower that looked like a smaller version of the one she'd handed over to the Marshall—wait, where had that come from?—aimed square between his eyes. "Drop it, kid." Corbett threw the maser away like it had just caught fire in his hands.

"Ranger, I didn't know he was wanted, I swear it! You gotta believe me! I...I don't want no part of this!"

"Doesn't matter, kid," Hawk replied, her voice deadly even. "You're in this up to your eyeballs whether you want to be or not." The little slugthrower's muzzle never wavered as she slowly got to her feet, tossed the marshal's gunbelt onto the desk, and sidestepped into the corner of the room. "Take off your belt."

"Wha—what?"

"Your gunbelt. Take if off and let it fall."

"Ranger..."

"I won't ask twice, and this doesn't have a stun setting. Take off the belt. Now."

Corbett frantically fumbled with the buckle before finally managing to undo it, and the belt tumbled to the floor, taking his empty maser holster and his stunstick with it.

"Good," Hawk nodded. "Now drag Taggert to one of the cells and lock yourself in with him."

"Wha—? But I ain't with him!"

"I don't know that, and I can't risk it."

"Ranger, I—"

"Look, kid, you're not doing yourself any favors here. Way it's sitting now, there's a good case against you for aiding and abetting a known fugitive. You do as I say and I'll do what I can to convince Judge McMurtie and The Company that you really didn't know your boss was a wanted fugitive. But if I lose William Taggert because of you stalling me, then your ass is grass. Got it?"

"Yes, ma'am." Corbett hurried over and began dragging his boss's unconscious form over to the closest cell.

"And if I was looking for William Taggert?" Hawk prompted.

"The Saloon," Corbett grunted. "Marshall called in a favor and got him a job dealing Lunar Stud. Rumor is he worked a deal with the manager for a quarter of his table's house take. You'll tell the Judge and The Company Reps that I told you that, right?"

"I'll be sure to mention it." Hawk didn't move, save to keep her gun trained on Corbett, until the deputy had dragged Fast Eddie Taggert into a cell and swung the door shut behind him. The heavy hatch locked with an authoritative electronic *CLACK!* Satisfied that neither Marshall nor Deputy was going anyplace anytime soon, Hawk moved to the evidence locker and opened it with the electronic fob she'd pulled from the Marshall's belt. She reloaded and reholstered her primary slughtrower, returned her backup piece to the holster clipped to the inside of her left boot, and then tossed the masers and stunsticks she'd taken off the two lawmen into the locker and closed it. Pausing just long enough to retrieve the two holopads from the Marshall's desk, she headed back out into the street and renewed the search for her quarry.

Finding the saloon wasn't difficult: at three stories tall, it was the biggest structure in the "town" part of Palladiumtown. Only the mining structures towards the far side of the dome dwarfed it. The interior was, to Hawk's mild surprise, brightly lit, but the place still reeked of cheap booze, sweat, and tobacco vape. More surprising were the table games: they were actual physical tables with actual physical cards, dice, and chips rather than holoconsoles where everything was digital. Which actually made sense: tables didn't break (and when they did, they were much cheaper to fix or replace than a holoconsole) and the dealers were probably all indents, so The Company didn't have to pay them much of a salary.

The direct approach like she'd taken with the Marshall wouldn't fly here. The crowd wouldn't take kindly to an offworlder, even a New Texas Ranger, throwing her weight around like she owned the whole damn colony, and if Taggert was using the same bullshit story here that he'd been using elsewhere, he'd probably have the crowd on his side, so Hawk played it cool and moseyed on over to the bar.

"What'll it be, stranger?" the barkeep asked after she'd grabbed his attention. He was a hatchet-faced man with a cybernetic left eye that glowed a disturbingly-unnatural shade of green. Hawk had to make an effort to look somewhere between his bald head and his good eye.

"Virgin Moscow Mule."

"Virgin?" He gave her an odd look.

"Don't drink anything hard when I'm workin'."

"Workin', eh?" The barkeep sized her up while he fixed her drink. "Never seen yous in here before, which means yous either a brand-new assignee here to this little slice of hell in the ass crack of the universe, or yous an offworlder visiting. Ain't no tourism 'round here, and yous don't carry youself like a miner or one of the indented girls..." He gestured vaguely towards a pair of young ladies in cheap synthlace lingerie—two of the well over a dozen that were cruising the gambling floor—who were starting to woo a miner who'd just scored a big pot at one of the poker tables. At least three of the girls looked far too young to legally be working in the saloon, but they, too, were probably indents. If you owed The Company money, it'd collect one way or another, and didn't care one iota how many lives got ruined in the process.

"... Er, no offense."

"None taken."

"So I's figuring yous ain't a brand-new assignee or intent. And if you's working and you's ain't drinkin', that must make you Law of some sort."

"Guilty as charged." Hawk discreetly opened her duster just enough to give the barkeep a clear view of her badge. The old man let out a long, low whistle as he placed the chilled copper mug on the bar in front of her.

"Damnation. Heard of yous, never thought I'd meet one of yous in person. Real honor, Ranger..."

"Hawk."

"Ranger Hawk. I's guessin' you's here for ol' Big Bill Taggert."

"I'm afraid so." She took a tentative sip of her drink. Not bad, and alcohol-free as requested. "Very good. Thanks much." She placed a credit chit on the bar and told the barkeep to keep the change.

"I's guessin' there's more to his tale o' woes than he been tellin'?"

Hawk let out a sad chuckle and shook her head.

"He still telling that same bullshit story? He found himself a girl and her daddy didn't approve, so they got into a tussle and he accidentally killed the old man, and it was self-defense but Daddy was rich so his family done sic'd the mean ol' New Texas Rangers on him, and the Rangers done run him offworld and have been chasing poor od' Big Bill all over the sector ever since, right?"

"That 'bout sums it up."

"Yeah, there's a lot more to it. And that's on top of the dozens of other charges he's facing. Assault, robbery, and murder."

"So his story 'bout the girl's just straight-up bullshit?"

"Not entirely, but like I was saying, he left out a bunch of pertinent details." It only took Hawk a moment to fill the barkeep in on those details, but his face had gone ashen well before she finished.

"Good Gawds!"

"Yeah."

"You's shartin' me!"

"'Fraid not. Wish to God I was."

"Shee-it! Never thought I'd be sayin' this, but I's glad you's here, Ranger. You want I should get the Marshall come back yous up?"

"Don't bother," Hawk shook her head. "Marshall's, ah, let's just say he's indisposed for the time being."

"Ind'spos'd? What happened to him?"

"He, ah, found himself on the wrong end of a warrant."

"He did whatnow?"

Hawk pulled the holopad from her duster pocket and showed it—in 2D mode—to the barkeep, who snorted in disgust.

"Knew there was somethin' wrong 'bout him, I's did! Never could unnerstan' why a lawman'd be so chummy-chummy wit' an outlaw, 'specially one 's bad 's Big Bill Taggert. So you's got Fast Eddie. An' now yous' gon' take Big Bill. Yous gonna do it 'ere an' now?"

"Can you think of a better place or time?" The barkeep considered that for a few moments, then shook his head.

"Naw. 'E's bragged 'bout all the hardware 'e's done got stored in 'is bunkroom. Which is upstairs. Don't hardly leave the buildin' anywho. Might 's well take 'im 'ere. You want I's should back yous?"

"Appreciate the offer, but I can take him."

"Yous' sure? I's got me an ol' scattergun back here. That'll make 'em think twice afore they does summin' stupid."

"Scattergun?" Hawk raised an eyebrow. "Slugthrower?"

"Yes, ma'am. Double barrel, sixteen-bore, single-aught buck."

"Thought Company Policy banned everything but stunsticks and masers, Class Two maximum."

"What lyin' idjit told yous that?" The barkeep gave her an incredulous look.

"Why, Marshall Teague, of course." Hawk's affection of a wide-eyed innocent schoolgirl elicited the desired guffaw from the barkeep.

"Should've figured. But I's serious. Big Bill's fast. I's seen 'im draw, I's has. An' he's done made lotso friends wit' that bullsheet sob story o' 'is. One of 'em might fix t' backshoots yous if'n yous tries takin' 'im in o' callin' 'im out. Two barrels full o' buckshot 'll make 'em think twice."

Hawk studied the man. He struck her as an honest sort, and his reaction to the truth about Taggert's crimes and his desire to get the outlaw out of the saloon and off Ganymede both appeared genuine. But at the same time, she hadn't stayed alive as long as she had by trusting every honest-seeming sort that crossed her path. The barkeep seemed to realize what she was thinking, so he decided to plead his case again.

"Look, Ranger, I gets it. Yous don' know me from Adam. But I's does my best to run a clean game here. Don' like bein' forced t' let 'im run a dirty table. An' I's gots three granddaughters back on Artemins Prime. Young 'uns." Hawk continued to think it over for a few moments, then gave the barkeep a somber nod.

"Consider yourself deputized. What's your name?"

"I's called Casper Johns."

"Pleased to know you, Casper Johns. If you don't mind my asking, what was that about you wanting a clean establishment?"

"Taggert cheats. 'E stacks th' deck 'n' deals dirty. 'E lets 'em win ever once in' a while t' keep 'em comin' back, but mostly makes sure they's gar'n'teed t' lose. I's seen 'im do it, so I's has. Tol' th' Marshall, he tol' me t' shut m' lip. Now I's knows why."

"And he gets a quarter of the house take from his table?"

"Yep. Taggert said either I's gets game to that or I's be findin' m'self outsides th' Dome sans m' envirosuit. Marshall tol' me t' shut m' lip 'bout that, too."

"Well, Mister Johns, how about you let me clean up the place?"

"Sounds like a mighty fine deal t' me, so's it does."

"Good. I'll take Taggert. You watch my back. Don't fire unless your life or mine or a civilian's is in imminent danger. And if you cross me..." Casper Johns threw his head back and laughed.

"Ma'am, I's may not be the smartest man in th' verse, 's how I's ended up 'ere after alls, but even I's ain't stupid enough t' try crossin' a New Texas Ranger."

"That's good to know. You got any way of keeping that scattergun out of sight?"

"I hides it unner mah apron."

"Why do I get the feeling you've done that before?"

"Might 'ave a time 'r two." Ranger and barkeep shared a knowing grin.

"Good to know. Keep back far enough to cover me, and stay frosty."

"How's they say it in New Texas? It ain't mah first rodeo."

"I thought not."

Casper Johns retrieved the shotgun—a handy little thing with barrels that had been cut down to a hair over 300 millimeters long—and moved out from behind the bar. By holding it down low with the stock between his arm and his chest, and sliding the stubby barrels into the side of his apron, the little hand howitzer became all but invisible to the casual observer. The barkeep fell in a half-dozen steps behind the Ranger as they headed off towards what both knew deep down was coming.

It wasn't hard to find Taggert's Lunar Stud table: it was in the far corner of the room, surrounded by a large crowd of onlookers. Taggert's deep, booming voice could be heard even over the chaos of the gambling floor as he regaled the assembly with highly-exaggerated, not-a-little falsified tales of his "exploits" and "adventures" on New Texas. It took a not-insignificant amount of Hawk's self-control to not scoff or roll her eyes. The way Taggert made it sound, he'd single-handedly blasted his way out of the ambush that the veritable army of evil Western Union agents had set up *and* saved a whole carload of widows and orphans from the ensuing hovertrain crash...a derailment that, in reality, he and his gang had deliberately caused to rob the Western Union car. Two of the three agents in the car had died in the crash, and Taggert had personally executed the third in cold blood. And while there had been some widows and orphans aboard the train, it hadn't been a carload of each, but still enough to make very convenient hostages and meat shields for Taggert's gang as they fled the New Texas Department of Public Safety's Rapid Response Unit that had descended upon the scene.

Casper Johns stopped a few paces short of Taggert's audience while Hawk muscled her way through to the table. All seven player seats were occupied by rough and rowdy-looking miners. Across the table in the dealer's chair, a big hand-mazer holstered on his right hip and a tiny girl with jet-black hair and gauzy purple corset on his left, was William "Big Bill" Taggert himself. He looked a little older than his mugshot, his face a little more worn and weathered from his time on the run, his body a bit softer from the seven standard months of easy living he'd had in Palladiumtown. But his eyes, they were still the same. Hawk would know those empty, soulless grey pits anywhere.

Hawk's timing could've been better: a game had just started, and everyone's attention —including Taggert's—was on the table. Bets had already been laid down and Taggert was dealing out hands. He dealt quicky and kept the crowd focused on his tall tales instead of the cards, but Hawk still managed to catch some false shuffles, and she was pretty sure he floated a card or two. And he definitely dealt the community cards from the bottom of the deck. But Hawk decided to let the game play out: if Casper Johns was right, Taggert would already have the crowd on his side going into this. No point in antagonizing them further. Not that it really ended up mattering all that much, because Taggert ran a quick game: lambasting players who dithered over betting or folding for more than a few seconds. The whole thing ended in less than three standard minutes. Of the seven players, two came away with push pairs, so they didn't lose their standard bets (though they didn't get paid, either) but did lose all of their bonus bets, while a third had a pair of Kings in his hand that turned into Triple Kings on the third community card, which netted him a cool thousand credits with all the bonus bets factored in.

Hawk was standing behind the winning player—named Charlie, if the whoops and cheers from the bystanders was anything to go by—and finally caught Taggert's eye when he was paying out all the man's bets. His forced smile (Charlie had just eaten into his daily earnings, after all) rapidly became genuine as he took the Ranger in.

"Well, hello, gorgeous," the outlaw drawled, completely forgetting the pretty girl already on his arm. "Ain't seen you 'round here before. You lookin' for a good time? Well, you've come to the best table at the best gambling hall on the whole planet. Have a seat, darlin'. Ah, there ain't no seats left. Charlie, stand up an' let the little lady have a go."

"Aw, c'mon, Bill!" Charlie whined. "My luck's just startin' to change."

"Stand up and give the lady your seat, Charlie." Taggert's jovial tone took on a definite threatening edge as he glared at poor Charlie.

"Find another table, Charlie," Hawk said, "That goes for everyone else, too. Go on home or find another game. This table's closed."

A confused murmuring washed over the crowd as a look of utter disbelief washed over Taggert's face.

"Look, little missy, I don't know who you think you are or where you come from, but *I'm* the dealer here. *I* say whether the table's open or closed, and *I* say it's *open*."

Hawk pulled open her duster, giving Taggert and the players (who'd all turned to watch the exchange) a clear view of her badge and her gun. Taggert's eyes went wide as he saw the unmistakable circle-in-a-star emblem.

"I'm Jacinta Hawk, New Texas Ranger," she announced in her no-nonsense "command" voice. "William Taggert, alias 'Big Bill Taggert,' alias 'Rusty Taggert,' I have a warrant for your arrest. Stand up and place your hands on the table."

Taggert recovered from the shock of Hawk's appearance in almost no time at all, and (as Hawk expected) addressed his audience.

"What's the Marshall got to say about that, Ranger?" he demanded.

"Don't take this wrong, but I'm not interested in what the Marshall might have to say about it."

"That so? Well, I reckon most everybody here is *mighty* interested in what ol' Earl will think. Charlie, be a good man and fetch the Marshall?"

"Don't bother, Charlie. Marshall's indisposed. Won't be coming here or going anywhere else for a good long time."

"You damned offworlder!" Taggert snarled. "You done killed 'im!"

"I didn't kill him, though he's gonna be in enough pain when he wakes up that he'll probably wish I had."

"Y'all hear this? This here New Texas Ranger's done bushwhacked the Marshall so she can to haul me back to the hangman!" That got the crowd murmuring louder. "And for what? Y'all know what happened! All I done wrong was find me a good woman who loved me more 'n words! Daisy Rose Willard was the apple of my eye an' I was hers!" But her rich ol' daddy didn't like his girl takin' up with a poor ranch hand, so he tried to kill me! It was self-defense by New Texas law! But there ain't no justice in New Texas for a poor ol' fool like me!" With each proclamation, the noise of the crowd grew louder and angrier. Taggert was spooling them up to drive Hawk out of the saloon or, better, tear her apart right where she stood. That's when Hawk played her two aces in the hole.

"Marshall Earl Teague's real name is Edward Taggert, aka 'Fast Eddie,' aka Big Bill's older brother. I got warrants out on him, too. And as for Daisy Rose Willard, I'd wager her father didn't approve because she was *nine standard years old*!"

The crowd around the table—along with the entire gambling hall—went silent. The color drained from Taggert's face as he shoved the saloon girl aside and lurched to his feet.

"That's right," Hawk continued. "And little Daisy Rose wanted to be with ol' Big Bill here so much that he had to drag her kicking and screaming away from her home. After he walked up behind her daddy and shot him six times in the back, that is. And then Big Bill spent five standard days and five standard nights violating little Daisy Rose before he got bored with her, so then he strangled her with her own undergarments and buried her in a shallow grave. Only must've worn himself out after five days and five nights, 'cause he didn't do a full job strangling her. She was still alive when he dumped her in that hole and filled it in on top of her."

"You lyin' wetback slut!" Taggert bellowed.

"That's 'featherhead squaw,' to you, Taggart," Hawk fired back. Taggert blinked.

"Huh?"

"I'm Comanche, not Mexican. If you're gonna be a racist asshole, at least be an accurate racist asshole. And as far as calling me a liar, I've got crime scene holos, I've got a sworn coroner's report that found *your* DNA inside of *her* body, and I've got damn near ninety standard hours of the sickest, most disturbing, most depraved holofootage I've ever seen." The crowd began muttering again, its rage and horror returning anew, but now aimed square at Taggert. "Yeah, he filmed everything he did to poor little Daisy Rose. Probably kept a copy for posterity. I wager that if you tossed his room *real* good, you'd find it." By now, Taggert's face had gone beet red, his nostrils were flaring as his chest heaved in a rage. "So that's what I have. What do you have, Taggert, besides more bullshit stories?"

"I got a Class-Five maser that'll flash-boil your insides faster 'n you can blink!" he snarled. Hawk gave him a slow, grim nod.

"You planning on using it anytime today, Rusty, or do you just want to keep standing there blowing gas?"

Taggert's face went dead pale, then flushed red, and then he went for it.

Nobody actually saw Hawk draw. One instant, her hand was resting casually on the butt of her slugthrower, then half an eyeblink later the pistol was in her hand. A pair of earsplitting reports echoed through the saloon and Taggert's angry war cry turned into a scream of pain as Hawk fired from retention and put two hollowpoints into the outlaw's guts. Taggert's legs gave out and he want to his knees, catching himself on the game table with his off hand. He began to haul himself upright, screaming obscenities as he raised the big, deadly maser up above the table. His screams turned into a sick, wet gurgle as Hawk raised her pistol in a two-handed grip and put a third bullet into Taggert's throat. The big man went down, weapon tumbling from his hand.

Hawk moved around the table and slid Taggert's weapon out of his reach with her bootheel, keeping her slugthrower pointed between the outlaw's eyes for long minutes until he finally expired.

There would be an inquest later. Two of them, actually: one from the Rangers and one from The Company. The latter party had come into their witch hunt wanting Hawk's head on a literal platter, but their aim rapidly shifted away from her to whatever corrupt, middle-management paper-pusher had allowed a known, wanted fugitive to obtain a position of authority at a Company facility, and allowed a second known, wanted fugitive to perform unauthorized labor in a Company facility and permitted said second known, wanted fugitive to openly and blatantly skim The Company's profits from said facility.

The Ranger's inquest, on the other hand, was an open-and-shut formality. Witness statement and the saloon's surveillance system proved that Hawk had announced herself as required and directed by NTDPS regulations and that Taggert had pulled first. As to why Hawk had shot Taggert in the guts and throat instead of chest and head as per Ranger training protocols, she'd just shrugged and explained that she'd rushed her shots, jerking the trigger just hard enough to pull the muzzle down. Back in New Austin, Captain Walker had given her a questioning glance when she'd told him that, then shook his head and let the matter rest. The warrant had read "Dead or Alive," after all. Either way, Cherokee Nation would get its pound of flesh out of Fast Eddie Taggert, and hopefully little Daisy Rose Willard and her daddy could rest easy now that Big Bill was in the ground.

Not that Hawk nor Walker had time to consider such philosophical musings, seeing as how the old-fashioned synthcork bulletin board in the

Rangers' squad room was still covered with wanted posters. There were plenty more fugitives that needed running down. Walker pulled down an especially nasty piece of work, handed it to Hawk, and sent her back out on the trail.

GIDEON'S WILD RIDE

Scott Slack

G ideon Neitzel sat erect in the saddle as the wind blew over the ridge. Five cows had gone missing in the night.

None of the other ranch hands had wanted to go looking. There'd been one excuse after another. Too tired, no idea where they were, saddlesore from the day before, and one who'd proclaimed, "There's nothing in it for us, they're the state's cattle." That last point had been a good one. Gideon's brother Aaron had said something very similar before he'd snuck over the border from Tyran into Sala. That was the last Gideon had seen of his brother.

That was four years ago. Gideon had only been sixteen years old when Aaron had left. He wished he could have gone, too, but State Security tightened their grip everytime someone made it over the border, and Aaron hadn't said anything to Gideon before he left. He still wondered why. The note Aaron had left explained that he'd been helping people over the border for years, and he was afraid State Security was onto him. But that didn't explain why he'd left Gideon.

Gideon looked down from the ridge on the ranch. There was a tall dust-cloud coming along the road. Several large cars were driving to the ranch. That was odd. It wasn't time for a delivery, and they weren't expecting anyone.

Then the cars came into view. They were painted in the dark gray of State Security.

Gideon dismounted and led Joey away from the ridge, then crept up to the ridge on his stomach, doing his best not to be silhouetted against the sky or mountains. The cars stopped, and the doors opened, disgorging more than a dozen State Security agents.

That was a bad sign. That was a raid. There were any number of reasons why they could be raiding the ranch, and none of them good.

Someone could have informed on David for his comments about the state's cattle, someone could have caught them skimming a bit of meat to supplement their allotments, or someone could have figured out that Gideon, like his brother before him, had been helping Tyrans slip away into Sala.

It had been a while since he had; the last time had been a family of three, a father and his two sons, nearly eighteen months before. They'd seemed normal enough, but the effort to track them down had been more intense than any before, and there were rumors that the Border Patrol had chased them onto the Salan side of the border, been ambushed by the Salan military, and sent back in shame without their weapons. Something had been different about that family.

Gideon laid there for another moment. No good could come of this raid, even if they weren't coming for him. He stood up and returned to Joey, mounting him again and spurring him forward. It was time to follow where he'd led others. It was time to go to Sala.

Joey took off at a trot. It made for a bouncy ride, but there were many kilometers to go, and while a faster gait would be smoother, he couldn't afford to let Joey get too tired. He'd need to reserve the speed for an emergency. He guided Joey along one of the many trails through the ranch. The fast route was, unfortunately, not an option. Not only was Joey physically incapable of rock climbing, but ever since he'd guided the Greens to the short route, it had gone from being nearly unpatrolled to being the most heavily patrolled border crossing in the area.

Gideon's first stop was a small stream. It was running well this time of year, and it was small enough not to show up on any of the maps. It had the added benefit of being the spot where Gideon had buried a cache of food and some other supplies. Gideon dismounted and led Joey to the water. While Joey drank, Gideon retrieved a folding spade from his saddle and began digging for his cache. After several minutes of digging, he was certain he'd dug deep enough. But it wasn't there. He stood up and looked around.

"It couldn't have moved itself," he said aloud.

Joey stopped drinking for a moment, made a brief snorting noise and turned to look at Gideon.

"Just keep drinking," Gideon said, scratching his head. He looked at the tree beside which he thought he'd buried the cache. *Perhaps it was the wrong tree,* he thought. He walked over to another, and looked at the rocks beside it. He did remember rocks by the tree. Perhaps this was the one. He dug again, and was rewarded when the spade contacted thick, rubberized canvas.

He pulled the cache from the ground and unwrapped it. The bags looked intact. No holes or tears, and the dried meat inside looked to be unaffected by its time underground. Unfortunately, his cache did not include horse feed. It wouldn't keep underground. He'd have to let Joey forage when they had the chance.

Gideon grabbed a bottle of water from Joey's saddle and drank from it. He made a habit of carrying some food and water with him whenever he had to go after missing cattle. It could take a long time to find them, so it made sense to carry supplies for both him and his horse. Those long times also made for good opportunities to scout out the area and become intimately acquainted with it.

That was why he made a habit of helping the cows slip out into the night. More than once, a cow had been released into the night to cover someone's escape from Tyran.

Gideon didn't know what happened to the people he helped escape. He imagined a fair number were shuttled to other countries by Sala. The two countries had not been friendly in the hundred years Sala had been independent of Tyran, and many Tyrans would struggle to adapt to Salan life.

Even before the collapse of global governance in the aftermath of Last Contact, Sala had not been the most obedient of subprovinces. The people of Sala were as rugged as their hills and mountains, and not given to taking orders from the people east of the Atlas mountains. That kind of culture would be difficult for many Tyrans to handle. Most Tyrans were taught to be obedient, do as they were told, and nothing more.

Even on a state-owned ranch, where independent thought was essential, and the individual and the collective had to coexist, Gideon had been taught from the youngest age to obey. It was little wonder that he snuck off as he wished, finding one excuse or another. And now he was sneaking away for the last time. His brother was in Sala, and his parents died long ago of treatable diseases. The only thing left for him in Tyran was an excruciating death.

He remounted Joey and resumed the ride, wondering how long it would take to find his brother once he made it into Sala. Somehow, he knew his brother would be there. Aaron wouldn't have gone to another country, which probably meant he was serving in the Salan military, conscripted like all the Salan men, but entirely of his own volition. Gideon wasn't so sure he wanted to be a soldier. His own experiences with soldiers had done little to earn respect for the job, or a desire to join them.

The kilometers passed quietly, the only noise the sound of Joey's unshod hooves on the dirt trail. Good farriers were hard to come by those days, so they had been forced to go through the long process of training the ranch's horses to go barefoot. The quiet kilometers gave Gideon ample time to think. He scanned the woods around him looking for threats, both human and animal, but there were none to be seen yet.

Finally, he encountered his first threat, something neither human nor animal. He came to one of the cleared lines, a swath of forest that had been clear cut, making a long line of grass. He knew that beneath the grass lay an oil pipeline, one which ran through Sala to the coast, and from there onto ships that carried it around the world. But what was beneath it concerned him less than what was above it: radars. Not the large radars that scanned the skies watching for Salan aircraft, come to bomb, destroy, or land infiltrators, but small radars designed to track smaller things moving on the ground. In other words: escapees.

Gideon halted Joey, and stared at the radar. He was already well within its range. If he could see it, then it could see him. And by now, his movement, utterly unlike that of a breeze moving the trees, or a mouse inching along, would have triggered its onboard cameras. At that very moment, a human could be staring back at him who knew where, and reporting his position to State Security. He hadn't planned on this. The last time he'd crossed the pipeline, there hadn't been a radar picket, just the occasional patrol. It wasn't illegal to cross the line, necessarily. He had a legitimate and legal reason to be there, as he had in the past: he was looking for missing cattle. But this time, the sudden presence of a picket bode ill for Gideon. There was only one thing he could do.

Gideon dismounted and led Joey into the clearing. One side effect of clearing away the trees was that grasses had grown in their place, and that meant forage for Joey. Gideon removed the bit from Joey's mouth and allowed him to forage. Meanwhile, Gideon drank some water and pulled a bit of dried meat from his supplies, and bit off a piece, letting it sit in his mouth to soften before he chewed it. It was spicy, having been flavored with onion and chile, both of which would reduce microbial growth, and smoky from the drying process. Sooner or later, a patrol would come to question him. Better to look innocent than like a man fleeing for his life.

The patrol took a good fifteen minutes to arrive. They drove up in a truck modified for use off-road, as well as modified for prisoner transport, the bed converted into a cell with the simple addition of a cage and bars. Gideon had never been inside one, and hoped to continue with a perfect record of zero arrests, even if his record were complicated by his many crimes against the state.

Two patrollers descended from the tall vehicle. Gideon breathed a sigh of silent relief. It was Tayler and File. He didn't like these two patrollers, but they liked him, or more precisely, they liked his bribes of food to supplement their less than satisfying rations.

"Well, Gideon, it's been a while since you've been out this way," Tayler said. "Looking for another poor old lost cow?" he added, condescendingly.

"Yeah, old May wandered off again with a few others. Hoping to find her before lunch," he said.

"You really need to do a better job keeping them in, you know," File lectured. "Those cattle belong to the state, and you're supposed to take good care of them." Gideon never did care for File, who was all too willing to take a bribe. Yet he had a strange sense of loyalty, and he was always willing to lecture Gideon, even on subjects about which he knew nothing.

"We're trying. Problem is we can never keep up with the fencing. It's always breaking, and we can never get what we need fast enough to keep them in," Gideon said defensively. It was almost true. The fencing was always falling apart; sometimes it was rotting posts or rusting wire, and sometimes it was bolt cutters hidden in Joey's saddlebags.

"And what about the times someone left the gate unlocked?" Tayler asked.

"Not my fault," Gideon answered. Fault implied a mistake, and Gideon had never made a mistake when he'd left the gate open.

"Well, be that as it may, you shouldn't be here. No one can just cross the pipeline without a legitimate reason, and I don't see your legitimate reason just yet," Tayler said.

And there was the solicitation. "I understand, sir. I can get you my paperwork from my saddlebags if you want to see it," Gideon offered.

Gideon withdrew his rancher's license, which gave him some privileges to go where others couldn't. Inside it, he slipped a twenty Mark note, and a good-sized bag of dried meat. It was a larger bribe than usual, but he couldn't afford to be caught today.

"Well, that's mighty generous of you, Gideon. But I'm afraid now we'll have to add bribery to the list of char..." He was going to say charges, but Gideon rudely interrupted him.

Gideon's hand shot under the saddlebags on Joey's left, and withdrew from concealment a cut-down shotgun he kept there for dealing with predators, both four-legged and two-legged. He cocked the hammer and discharged the single barrel into Tayler. The heavy load of buckshot took Tayler just above his armored vest. Tayler fell to the ground heavily as the sound of the shot echoed off the trees.

File stood there fumbling for his sidearm as Gideon charged at him and struck his face with the butt of the now-empty shotgun. File grunted in pain and doubled over before he tried to shove Gideon away. His shove was ineffectual. Gideon smashed his head in with the butt of his shotgun, and File fell to the ground. Gideon grabbed a knife from his saddle, knelt on File's spine, and pulled File's head up by his hair and cut his throat. He wiped his blade off on File's shirt, and remounted Joey and spurred him on at a gallop. Someone probably heard the shot and would send backup to the location of the last radar alert. His mad dash away on Joey was already telling them he'd fled the scene, and it would also tell them in which direction he'd gone, but it was better than waiting to die.

An hour later, he regretted his haste. Tayler and File had both been armed, and he'd left his papers with them. If he'd not panicked, he could have taken their sidearms and his papers. Now he had only two shots left for his shotgun, and State Security and the Patrol knew exactly who to look for.

Gideon slowed Joey to a walk, and broke open his shotgun and inserted another shotshell into the chamber with suddenly clumsy fingers. It wasn't likely to help him, but it might. He closed the action again, and moved the shotgun's scabbard from under his saddlebags to where he could grab it while mounted. There would be no bluffing or bribing his way out now. He'd killed two men, and crossed his own personal Rubicon.

In the distance he heard sirens. It was time to make a turn. The radars would have shown his initial direction as he ran, and he'd continued that for a bit, just to make good headway, but now he needed to throw them off his path. He applied a bit of boot to Joey's side to veer southwest off the trail. This deep in the forest, there was little undergrowth to block the way. The thick canopy kept undergrowth from sprouting, and periodic fires cleared away the dead branches and trees that littered forests closer to the farms and ranches.

He crossed another creek, and stopped Joey for a break. He gave him time to drink from the creek while Gideon drank from one of his bottles. He wished he'd brought more water with him. It would be more weight, but he needed to drink, too. The bottle in his hand ran dry, and looking down at the creek, he dipped the bottle in and filled it, then capped it tightly and moved it to a bag on Joey's saddle. He had two more bottles of clean water left, but if it came to it, he'd drink the creek water.

Gideon looked up at the thick canopy above him, searching for the sun to judge the time. He wanted to keep Joey moving at a trot to get as far away as he could, but he'd ridden Joey for hours. Rather than mount, he led Joey away from the creek, walking beside him. It was slow, but some distance was better than none. The sirens faded away to silence, and he faintly heard the chopping noise of helicopters. Military or civil, he couldn't tell this far away. Civil would be bad enough, with their sensors and cargo of border guards, but military would be a bigger problem. He would want to keep to the forests as much as possible, and hope they never got close enough to see through the canopy. A man and a horse would shine brightly on thermal sensors.

He and Joey walked for half an hour, before Gideon remounted and pointed Joey towards one of the many narrow river valleys running through the Atlas Mountains. He knew which one he wanted. Dense tree cover, and not a single road. Despite that, every time he'd been there, he'd found the tracks of humans wearing boots carrying heavy loads. But he'd never seen State Security or Border Guards there. A smuggling trail, he imagined.

The now-omnipresent sound of helicopters drew gradually closer. It was a bad sign for Gideon. He spurred Joey to move just a little faster. He couldn't outrun the helicopters, but he could at least delay being spotted, and perhaps find better concealment.

Several hours later, he was forced to stop. The sound of helicopters behind him had faded, and now he heard helicopters ahead of him. These helicopters were definitely military. That meant that the military had probably also scrambled drones to track him.

This was a very bad sign. Now he'd have to find a way through the military's net rather than outrunning the border guards and State Security.

He checked the sun. He'd have another hour and a half of daylight. That was enough time to make it further before night. He halted Joey and began thinking, looking around as he did. Night would be particularly dangerous, because the thermal optics that worked decently in the day would work very well at night. File had been too talkative once, under the influence of delicious, dried meats provided by Gideon, and he'd let slip some information about the various means used to patrol the border.

He'd also let slip one interesting detail. Around sunrise and sunset there was a period in which thermals were close to useless, where everything was close to the same temperature as it warmed or cooled. That would give Gideon a window.

Unfortunately, File hadn't been too clear on how long of a window it was. Gideon would just have to hope, and pray. He wasn't typically given to prayer. He'd never even been inside a church in his life, but every now and then a little something slipped out, if only in his mind.

He spurred Joey towards the same valley as before. He didn't have a good backup plan, there were only so many viable ways of making it across the border with a horse, and he hoped he could get the timing right to make it across unseen.

Gradually, the sun set, and the day cooled. Gideon spurred Joey faster again, hoping to make up ground during the window. Finally, the sun had dipped below the mountains, and Gideon again dismounted and walked Joey.

"Good work today, Joey. I couldn't have done this without you," he said, stroking the horse's neck affectionately. "When we get to Sala, I'm going to let you eat plenty of good grass and cool, clear water. Might even get some sugar cubes. You've been great."

Joey chuffed in reply.

"Now let's see if we can find someplace to rest for the night," Gideon said. They hadn't made it to the valley the way he'd hoped, but they would be able to make it later that night, or early in the morning. Gideon had an idea what he was looking for. If he was lucky, there'd be another creek, or at least a deep gully around. If he could find a dry creek, then he'd have a perfect place to wait out the darkness. If he couldn't, he'd have to make do.

After another half-hour of searching, Gideon gave up. It was time to improvise. He unsaddled Joey and grabbed his blanket, as well as the saddle blanket he'd used as a saddle pad, and unrolled both. There was a fallen tree with a huge root bulb fully exposed to the air. He tied Joey to one of the roots, then he hung the blankets to form a partially enclosed shelter for Joey. It would keep Joey dry if it rained, but more importantly, it would shield him and Joey from the prying eyes of any Tyran drones or helicopters. As long as the blankets didn't warm up, all the thermal optics would see there would be wool blankets at the same temperature as the surroundings, if Gideon had gotten the angles right. It wasn't an invisibility cloak, but it was as good as Gideon was going to get. A true invisibility cloak would be handy, and while there were rumors that the Salan military had such cloaks, Gideon was not a believer.

Gideon took the opportunity to rest for a while. He'd kept on the move as the police and military had begun their shift changes, going back to their homes and barracks and their wives, mistresses, girlfriends, and dinners. That had given him some time with no one looking for him. After he slept a little, he would continue to make his escape, once the night watch had had enough time to become tired and lazy.

He unwrapped a bit more of his rations and began eating his own dinner. It wasn't much. It wasn't even close to much, but it would do. The next day he would be in Sala, and he would surrender himself to the first Salan he saw. Then he would have plenty of time to eat. For now, he just needed to eat enough to make it that far.

He began thinking about the ranch, and the people he'd left behind. It hadn't been the worst life. It had been full of hard work, but it wasn't terrible. Sometimes he could even forget where he was while he was out on the land.

A cool wind blew around the blankets and through the trees, making Gideon shiver slightly. He inched closer to the blanket to stay out of the wind. The next few hours were likely to be windy as the mountains and the valley cooled unevenly, pulling the air through the canyons. Once the mountains cooled to the same temperature as the land below, the winds would die, and it wouldn't be so bad.

Gradually, Gideon fell into a light sleep, the saddle his pillow, every little noise rousing him as he determined if the source was natural or human. He didn't plan to sleep the entire night. In a few hours, he planned to wake up and resume his march west. Around two in the morning would be ideal. He'd be exhausted, but the searchers would be asleep. No one wanted to be awake so early, not even Gideon. But his life depended on it. The searchers, at most, would be yelled at if he escaped.

Gideon awoke to Joey stomping his feet and pulling on his tie. Gideon was instantly alert, but he did not bolt to his feet yet. He didn't know what had frightened Joey yet. The night was dark, with only the faint light of one of Freya's moons providing any light. Gideon listened intently, and carefully rose to his knees.

"Quiet," he whispered to Joey, who continued making noise and attempting to run off. Joey reluctantly held still. Somewhere out in the dark something had startled Joey, and Gideon still didn't know what. It could be any number of things. There could be soldiers stalking up on him, but there was something more likely out here at night: coyotes. He slid his shotgun from its saddle scabbard, and placed his thumb on the hammer. He had two shotshells left, but he'd likely not have time to load his second shot if they did attack. He heard rustling in the bushes. He silently regretted untacking Joey for the night. He'd wanted to give Joey time to rest well, but if he hadn't, he could have mounted and ridden away. Now, he had to hope that one gunshot would scare off the entire pack.

He could see the coyotes now. There were at least six creeping up in the darkness.

"Leave!" Gideon shouted into the silence. The coyotes paused briefly, then continued their slow advance, and they were growling. They weren't afraid of humans. That would be a problem. He thumbed back the hammer. He would only have one shot. He raised the shotgun to his shoulder, taking aim at the nearest coyote. The small bead sight had been cut off when the barrel had been cut down, making point-shooting his only option. He could either shoot while he still had some range, and hope he scared them off even if he missed, or wait until they were closer, and risk having to shoot at a running target already committed to the attack. He made his choice.

The blast echoed in the woods, the muzzle flash briefly lighting everything like lightning before the darkness came crashing back. There was a howl of pain, and the pack scattered, abandoning the wounded coyote, which limped away with one leg in ruins. Gideon released a breath he hadn't realized he'd been holding, and lowered the shotgun, ejecting the spent round to fly into the dirt, and placing a fresh round in the chamber before he closed the action sharply. He waited a moment to see if the coyotes were returning. When he was sure they were gone, he quickly slipped his shotgun back into the scabbard and began tacking up Joey. The sound of a single shot could travel quite a distance in the night, and if there were anyone nearby, they would be looking for him now. He checked his watch, and quickly realized it was broken. He didn't know what time it was without it.

Gideon disassembled his blanket enclosure and returned Joey's saddle blanket to its place before laying Joey's saddle on his back, double-checking everything as he went. Today would be a bad day to lose a stirrup or for a cinch to come loose. He'd tacked Joey in the dark before, but today was more difficult. The weather was just cold enough that Gideon's hands were stiff and clumsy, and he was used to checking the tack visually. He could still check it with his hands, but it was slower.

He remounted, and spurred Joey on again at a canter. He would have preferred to leave at a walk. Joey could see better in the dark than Gideon, but Gideon still wanted to avoid being knocked off or scratched by low-hanging branches.

The two of them made slow progress along Gideon's desired route. Joey stopped from time to time as he heard something in the darkness; horse hearing was better than human hearing, and they thought like prey animals. Ordinarily, that might be a disadvantage, but Gideon was no predator, not right now. He was the prey of State Security. He intended to ensure they end that day emptyhanded.

Somewhere in the distance, Gideon again heard helicopters. They were very persistent. Most dissidents didn't get such a vigorous manhunt. Perhaps it was because of the way he'd killed Tayler and File, but this response seemed disproportionate to what he'd done. Perhaps it was about that family he'd helped escape. The Greens, they'd been named. Clearly there'd been something more to them than he'd known. The military's pursuit of him would make sense as revenge for their escape, compounded by the deaths of Tayler and File.

He and Joey entered the narrow valley leading closer to Sala. The valley was only a few hundred meters wide, and partially taken up by a river. Gideon had to duck under trees repeatedly, and guide Joey around undergrowth. This valley was particularly green thanks to the river, and it managed to get plenty of sunlight most of the year. The natural conditions made it ideal for sneaking through on foot, though perhaps less ideal for sneaking through on a horse.

Somewhere in the darkness, barely audible over the small river, Gideon heard a noise like a rustling. He halted Joey and looked around. He couldn't see anything, and guessed it was a squirrel. He was about to spur Joey on again when he paused, the hair on the back of his neck standing up, and feeling eerily like he was being watched.

He looked around once more, slowly scanning his surroundings. There wasn't a soul in sight. Just empty forest in a narrow canyon. On his second scan, he stopped. There was something that caught his eye. A horizontal line extending low from one of the tree trunks, illuminated by a solitary beam of moonlight. At first, he wanted to say it was a branch, but it was too straight. Whatever it was was manmade. He was certain of it.

He swallowed silently. He looked away from it, and spurred Joey. If it was one of his pursuers, he could expect a gunshot any moment now. If it wasn't, well then, he wasn't sure what would happen. Smugglers might shoot him, or they might not. He looked back, and the line was gone. He'd thought it might be someone wearing a hat hiding behind the tree, but now there was nothing there, except he almost thought he could pick out a vague human silhouette in the darkness, barely visible, and very broken up. Like someone wearing camouflage, perhaps. He squinted, and even that silhouette was gone. He thought he must be imagining things. Lack of sleep, combined with paranoia and adrenaline, made him see nonexistent threats. He moved Joey into a trot, wishing to put the apparition behind him.

Gideon and Joey rode hard through the hours, riding through the sunrise, picking up speed as it grew lighter and they could both see better. The helicopters had been mostly quiet through the night. Gideon hadn't heard them fly at night often before, though he wasn't sure if this was due to laziness or lack of training. There might have been drones after him, either of the large variety that could fly for hours on end, or smaller drones that were light enough to be moved by men on foot and deployed as needed. But he was still alive, so either there were no drones, or they weren't sure it was him or they wanted him alive. He suspected it was the former.

He drank the last of his clean water sometime in the midmorning. That left Joey able to drink whenever he wanted as long as they followed the river, while Gideon's thirst only grew from hearing that same river.

After many hours of following the valley, they arrived on the plateau. The only thing separating Gideon from Sala was distance. He'd have to cross kilometers of open field to be free. It was excellent country for riding. It was also great for vehicles, and he had no concealment. And at the end of the plateau, he would have to cross the firethorn hedge, the seemingly endless hedge planted by Tyran marking the border between Tyran and its former holding, Sala.

He looked to the south, and he saw a long dust-cloud rising into the sky. Anyone who had ever seen it would recognize it: vehicles driving off-road. And here, that could only mean Tyran military or police. Had they spotted him or was this just bad timing? He didn't intend to find out. Once more he spurred Joey. There would be time for rest when they were in Sala or dead.

Adrenaline blurred the passage of time. Gideon could watch as the dust-cloud grew closer. He was fortunate in one thing: he was closer to the border than the cloud. It was unfortunate that whatever it was, it was moving faster than him.

"Come on," Gideon murmured through gritted teeth. He still had a way to go, at least half an hour before he crossed the border. His heart pounded in his chest. He wasn't sure he'd make it. His thoughts became almost a chant, praying over and over for deliverance.

Behind him, he heard helicopters again, choppy, loud, and deep. Definitely Tyran military helicopters, either Stalwarts or Sentinels. Either was bad. Stalwarts could carry an entire infantry squad, while Sentinels could rip him to pieces without a second thought, either with guns, rockets, missiles, or even the defensive laser typically reserved for dealing with small unarmored targets like missiles or drones.

Soon, he heard another disheartening sound over Joey's thundering hooves. Fighters had joined the hunt. That could not be good for him.

In the distance, he thought he could see the firethorn hedge. Why they'd brought pyracantha with them from Earth when they'd colonized and terraformed it, Gideon could not say. It was a pest, a pox on all houses. But it did serve its purpose by making it very painful to cross the border.

The dust-cloud was getting close now. He could make out the large truck at its head. He turned his head, and could see the helicopters coming straight for him.

A noise like the ripping of canvas and angry hornets ripped behind him, the Freyan earth north of him erupting in explosions and smoke as the helicopter fired on him. Joey ran faster, and tried to turn away from the explosions. They were trying to drive him towards the truck. Gideon applied one spur gently to bring Joey back on track. The helicopter fired one more time, trying again to flush Gideon and Joey to the south. Gideon again guided Joey towards the hedge. He doubted he'd get another warning shot.

The noise of the fighters grew suddenly, and before Gideon knew it, there was a loud double-boom that startled him. He looked towards its source, and realized that it wasn't a Tyran fighter making the noise. The fighter was to the west of him, heading north.

It was a Salan fighter paralleling the border. It wouldn't do him much good. Not now. And he was so close.

Any second now, and the helicopter would shoot. Any second.

Without warning, there was another sonic boom. It was another Salan fighter. It had come out of a canyon still on the Salan side of the border, flying low to the ground and straight at the Sentinel, and suddenly pulling back on the stick, it flew straight up, still breaking the sound barrier, barely staying within the Salan border.

The Sentinel veered off, startled by the fighter appearing from out of nowhere. The fighter didn't shoot, but the surprise of it gave the Sentinel's pilot pause. They were all within shouting distance of the border, and now there were witnesses to whatever the Tyrans did, witnesses capable of strenuously objecting kinetically.

With the Sentinel forced away from its pursuit, it all came down to who could make it to the border first. Gideon heard a cracking noise over his head, but barely registered it. He was almost there. Now the only question was if Joey could jump the hedge.

They were getting closer and closer. The hedge seemed fifteen meters high, though Gideon knew it was closer to two. He spurred Joey forward one last time, and gritting his teeth, he signaled Joey to jump. Gideon ducked low into the saddle as he did, his saddlehorn striking his chest as he did, and with a whisper of hoof against thorn, they flew over the hedge.

"Good job!" Gideon shouted before he knew he'd said anything.

He looked back to see the truck. There were armed soldiers atop it, pointing rifles at him. Bullets cracked around him. Through some miracle, they hadn't hit him or Joey yet, but in Gideon's experience, miracles rarely lasted.

Suddenly, the soldiers and their truck were bathed in bright red light. The soldiers shielded their eyes and stopped firing. It was like a bolt of fire had descended from Heaven and surrounded them. But they were not consumed.

Gideon traced the path of the laser as it illuminated scattered dust particles, and not far in the distance, spotted another aircraft. It didn't have the sleek lines or high speed of a fighter, but it did apparently have a very bright laser, and was reminding these soldiers that they were firing into Salan territory.

The soldiers ceased firing, and sheepishly reentered their truck and drove away. Gideon kept riding, though with less sense of urgency as he did.

The stout aircraft, some kind of bomber, turned away from the border, and flew back into Sala. As it did, its laser reactivated in front of him, moving in a straight line, pointing west by northwest, just slightly off Gideon's course. Gideon raised a hand high in the air, his thumb up to indicate agreement, and he guided Joey along the path the laser had marked. The plane deactivated its laser, and waggled its wings as it departed.

Another bomber arrived, making lazy circles in the sky, keeping an eye on Gideon and the border. Once Gideon was a few kilometers from the border, he descended from Joey's saddle and the two of them walked together, Gideon walking with a bit of a sway, his legs stiff and exhausted from long, hard riding. Joey appreciated the break, too. It was only through some miracle that Gideon had ridden him so hard without laming him.

After a half-hour of walking, they came to a dirt trail. The bomber, still circling overhead, activated its laser again, and traced a circle around him. Joey was clearly confused by the circling light, watching it as it moved.

Gideon, for his part, raised his hand high in the air with his thumb up again to signal understanding.

The laser switched off. Gideon wondered what kind of reception he'd receive. Whatever it was, he hoped they hád water. His mouth was simultaneously dry and sticky from the lack of water, and he wished for shade.

After what felt like a long while, he heard engine noise. A group of small, single-man four-wheeled vehicles drove up. They were low to the ground, with large, lattice tires, and a weapons rack over the engine. The riders wore dusty camouflage uniforms and sleek, sturdy boots in brown leather. They came to a stop in front of him, and Gideon could imagine the lead rider's eyes searching him up and down behind the darkened ballistic goggles covering his eyes.

"You the one they told us about?" he asked behind the balaclava keeping dust and bugs out of his mouth.

"Probably," Gideon answered.

"How attached are you to the horse?" he asked.

"Joey's not for sale," Gideon answered.

"Not interested. No one mentioned a horse. We don't have a way of transporting him. Is he still good to ride?" the rider asked.

"Might be, with a little more rest. You got any water?"

"Sure. For you or for him?" the rider asked.

"Both, if you have it," Gideon requested.

The rider pulled a bottle from a rack on the back of his ATV and tossed it to Gideon. He uncapped it and took a long drink. It wasn't cool water, but it was clean. "Thanks," he uttered. "Got a bucket we can fill for Joey?" he asked.

"No bucket, but there's a stream just over there," he said, pointing west with his thumb.

"Good," Gideon said.

The lead rider and two others dismounted their ATVs and grabbing their carbines, accompanied Gideon to the stream. Gideon let Joey drink his fill while the soldiers watched him and watched over him, their carbines held high, ready to drop down and open fire, either on him or on a threat. These soldiers were cautious.

"Is there any chance we can get a truck and trailer up here for Joey?" Gideon asked.

"No," the heretofore silent soldier replied laconically.

"Okay. Going to take a while to ride there," Gideon mentioned.

"We know," the soldier said again.

They returned to the dirt road again, and began the trek through the Salan side of the Atlas Mountains. It took the better part of the day. Gideon was careful to rest Joey, which made for a much slower pace than the soldiers would have liked. There were jokes, some of them good-natured and some less friendly about horse people and the cavalry. Gideon shrugged them off. Joey had saved his life, and he wasn't going to repay his steed with malice or neglect. Joey was an old friend, and that meant something.

They made it to a Salan camp late in the afternoon. They fed Gideon a good meal, and to Gideon's surprise, they had horse feed on hand, and a water trough and hitching post.

"We'll be holding onto this," one of the soldiers said, gesturing to Gideon's shotgun.

"You can hold onto it, for now, but I'll want it back," Gideon said, his voice not exactly threatening. He wasn't in a position to make or follow through on threats.

They brought Gideon into a room and sat him down at a table. To Gideon's surprise, he realized they hadn't taken his knife. A man stepped into the room, another soldier, and sat down across from him at the table. He was wearing the same uniform as all the other soldiers around, though unlike the patrol that brought Gideon in, his uniform was clean and neat. He removed a pair of brown leather gloves as he sat down.

"I'm Lieutenant Thorsten. I'll be interviewing you about recent events, and your entrance into Sala. And your name is?" he said.

"Gideon Neitzel," Gideon answered.

The officer paused before responding. "The Gideon Neitzel?" he asked.

"The only one I know," Gideon admitted forthrightly.

"Have you helped anyone else cross the Tyran-Salan border before?"

"Many," Gideon said.

"Can you name any?" the officer said intently.

"The last ones were a family named the Greens. A father and two sons. No mother. I don't recall any first names," he answered.

"I see. Do you have a brother?"

"Aaron. He escaped to Sala years ago. Is he still here?" Gideon asked.

"We'll get to that. Why did you come here?" Thorsten asked.

"To escape. State Security came for me. I think they figured out I was the one helping people across, especially the Greens," Gideon answered. A part of him whispered that it was not a good idea to be so open with anyone in government. Another part whispered to answer every question, because this man held Gideon's life in his hands.

The conversation continued for a long time. They finished their chat, and they took Gideon's picture and recorded his biometrics, then took him to a small room with a bed and a bathroom on the third floor of a dormitory.

"We'll come and get you in the morning. Do not leave this room without permission. Understood?" Lieutenant Thorsten said.

"Yes, sir," Gideon answered. "What about Joey?" he asked.

"Joey?"

"My horse," Gideon explained.

"We'll move him to the stables," Thorsten answered.

"You have stables here?"

Thorsten responded in the affirmative.

Gideon walked into the bathroom and turned on the shower. It worked the same as any other shower he'd used, albeit taking much less time to begin pumping out hot water. He disrobed and rinsed off layers of dirt and dust. He watched as the dirt flowed off his body, across the white shower tile, and down the drain. He turned off the water, and grabbed a towel from the rack.

Gideon finished drying off, and changed into the same clothes he'd been wearing before collapsing onto the bed and falling deeply asleep, a guard outside his door, and patrols circling the building. When he awoke the next day, they brought him a large breakfast of simple food, much like he'd eat on the farm: sausages, eggs, and corn grits, which he devoured. Hours later, Gideon knocked on his own door, then opened it. The guard had backed away from the door, ready to raise his weapon.

"Got any work I could do around here?" Gideon asked.

"No. I'll tell them you asked," the guard responded curtly.

Gideon laid down on top of the bed and went back to being bored. A few minutes later, there was a knock at the door.

"You can stay here, or you can muck the stables. Your choice," the guard said.

"I'll muck the stables," Gideon said, swinging his feet over the side of the bed and putting his boots back on.

"Those boots are looking pretty ragged," the guard commented.

"It's hard to buy new things in Tyran. You use what you got until it falls apart," Gideon said.

"Well, might as well use old boots if you're going to be walking in shit," the guard said, leading him to a walking path. When they arrived at the stables, Gideon quickly set to work. Joey was there, happily eating and drinking, and licking Gideon when he had a chance.

"Lotta mules in here," Gideon commented. "Sala have an issue with horses?"

"Mules work well for what we do, or so they say," the guard said.

"We do say, humper," someone else said, walking up. It was another soldier, but unlike the other soldiers Gideon had seen, he was wearing a pair of tall leather boots to his knees. Gideon recognized them as riding boots, though more of the sort worn by those who played with horses rather than worked with them.

"You use mules in your military?" Gideon asked.

"We do. Salan mule cavalry is the best cavalry on all Freya," the newcomer answered. "This horse yours?" he asked, gesturing to Joey.

"He is. Been mine for years now," Gideon said.

"He's a good horse. Took you all the way across the border?" he asked.

"Yeah. How'd you know about that?" Gideon asked, surprised.

"Word travels fast around here," the soldier, his nametape read Lucas, said. Lucas grabbed a bag of apples and began feeding each mule one as a treat. "Your horse like these?" he asked.

"Sure, Joey likes apples. You're not giving him one, are you?"

"Only if you're okay with it," Lucas said, giving Gideon a quizzical look.

"Sure. But he's not one of yours," Gideon said, sounding a little confused.

"It's no matter. He looks like he could use an apple," Lucas said, offering it to Joey, who took it eagerly. "Good horse," Lucas said, rubbing Joey's neck tenderly.

Other soldiers in tall boots came and went, taking mules and tacking them up to ride or returning from rides. At first, he mostly got quizzical looks as an unfamiliar person in their stables, but gradually word spread, and the soldiers began starting friendly conversations. He felt comfortable where he was, even doing menial labor, and these soldiers were friendlier than he'd expected. It was almost time for dinner by the time Gideon was done, and the stable was immaculate. His guard, who'd been watching all day while Gideon worked, told him to put up the equipment, and follow him. They returned to the small room where Gideon had first been interviewed by Lieutenant Thorsten. The officer was there again, waiting.

"We've spoken to Immigration about your case, and they've agreed to hold a hearing—a formality—and grant you asylum and a path to citizenship. You are aware of our military service requirement, correct?" Thorsten said. Gideon nodded. "And is this situation to your satisfaction?" Gideon nodded again. "Excellent. Now, we have a whole system set up to help you acculturate to Salan life. Everyone who comes here from Tyran has a lot of trouble with it, but I've not known any that would go back. Usually there is a whole process for determining your career field. However, I am given to understand you know your way around equines, and Lieutenant Lucas already speaks highly of you," Thorsten explained.

"Are you suggesting I join your cavalry?" Gideon asked.

"If you'd like to," Thorsten answered.

"Sign me up," Gideon said matter-of-factly.

"Excellent. We also have another surprise for you," Thorsten added. Gideon stayed silent. The other door to the room opened, and in walked another soldier. The man's face was expressionless, but he looked very familiar. He stopped in front of Gideon and looked down at him with intense blue eyes.

Gideon rose to his feet with a start. "Aaron!" he said, startled. Sergeant Aaron Neitzel's blank expression broke into a wide grin, and he wrapped his little brother up in a bearhug.

"It's good to see you again, Gideon," he said.

"You, too, Aaron. But you've got some explaining to do," Gideon replied.

"Sure. I'll tell you all about it at dinner," Aaron said. "I wondered how long it would take you to get here. Glad you finally did it."

"I think I am, too," Gideon said.

Reunited at last, the two brothers walked out into the sunset.

NO HOME ON THE RANGE

Rick Cutler

The funeral was set for tomorrow, and Colt Ostergaard wasn't going to miss it. He pulled back on the reins and stopped his six-legged yima before riding it down the slope into the valley. The yima growled and stamped its feet. He'd ridden it hard for three days. They were both tired and hungry.

"Eat-eat!" The yima turned its fuzzy, ostrich head to look at him and gave Colt the stink-eye.

"Soon, big fella, soon." He swung down out of his saddle and patted the yima on its front shoulder.

Winter on Fenris runs some forty-odd years, followed by the Thaw and then the Spring boom, where trees sprout overnight and the animals go into a frenzied heat to spawn their broods. The last time he'd crossed this valley, it was still covered in hard-packed snow. Now it was covered with tall, golden-green grass. He pulled a pair of field glasses out of his saddlebag and scanned the valley.

"Damn."

The glasses picked up a maze of shallow mounds and open pits. A fur-snake had made itself at home there. It looked like a big one.

It would take an extra day to circle around the valley, or he could be stupid and try to go through it. He didn't like being stupid, but come hell or high water, he was going to make it in time for his father's funeral.

He put the glasses away, pulled out the yima's muzzle and then a handful of bacon bits from the feed bag. The yima eyed the bacon greedily.

"You want a yum-yum?"

The yima plunged its beak into the palm of his hand and sucked up the bacon. It chewed the hard bits rat-a-tat fast and when it swallowed, Colt slapped the muzzle over its beak and pulled it tight before the bacon made its way down the yima's long neck.

The yima didn't like the muzzle, but the breed barked like a gunshot when they got excited or scared. It sounded like a gunfight when a herd was on the move, and there was no good to come of rousing the fur-snake with a random bark. A medium-sized one could swallow a small child.

Colt checked the six-gun strapped to his leg, the Foster 12-gauge in the riding scabbard, then pulled down the brim of his flat-crowned hat.

"Follow the leader, big fella." He picked up the reins and worked his way down the slope.

It took several hours to work their way across the valley. Walking over the mounds wasn't an option. They'd collapse and then he'd be trapped in the pit until it was time for the fur-snake's dinner. They worked their way through the maze, keeping to solid ground, back-tracking when they hit a dead end, and always moving forward. They were almost out of the valley when the ground started to shake.

Behind them, a new tunnel was being dug, directly headed their way. Colt jumped into the saddle and spurred the yima. The beast reared up, then bolted the last three hundred yards, jumping mounds and clawing its way onto solid ground when they didn't completely clear a tunnel.

They made it to a rock outcropping, and Colt reined him in. Behind them the long mound of dirt stopped short.

"Not today, snake-eyes," he whispered, then patted the yima. "Good boy. Let's go." He kept an eye on his back-trail. Fur-snakes were nocturnal, but he hadn't met one yet that would turn down a midday snack.

The funeral was scheduled for noon. His mother insisted on the time, since it was Sunday and she wanted to go to church first. Nate, his younger brother, stayed behind to watch as Colt built the funeral pyre.

"You got in late." Nate hobbled on crutches over to a stump and sat down. One leg had a brace on it, the other a cast.

"That I did. What happened to your legs?"

"Alphie work camp for the POWs. I was with the Greensborough Militia at Hilltop Pass. The Alphies didn't take kindly to how many of them we killed before we surrendered."

Colt felt a twinge in his gut as he picked up an axe. "Heard about Hilltop. You held the pass for a couple of days."

"Yeah, when we were down to throwing rocks at the Alphies, the commander ordered us to surrender."

"You gonna be okay?"

"Mostly. Doc Arturo had to rebreak my legs and set them straight."

Colt set to cutting the stack of tree trunks down to size and trimming them. It was going to take a lot of wood to give his father a proper send-off.

"How'd it happen with Pa?"

Nate looked away.

"A snarlie came calling when Pa was out in the field. A big one. They went at it till Pa finally put him down."

It was quiet except for the sound of the axe chopping wood.

"I told him, you know. Told him not to go without me to spot for him. But he wouldn't have any of it."

Colt stopped and leaned on the axe. "Nate."

Nate wouldn't look at him.

"Nate, you know how he was."

"Yeah."

Up past the stone-walled house and barn, a buckboard pulled by a hefty work-yima topped the ridge.

"Ma's home."

Church must have let out early. She was followed by a long line of folks in buggys, buckboards, and on riding yimas. There was even a hover car, like he'd seen in Port Skaaldi.

Colt dug into the woodpile with a fury. He wasn't even half-done.

His mother parked the buckboard up by the house and walked down to the growing pyre. It looked like all the oldsters in Greensborough came with her. Even Clan-folk from as far away as Mt. Dugg and Stenberget showed up. They came with wedges, sledges, axes and chainsaws, shucking their coats and rolling up their sleeves to pitch in.

When the pyre reached four feet high, his mother put her hand on his arm.

"It's enough, Colton. Go on up to the house and get cleaned up. I ran your good shirt and Sunday suit through the 'fresher before church."

"You got time." Mr. Drukker, the Greensborough grocer and Post Master, wiped the sweat off his bald head with a red-print kerchief. "We won't start without you. Go and do as your ma says."

Colt looked around at the men and women helping with the pyre. They mostly ignored him. Nate was up on his crutches talking with the neighbors. He caught Nate's eye and nodded. Nate looked at the pyre and nodded back.

"Won't be long, Ma. Promise."

Good to his word, he was showered, shaved, and in his Sunday suit with hat and string tie in twenty minutes.

Six men, including Drukker, Sheriff Larsson, and the preacher, helped carry his father out of the barn on a funeral board. He was wrapped head-to-toe with linen strips. Colt could smell the bio-diesel soaking the wrappings.

The preacher said some nice things about his father. So did the neighbors and a few people he didn't know. They sang hymns when the pyre was lit. He knew the songs but kept his mouth shut. He wasn't in the mood.

After an hour, they started saying their goodbyes to his mother and drifted away. A tall scarecrow of a man in a fancy suit gave Colt a long look, then climbed into the hover car and drove off. Mr. Drukker watched him go, then turned back to Colt.

"So what are your plans? Are you back for good?"

"Likely not. Figured I'd help with the farm and all till Nate gets back on his feet."

"A lot of folk, not me, you understand, but a lot of them didn't like what they read about you and your court-martial. They came out for your pa today. But..." He looked down and rubbed the back of his head. "Sticking around to help your ma, your family, that's a good thing. And you're free to go where you will. But it's one thing for folks to know you're out here, and another to see you around town. They might not take kindly to seeing your face instead of the kids and kin they lost in the war."

Colt looked past Drukker, watching his mother and Nate walking back up to the house.

"I hear you, Mr. Drukker. If nobody brings trouble to my door, I won't be bringing none to theirs."

———————◆○◆———————

Colt shifted gears on their electric wagon and headed up the ridge towards Greensborough. It took him the better part of a day to pull it out of storage, lube and oil it, dust off the solars, and get the battery charged. Electronics were useless in the sub-sub-zero winter, but good for a sunny Friday afternoon.

"When did you learn how to do all that?" Nate grabbed hold of the railing when they bumped over a pothole.

"The 51st Regiment."

"Oh. You know Ma and me, we read about the trial when the net got restored."

"Figured."

"You could have just turned them over to someone else if you didn't want to do it yourself. They were murderers and rapists."

"Not all of them."

Colt checked his pocket watch. Thirty minutes to town, maybe another thirty or more for the Doc to x-ray and hopefully cut the cast off Nate's leg, then home in time for dinner.

"When the Greensborough Militia surrendered, y'all got put in one of those POW camps. With lots of other militia and units, right?"

"Yup." Nate frowned.

"So was every one of them an angel? No war crimes? No raiders?"

"I— We didn't talk about that. I suspected, but those weren't my people."

"Uh huh. So would you have been good with the Alphies killing all of you because of those bad apples?"

"No. Of course not."

Colt nodded. "Neither would I."

"But—but—"

Colt gave him a side-eye till Nate looked away. That wasn't the whole story, but it would do. Nate was quiet the rest of the way into town.

They pulled up outside of Doc Arturo's clinic, and Colt started to get out.

"Nope." Nate waved him back to his seat. "I can do this myself." He pulled his crutches out of the back and slid down. He shuddered when his feet hit the ground, then limped into the clinic.

Up and down Main Street, folks were busy spending their credits and loading up carts, buckboards, and wagons. A few stared at him, then quickly looked away when he stared back. His pocketwatch said it was nigh up three. He could stop by the saloon for a drink, and damn but he could use one. Or he could head over to Drukker's to pick up a few things. Ma was down with her Rheumatiz and could use something to take the edge off the ache in her joints. He pulled out and headed for the grocery.

The bell over the door jingled when he walked into the store and Drukker did a double-take when he saw Colt. He was up on a ladder shelving a box.

"Afternoon, Colt." He marked the box with a pen then stuck the pen over his ear and climbed down. "What can I do for you?"

"Need some yima-chow, bacon bits if you got 'em, flour, syrup, maple if you got it, some of that red licorice Ma likes, and something for her Rheumatism. It's acting up again."

"Sure thing." Drukker started piling things on a cart. "You know you could have ordered this online and I would have droned it out to the farm."

"Nate had an appointment with the Doc. I needed to kill some time."

The bell over the door jingled again. A young man poked his head in the door, looked at Colt, then ducked back out.

"Well now, don't that look suspicious." Drukker frowned and shook his head. "That was Jesse. He's a ranch hand for Ted Newman, the fella who had the car at your pa's funeral."

"What's Newman's story?"

"He bought the Johansen place after the war. He's from Port Skaaldi, if I recall. Kind of a pushy fella."

"How so?"

"Says we need some law and order out here, as if we needed more rules and regulations. He's not been getting much traction, but he's been stink-mouthing you all week, saying you're a bad element. I wouldn't put it past him to stir something up and blame you to make his point."

"Real neighborly of him."

"Maybe you ought to go out the back door. I can drone all this out to you."

'Wagon's out front."

"Can't you call it up and have it pull around back?"

"No phone. No computer." And no way to track him using GPS. "But I'll take you up on having this stuff delivered. Does Ma have a pay token going with you?"

"Yep."

"Then that's about it." He eased his six-gun in its holster and turned to the door.

"Hey, Colt."

"I don't mean to start nothing, Mr. Drukker, but I sure as hell will finish it if someone else does."

The bell jingled again as he stepped outside.

Three men, young guys in Stetsons, vests, and denims, leaned on his wagon.

"Gentlemen."

Two of them looked at Jesse, the one in the middle. He wore a two-gun rig slung low. Colt crossed his arms and nodded at him.

"What can I do you for?"

"This is a good town with good people." He stalked up to Colt and got in his face. The man stank of cheap cologne and beer. "Trash like you ain't welcome here."

Drukker's door opened and closed behind Colt. The walkboards creaked as Drukker stepped aside, out of the line of fire. He wasn't the only one who stepped out to see what was going on. A crowd was growing off to one side, and Newman sat across the street in his hover car. He wore one of those new translucent, wrap-around comms glasses that connected to the net. The red dot on the bridge of his nose meant it was recording, or maybe even streaming.

"Well?" Jesse couldn't have even hit twenty years yet. He for sure didn't know enough to keep his distance. He was too close to draw. "I said you were trash. A traitor. And you're too yellow to do anything about it, ain't cha?"

Colt tilted his head to the side, as if he were watching a funny bug. Across the street, Newman scowled and squirmed in his seat.

"Mr. Newman." Colt raised his voice and looked over at the man. "These nice fellas work for you?"

Newman jumped, then readjusted his glasses. He didn't seem inclined to answer. Drukker cleared his throat.

"Yes, they do. They're Jesse, Diki, and Matias, Mr. Newman's ranch hands."

"Mr. Newman, I would take it as a great kindness if you asked your boys to step aside and let me leave. They say I don't belong here. I'd be happy to oblige them by leaving."

Some of the crowd was watching Newman now. Sheriff Larsson arrived late to the party with a deputy in tow. Newman scoffed and took off his glasses.

"Yes, yes of course. The boys are high-spirited and it gets the best of them sometimes." He glanced at the sheriff, then straightened his lapels. "Come on, boys. There's work to do at the ranch and I want you to get right on it."

Colt tipped his hat to Jesse. "Pleasure to make your acquaintance, Dik."

"It's Jesse, and you best be remembering that name." He curled his lip and backed up.

"My apologies. I took you for a dick."

Jesse stopped and slapped his hands on his gun butts. Colt had his six-gun out and pointing at Jesse's nose before he could draw. His finger was on the trigger.

Jesse froze.

Colt spun his gun back into his holster, then looked around at the crowd. He smiled and stuck out his hand.

"But we're good, right? 'Cause you got no hard feelings."

Jesse frowned, as if he wasn't sure he should be embarrassed about being out-drawn or because there was a joke he wasn't getting. He turned around and pushed through the crowd. Matias and Diki followed him.

"Colt?"

"Yes, Mr. Drukker?"

Drukker opened and closed his mouth. "Never mind. You best be picking up Nate and headed home."

"Yup."

Nate met him out on the street. The cast was off, and he had a brace on both legs now. He climbed up on the wagon and didn't say anything till they were out of town.

"I heard some things about you and the Newman ranch hands." He looked behind them, then shook his head.

"News travels fast."

"Small town. You know, sooner or later, you're going to take off. You always do. Then I'm going to be stuck with whatever bad blood you leave behind."

"I'm thinking you're right about that." He bit the corner of his mouth and scowled. "Guess I'll have to make sure I don't leave you with my problems." Without killing anyone, if he could. This would take some hard pondering. "Mind if I use your computer after dinner? Been a while since I checked my messages." Yep, hard pondering, and some research.

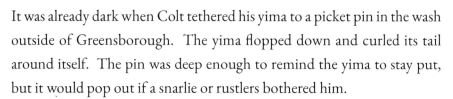

It was already dark when Colt tethered his yima to a picket pin in the wash outside of Greensborough. The yima flopped down and curled its tail around itself. The pin was deep enough to remind the yima to stay put, but it would pop out if a snarlie or rustlers bothered him.

"Eat-eat?"

"Sure." Colt fed him some yima-chow, then hung his spurs on the saddle. "Stay." He stroked the yima's head and scratched the back of its neck. "Good boy."

Colt headed into town, working his way toward Sheriff Larsson's office, picking deserted streets and alleys to stay off everyone's radar. The office was dark and locked up when he got there. It was only half-past eight, according to his pocket watch, and there were no lights on in the upstairs loft where the sheriff stayed.

"Damn."

The Barren Hare Saloon and Rooming House was just down the street. It was the place to socialize on a Saturday night. If he wasn't home, Larsson would be there keeping an eye on things.

The saloon didn't go silent when he walked through the door. The piano player kept playing, the dealer dealt cards at the poker table, and men and women kept drinking and telling each other lies. A few folks turned on their personal recorders. The others pretended not to notice him.

Sheriff Larsson and his deputy stood at the long bar, leaning on their elbows and using the mirror behind the bar to watch the room. Colt walked up and leaned on the bar next to Larsson.

"Colt."

"Sheriff."

The barman, a short, auburn-haired man with a friendly smile, raised his eyebrows.

"What can I do for you?"

"I'll have the same." He pointed at the sheriff's empty shot glass. "And another round for the both of them."

Larsson kept watching the mirror.

"Mighty bold of you to come in here after that stunt yesterday." He glanced down at Colt's six-gun.

"Can't change where I've been, Sheriff. Only the direction I'm headed."

"That would be Hell, I'm guessing."

"Most likely."

The barman sat his drink down and refilled the empty glasses. Colt saluted Larsson with his and took a sip. It was homemade whiskey that tasted like burnt sugar, tobacco, and raw alcohol.

"Mr. Newman doesn't like me much."

Larsson nodded.

"I'd like to have a sit-down. See if we can't hash it out or at least come to a peaceable agreement. I'll be leaving after a spell and I don't want there to be any trouble for Nate and Ma after I go."

"He's got no clan. There's no guarantee that he'd keep any bargain you two make, and no consequences if he goes back on his word."

"I know." He'd looked Newman up on the net the night before. He was convicted of racketeering, tax evasion, and sedition on Alpha Lympos, the inner planet. He might be guilty, he might not. It was a pretty common way to get rid of folks with the wrong political persuasion. He, his wife, and his two daughters were shipped out on one of the last convict barges before Fenris declared her independence and refused to take anymore of the deportees.

"Maybe it's a waste of time. Maybe it gets settled. Won't know if I don't try."

"I suspect you're right. Sean?" He waved the barman over. "Sean, you got a room open where we could do a sit-down?"

"Upstairs. Give us ten minutes and Luile will have it set up. She can referee, if you like."

"That works." Larsson turned to his deputy and pointed at one of the private rooms in back. "I believe Mr. Newman is holding court with the usual suspects. Invite him to meet with Mr. Ostergaard and explain the rules to him."

"On it, boss."

"Good." He focused back on Colt. "Who's your second?"

"Ah, I don't rightly have one." He made a show of looking around the room then settled back on Larsson. "I was hoping you could be. That might put some teeth into it if Newman knows this is sanctioned by the Law."

"Or make him think we're ganging up on him. Keep looking. Maybe someone else will show up that wouldn't mind giving you a hand."

They stood and nursed their drinks until Sean told them the room was ready. Larsson upended his glass and drained it. "Hell. Let's just go. Deputy Hicks will keep an eye on things down here."

A lot of eyes watched as they crossed the room and headed upstairs.

A woman in denims and rolled-up sleeves, Luile, he supposed, met them outside a room. Two empty side tables were set up on either side of the door. Newman and Jesse came up the back way a few minutes later. Newman was already recording with his glasses.

"The room is clean," Luile said. "No weapons, food, drink, or recording devices allowed inside."

"I'll go first." Colt unbuckled his gun-belt and laid it on the side table. Newman's eyes got large when he saw Colt add two knives, brass knuckles, a sap, and his ankle-gun to the pile. He stepped aside and held his arms out.

"Jesse?" Luile pointed at Colt.

The boy patted Colt down. He missed a couple of spots, but Colt didn't mention it. He wasn't holding anything out.

"Mr. Newman?"

"I—I don't carry any weapons."

"The ban includes recording or communications devices. Your glasses, if you don't mind?"

"Oh. Yes." He put the glasses on his side table and Larsson patted him down.

"We're good."

"Mr. Ostergaard, you requested the sit-down, so you'll enter first. Mr. Newman will follow." She stepped away from the door. "You may discuss your concerns for as long and as loud as you wish; however, I will remind you that if I hear anything else, I am authorized to take any measure to ensure the safety of the participants, up to and including deadly force." She laid her hand on the butt of her pearl-handled .45. "You may begin."

The room was bare except for two wood chairs facing each other. Colt sat in one and waited. Newman looked around the room before sitting down in the other one. He crossed his arms and glared at Colt. The man was skin and bone, except for the bags under his eyes and the turkey wattle under his chin. It looked like he had lost a lot of weight.

"Mr. Newman, I don't know you. Never seen or heard of you before the funeral. But I seem to have got on your bad side. I'd like to make amends if I've done you wrong."

"You can't." He spat the words out.

"And yet here I am." He leaned back and crossed his arms. "Tell me why. What have you got against me?"

Newman flushed and clenched his fists.

"You let them go."

Colt suspected it was something like that. He didn't interrupt.

"Those bastards harassed me on Alpha Lympos. Took away my business. Kicked us to the curb. And then they came here and—and—"

"And?"

"They did what they couldn't do at home! They killed them." He jumped to his feet. "Killed them. Raped them. Just pulled them out of a supermarket one day and—and—" He ground his teeth together. "And you let them go."

He was bright red and sweating. He started to shout.

"You let them go. Go home to their nice little wives and nice little children with blood on their hands. They should have been punished, they should have been killed, and you let them go, you son of a bitch!" He grabbed his chair and swung it over his shoulder, ready to hit Colt with it.

Colt bowed his head.

"You got the right to hate me. Just like hundreds of other folks. I don't blame you." He looked up at Newman. "What do you want from me?"

"I want you to suffer. I want you punished the way they should have been punished, and then I want you dead."

"Mr. Newman, you can hit me with that chair. Maybe even kill me before Luile gets that door open, but I can by God guarantee she will shoot you dead before my body hits the floor."

Newman huffed and puffed, then threw the chair across the room. No sooner had he done that than the door flew open and Luile charged into the room, her Peacemaker at the ready.

"We're good, Luile. Mr. Newman was just making a point."

Newman was bent over, his hands on his knees, catching his breath. He raised a shaking hand and nodded. Luile looked him over, then backed out of the room and shut the door again.

"You know, there's no way to know if those men were the ones who did that to your family."

"It doesn't matter. They were complicit. Just like you. I don't know who you bribed to get off so easy, but you're just as guilty. Maybe even a collaborator." He stamped over to the chair, righted it, and sat down.

Nothing he was allowed to say was going to make a difference to Newman. He took a deep breath and tried the next best thing.

"Your wife, your girls. Did they deserve what happened to them?"

"Of course not, you bastard!"

"Neither does my family. I've got nothing to offer you, but I'm asking that you leave my mother and brother out of it. This is between you and me."

Newman squirmed in his seat, as if he were at war with himself.

"I'll think about it."

"Maybe you can think about this, too. It's a chance to prove you're a better man than me."

"Don't you dare try to manipulate me!" He stood. "Are we done here?"

"I suppose we are."

"Good." He threw the door open and left, taking Jesse with him.

Luile and Sheriff Larsson looked in on him.

"Well?"

"Sometimes I just say too much." Colt shook his head. "We didn't come to any agreement. I asked him to leave my family alone."

"Think he will?"

"Don't know." It looked like there wasn't any way around it. There was going to be blood.

Colt heard the shot before the bullet splintered the doorframe next to his head. He hit the floor and rolled back into the house.

"Get down! Take cover!"

The side of his face stung, and it hurt when he touched it. His fingers came away bloody.

A red dot squiggled across the threshold, disappeared, then came back, holding steady on the floor.

"Nate—"

"Calling the sheriff right now," he shouted. There was muffled conversation, then Nate shouted out again. "He says to—"

One, then four more shots hit the front window, shattering the insulated glass.

"He says to stay away from the windows and shelter behind something solid."

This wasn't an experienced sniper. He didn't have the radar-penetrating equipment to see past the stone walls, and at most, he was shooting a hunting rifle, most likely a .350 Mag, made for taking down huge woolies.

Colt crab-walked back into the hallway where Nate and his mother were on the floor. Nate was strapping his gun-belt on and his mom had her Burke shotgun across her lap.

"Colton! You're hurt!" She crawled over to him and pulled him up by his chin.

"Ma!"

"Sit still. You got some splinters."

"Ma, there's a sniper out there trying to kill us."

"He's just going to have to wait. There. Now I'm going to get some bandages and alcohol out of the—"

"No!" Colt and Nate both shouted at the same time.

"Don't you be yelling at your mother." She tore off her house slipper, not sure which one of them to hit.

"Hit him first. I'm still bleeding."

"What?"

Colt loosed his six-gun and rolled into a crouch. "Stay put until you hear Larsson give you the all-clear."

"Ya think?" Nate flicked the cylinder of his S&W out, checked the chambers, then clicked it back into place. "Hey, where are you going?"

"The shooter's not going to stick around. He'll be gone by the time Larsson gets here. I'm going out the back door to the barn, then mount up and chase him."

"And if there's someone covering the back?"

"Then I best be a fast runner. Tell Larsson what I done. Don't want him shooting me by accident."

Colt bolted out of the back door, zig-zagging for the barn. Nobody took any more shots. Inside he threw his saddle over the yima's back and cinched it.

"Time to ride, big fella."

"Run-run?"

"Yep. Run-run." He set the yima's bit and bridle, then legged up onto the beast. The yima let out a gunshot bark and burst out of the barn. They laid tracks for the ridge facing the house. A yima at full bore is like riding a meteor. They were up on the ridge in minutes.

"Whoa, whoa, big fella."

"Run-run!"

"Whoa, now. I don't want to hit my head on a branch or run us into an ambush." He swung off the yima and led him through the new trees. He'd been stupid lucky so far. Now it was time to be smart.

He kept an eye on the house below, looking for the spot where he would have nested down if he was going to take those shots. When he found the crushed undergrowth and spent casings, he knew he'd found it. Larsson should be able to get DNA and fingerprints off the brass if he was worth his salt. More crushed undergrowth led down the other side of the ridge, away from the house. So far, the shooter was on foot. He tied the yima to a tree and followed the trail.

The trail disappeared in a clearing. He was halfway across it when he heard a trigger click.

He drew and spun around. No one was there. In the trees behind him a rifle bolt got recycled. The shooter had to be close if he could hear that.

Click.

They definitely weren't a pro or even a veteran if they were pulling on a dry magazine. He holstered his gun.

"Whoever you are, give it up. You got a dry mag and if I found you so easy, you know the Sheriff will, too."

Branches and leaves rustled, then Jesse stepped out from behind a tree with both six-shooters in his hands.

Damn.

"Draw, traitor."

"You sure you want to die today?"

"The only—"

Colt drew and fired.

Jesse staggered back. He fired both guns. The shots went wild. Blood bloomed in the middle of his chest, and trickled out of his mouth.

Jesse, no last name, fell and died.

Colt reloaded and holstered his six-gun. Then he stuck his shaking hands in his pockets. The sheriff would be along soon enough.

Sheriff Larsson studied the antique computer screen sitting on his desk.

"It was a righteous shoot," he said.

Colt sat on the other side of the desk, waiting for him to finish.

"Righteous, but dumb. You shouldn't have chased him."

"Maybe. He did have a yima with a month's worth of rations down by the creek. He could have disappeared into the high plains or mountains and you never would have found him. Not until he came back and took another shot at me or my family."

"But you didn't know that when it happened."

Colt kept his mouth shut this time. Larsson shook his head and tapped the "Enter" key.

"The results of the inquest are public now. The suit Newman filed against you for loss of a contract employee is voided."

"Was there anything tying Newman to the shooting?"

"Nope." He leaned back in his chair. "On the other hand, most folks will put two and two together and figure it out. The ones that don't like you won't care. Other folks, like the clan families, won't hold it against you. They may not like you, either, but they'll like Newman even less. His man shot at you while you were under your mother's roof. That's a major violation of their sanctuary law, and they'll remember that the next time he starts talking law and order."

"Which still leaves me hanging in the wind."

"I'd say it's about time to start moving on. Newman's got a grudge and he won't let it go." He pulled Colt's rig out of a drawer and slid it across his desk. "Righteous shoot, but I'd watch my back."

"Yeah." Colt stood and strapped his rig on. It felt good to be wearing it again. "I'll be saying goodbye to my family and then heading out in the morning."

"Where to?"

Colt shrugged. "It's a big world out there since the Thaw. Guess I'll follow the sun and see where it takes me."

"Good luck." Larsson stood and shook his hand. "And don't come back."

Colt's mom hugged him and cried a lot. Nate did a lot of blinking and rubbing his eyes.

"Just got you back and you're gone again."

Colt freed up one hand and put it on Nate's shoulder.

"You're the head of the house now. Find yourself a good woman and have lots of kids. Fill this place up and send me lots of vids. I'll check the net from time to time to see how you are doing."

Nate gave him a half-hearted chuckle.

"I'll see what I can do about that."

Colt mounted up and headed back west, the way he'd come. The last he saw of his family, they were standing outside the house, waving goodbye.

"Giddyup." He didn't run the yima full out. They had miles to go and they were in no hurry.

He was a half-day out from the farm when he pulled up at the top of a hill and looked back. Something was riding hard on his trail and that didn't bode well. He took out his field glasses and confirmed his gut feeling. It was two riders and a hover car. He stuffed the glasses back into his saddle bag.

"We need to cover some ground, big fella. Time to run."

"Run-run!"

They ran hard until they reached the fur-snake's valley. It put them maybe two hours ahead of Newman. He reined the yima in and slid out of the saddle. There looked to be twice as many mounds crisscrossing the valley as there had been before. The fur-snake had been busy.

"Got to slow-walk it now, buddy." He muzzled the yima led him down the slope into the tall grass.

It was hard going. They kept hitting dead ends and having to backtrack just to move forward on solid ground. When he turned around at the latest dead end, he saw their lead over Newman was gone. Newman, Diki, and Matias were up on the edge of the valley. He pulled out his field glasses and watched them.

They were too far away for him to hear what they were saying, but Newman was obviously agitated. The ranch hands kept shaking their heads.

"Walk away," he said under his breath. "I'm not worth it."

Whatever Diki and Matias were telling him, Newman wasn't having any of it. He threw himself into the car and drove down into the valley.

Mounds collapsed where he drove over them, which made no difference to the hover car. Newman kept coming. Diki and Matias just watched.

Colt picketed the yima and waited.

Newman broadsided the car when he was in shouting distance and dropped it on the ground. It didn't look like anyone was inside it until the door on the other side opened and closed. There was rustling in the grass and Newman's head popped up over the hood for an instant.

Colt stuck his thumbs in his gun belt.

Newman's head popped up again and stayed up. He steadied an unusually large Ruger on the hood of the car with both hands. He wasn't wearing his comms glasses now.

"Don't move."

"Go home, Newman." Colt spoke quietly. "You don't know what you're doing."

"Yes, I do. People like you can't be allowed to run wild, shooting whoever they like. Jesse was running away. You should have let him go, just like you did with those soldiers."

"So you're going to be judge, jury, and executioner now?"

"No more than you've been. But you'll be gone and I'll still be here. Now draw." His hands trembled.

"Do you want to know the whole story?"

"What?"

"About that day. About what happened. Why I let the Alphie soldiers go home?" The court-martial made his silence a condition of his release, but either he or Newman were going to be dead at the end of the day, so it didn't seem to matter much anymore.

"What do you mean?"

"The war was over. We won. My men rounded up all the Alphies in Port Skaaldi and there were quite a few. Then the order came down to kill them all."

"But you didn't."

"Nope. I disobeyed my orders."

"Why? Were you a sympathizer? Didn't you have the guts? Did they bribe you?"

"They did bribe me, of a sort."

"I knew it."

"There was a lot of propaganda and lies going around at the end. Maybe I didn't know who, but I knew at least some of them had raped and murdered our people just to try and cow us, scare us, make us give up."

"You knew, you son of a bitch. You knew and you still let them go. What did they bribe you with? Money? Women? Drugs?"

"Our sons and daughters."

"What?"

"They still had hundreds of our people in work camps, our soldiers in POW camps. Their orders were to scorch the earth if they had to evacuate. Kill everyone and burn it all down."

He closed his eyes, pushing back the memories of camps where he'd seen just that.

"Their General, they called him the Peace Commander, offered me a deal. He'd call off the order if I let his men go home."

"And you took the deal."

"Not right away. I ran it up the chain of command. Our Regimental Commander rejected it. He said no."

"And you did it, anyway."

"Yeah."

"You could have killed them after he gave the order. You had them all under control."

"Could have. Didn't. So they cashiered me." Cashiered him, pretended there wasn't ever a deal, and retired the Commander who gave that order. All to save face. "You think I was wrong to let them go."

"Yes."

"What if it was your family, your wife, your daughters? What if they were in one of those camps?"

"But they weren't."

"But—"

"We're done talking. Draw."

"No."

"Draw, or I'll just shoot you."

"You don't want to do that. Not here."

Newman bared his teeth and fired. He flinched and missed. The sound echoed across the valley. The yima raised his head and looked around.

"Draw!" He screamed and fired again.

"You don't understand."

He shot again. And again.

The ground started to tremble. The yima buried its head between its legs.

"Newman, I'm trying to save your life."

"Liar!"

The fur-snake burst out of the ground behind Newman. It was enormous, at least thirty feet long and big enough to swallow a man. Hundreds of tiny feet lined its long underbelly and all that was left of its winter coat was the shaggy mane around its neck.

Newman shot the last of his rounds at the fur-snake. Some might have even hit it. The shots, sounding so much like a yima's bark, made the fur-snake shake with anticipation.

Newman ran, screaming.

The snake lunged and scooped him up in its jaws.

Bones cracked.

Blood gushed out of the fur-snake's mouth.

Newman was still screaming.

Colt looked away. When the screaming stopped, Newman and the fur-snake were gone.

"Damn."

At the edge of the valley, Diki and Matias had seen the whole thing. No telling what story they were going to tell.

"Come on, big fella." He got the yima up on its feet. "The snake's been fed. Time for us to move on."

TIN BADGE, TIN DOG

Daniel G. Zeidler

Master Boarding Sergeant Tass ke'Dolh (Makhtari Commonwealth Marine Corps, Retired) felt he had earned the right to sit on his front porch in the morning and enjoy a quiet cup of *zahrah*.

The Universe disagreed.

The approaching rider was clearly in a hurry; he was crouched low in the saddle with his horse at a gallop as they raced up the road to Tass's ranch house. Tass indulged in a cautious sip of hot *zahrah* and considered the rider through narrowed eyes. Each of the Septisolaran's seven Houses had specialties, and House Ain's specialties were agriculture and animal husbandry. The Ain homeworld almost seemed to consist solely of endless pastoral landscapes, and Tass was certain there wasn't a single son or daughter of the House who did not know how to ride a horse. That being said, they normally only did so for ceremony or pleasure; for all else, they drove gravitic repulsion speeders just like everyone else on every other world in the Commonwealth. His gut told him, however, that it was trouble that urged the rider forward at such a reckless pace, and it would be a strange trouble indeed that came to his door on horseback.

Tass looked regretfully down at his *zahrah* mug and sighed. It was a shame that it would go to waste, but such was the life of a Commonwealth Marshal. He stood up and reached through the open kitchen window to place his mug down beside the *zahrah* machine, then slid the window shut. A sound came from within the house; it had the rhythm of an approaching dog's claws clicking against the floor, but the sound was off slightly. Tass opened the kitchen door before it was headbutted open and let what looked like a metallic wolf out onto the porch.

The concept of military working dogs went back in human history to the prehistoric times prior to the Nomad Wars, but no amount of training or genetic manipulation had proven capable of producing a biological dog that could function comfortably and effectively in the unique environment of deepspace, ship-to-ship boarding actions. Centuries of development had resulted in the first *Mech-sent, semi-autonomous, armored, boarding support, canid form* being produced during final decades of the Nomad Wars. After that, the Terran Imperium has gone on to improve the design, and centuries later, the Makhtari Commonwealth, in Tass's not unbiased opinion, had perfected it. Zdrev was a mechanical sentient, but he was also most assuredly a Good Dog.

Tass recognized the approaching rider as Ain Koto, a tall, stocky twelve-year old whose family had sold Tass the land where he'd built his home. Koto slowed his horse from a gallop to a trot before bringing him to stop when he reached Tass's porch. He slid out of the saddle and, breathing heavily, bowed his head and placed his open hand over his heart. "Greetings—greetings, Noble ke'Dolh! The Sept Leader— Sept Leader requests—"

Tass made a calming gesture with both hands. Koto's family had their own surname, but it was the custom of the Septisolarans to use one's House name in the place of the clan surname when speaking with those who were not of the same House. "Easy now, Ain Koto. Take a moment to catch your breath, then go ahead and tell me."

Koto nodded, took a few breaths, then squared his shoulders as he assumed a position of attention. "Sept Leader Ch'Kaya requests the honor of your presence at your earliest convenience, Noble ke'Dolh. She also asks that you bring the Noble Zdrev, as well."

Twelve years earlier, when Tass had needed to come up with a name for his canid mech-sent companion, he'd chosen *Zdrev* because the Septisolaran word had sounded exotic and tough, and he'd thought that it referred to the fierce wild dogs that prowled the remote territories of the Septisolaran worlds. When he'd arrived on the Ain homeworld, Tass soon discovered that in Septisolaran-variant Standard, *zdrev* actually meant *domestic dog,* with connotations of being notably tame, friendly, and not at all dangerous. This had led the adults to suspect at first that the Commonwealth had perhaps not sent their brightest Marine to serve as one of Ain's first planetary marshals, but the children had found, and *still* found, an advanced combat mech essentially named *Big Friendly Dog* to be incredibly amusing. Koto, however, hadn't even shown a hint of a smile when he'd addressed Zdrev.

"This sounds serious, Ain Koto. Did the Noble Sept Leader give you anything else to say?"

"More serious than anything I've ever seen in my whole life, Noble ke'Dolh! A Divine Right Raider decloaked over town and hit us with a suppressor pulse. Then they set down in the old smuggler's field south of town and the captain came out and said we'd better load as many cattle on his ship as could fit in the hold or he'd blow the whole town up!" Koto said, his eyes growing wider and his words tumbling out faster as he spoke. He pointed to Tass's badge. "Sept Leader Ch'Kaya also told me to let you know that she doesn't need the Marshal—she needs the Marine."

"I see. I'll be needing my armor, then, and while I'm getting it, please feel free to see to your horse's needs, Ain Koto. You can keep Zdrev company while I gear up," Tass said. Then, remembering how formally Koto had begun their exchange, he inclined his head in the formal manner of the Seven Suns and added, "Honor to House Ain."

"Honor to your House, as well, Noble ke'Dolh," Koto replied with a salute. His attention quickly shifted to the mech-sent and he grinned broadly. "C'mon, Zdrev. Let's head over to the stable."

Tass, knowing that Zdrev would keep Koto safe on the off chance that any of the Divine Right raiders were foolish enough to follow the boy to his ranch, went inside and made his way to his small armory. He changed out of his work clothes and into a tac suit, then quickly donned his light boarding armor. He deployed the helmet, confirmed the suit seals and power supplies were at one hundred percent, then retracted the helmet. Tass turned to his weapons rack and without hesitation grabbed a needler pistol and a utility cutting tool. He reached out to grab his energy rifle, but paused. A rogue Divine Right ship crew wasn't much of a threat on the ground, but Divine Right Naval Infantry, rogue or otherwise, were always foe to be treated with respect. He picked up a brace of spare power packs, a spool of breaching cord, and his inertia carbine.

Inertia weapons (originally INERTIA, but the meaning of the acronym had long since been lost to time) were anti-armor weapons loosely based on the same technology as a starship Jump drive. The weapon first fired a targeting beam to lock on to a portion of the target, then it used a particle burst to attempt to accelerate that portion of the target out toward infinity. In the case of the inertia carbine, the area affected could be set by the user to as small as zero point five inches or as large as fifteen inches in diameter. At lower settings, inertia weapons were useful for dealing with individuals in combat armor, while at higher settings, they could be used to breach bulkheads and hatches, or to just generally wreck the enemy's toys and gadgets.

When Tass went to the stable, he was surprised to find that Koto had Tass's own horse, a brown Ain Saddlehorse named Racer, saddled and waiting for him. Taking a speeder would have been faster, of course, but it would have been more likely to be detected by the raider's sensors; something twelve-year old Koto had known. Before the Septisolarans had joined the Commonwealth, indeed, one of the main reasons they had joined the Commonwealth, raids between the seven Houses were common. After the Seven Suns joined the Commonwealth, they maintained a considerable amount of autonomy with the original worlds of the Commonwealth, essentially serving as an eighth House responsible for patrolling the space lanes, resolving disputes between the Seven Suns, and law enforcement in the form of a frontier marshal service. The frequency of raids had dwindled to almost nothing, but memories were long in Septisolaran space, and children were still raised to know what to do and what not to do during a raid.

"Thank you, Ain Koto. You've done well," Tass said after greeting Racer and making a quick inspection of the tack and saddle. He slid his inertia rifle into the saddle holster, then swung up into the saddle. "I imagine the Noble Sept Leader has already instructed you to remain here?"

Koto nodded solemnly. "This is my duty station for the duration of the raid, Noble ke'Dolh. I am to hold this position and assist any others who might arrive to take shelter here until relived by yourself, my Deck Officer, or the Sept Leader herself."

"Very good," Tass said, then saluted him in the Makhtari style. "Honor to your House, Ain Koto."

Koto responded with an impressively crisp salute. "Glory and honor to you in battle, Noble ke'Dolh!"

Tass urged Racer forward and whistled for Zdrev to follow. He focused a moment on the thought patterns that boosted his cybernetic link with Zdrev into combat mode. He smiled at the familiar sensation of Zdrev's neural network practically humming with excitement. Most of that network was dedicated to interpreting the vast array of sensor data Zdrev constantly took in with very little, percentage-wise, left over for communication. Zdrev could communicate along normal canine channels such as body language and auditory cues, but he could also communicate simple messages via text that appeared in one corner of the virtual heads-up display Tass saw when his cybernetics were in combat mode.

>>QUERY: PLOT COURSE TO (RONDEZVOUS COORDI-NATES)?

"Let's approach the old smuggler's field from the southwest and do a little reconnaissance first, Zdrev. Keep it low-key, though," Tass replied out loud, though he could have just as easily sent the message over his link. When he'd first been paired with Zdrev, the medico had told him that mech's neural network both responded to and was shaped by Tass's own mind. If he wanted his mech to act like a machine, he should treat it like a machine, but if he wanted it to act like a dog, then he should treat it like a dog. There were arguments to be made for either approach, but the decision had been an easy one for Tass to make.

>>ACKNOWLEDGED. MISSION PARAMETERS UPDATED.

>>COURSE PLOTTED.

>>ENGAGING (STEALTH) MODE.

Zdrev calculated the best route for them to take to minimize their chance of detection, then shimmered into near invisibility as he activated his stealth field. Racer shook his head in mild disapproval of a combat mech that could disappear, but was otherwise unimpressed and continued on-ward at a casual trot. While Tass appreciated Racer's ambivalence toward combat mechs and weapons fire, he did wonder from time to time how his horse had acquired that ambivalence. The answer that struck him as most likely was that the Ain were actually crazy enough to breed and train horses they could bring along while raiding the homeworlds of the other Houses. Not that any of the Ain would ever even dream of conducting a House raid these days, no sirree, Marshal; thanks to the Commonwealth, that sort of thing was in the past.

Another Seven Suns tradition that had been theoretically relegated to the past was smuggling. By its very name, the *old smuggler's field* boldly attested: *there's no smuggling going on here anymore—honest, Marshal.* To give credit where credit was due, it was a true statement: no smuggler's ship had landed in the field south of town since the Seven Suns had joined the Commonwealth. All of the smuggler vessels now landed *north* of town in the *new* smuggler's field that was equipped as well as any military forward operating base, complete with a mobile ship cradle and camouflage screens. So long as certain clearly defined lines were not crossed, the *scourge*, so-called, of smuggling was an internal Septisolaran concern, so Tass politely pretended that he was unaware of the north field and its curious assortment of military "surplus" hardware. The Ain respected politeness, and so they politely scheduled their smuggling operations for times when he was busy elsewhere.

The course Zdrev had plotted had them following a faint trail which Tass suspected more than one smuggler had used in the past, that wound its way through forested hills and stopped just out of sight from the old landing field. Tass dismounted, removed his inertia carbine from its sheath, and sent Racer back home to his stall with a pat on the shoulder and a whispered command; the Ain had high standards for what they considered an acceptably trained horse. He deployed his suit's helmet and tapped his wrist comp to synchronize his stealth field with Zdrev's field.

Tass did a quick check of his weapons and looked down at Zdrev, who responded with a wag of his tail. "All right, buddy, I'll bet there's a little concealed spot up near the top of this hill that has a clear view of the landing field, isn't there?"

>>CONFIRMED.

"You have to love the Septisolarans, Zdrev. They are both consistent and efficient in their distrust of one another. Let's go have a look at what these Divine Right raiders have brought to the table, shall we?"

>>QUERY: PROTOCOL (SADDLE UP)?

Tass wasn't sure if Zdrev had picked up a rudimentary sense of humor or if he simply liked the phrase. "Yes, Zdrev. Saddle up."

Tass followed Zdrev up the slope to the concealed entrance of a narrow passage cut at an angle into the hill and lined with durcrete. The passage ran straight for several yards, then turned sharply at a right angle, and when they approached the turn, Zdrev dropped into a low crouch.

>>ALERT: DIVINE RIGHT (INTRUSION DETECTION) SENSORS DETECTED

Tass dropped down to one knee and studied Zdrev's scan data on his helmet HUD. To his relief, the Divine Right crew hadn't set up any sensor relays in the passage; the sensor emissions Zdrev was "scenting" were from a ship-based system. He saw Zdrev tip his nose up, as if he were trying to catch more of the scent, and the data on the HUD updated to show the type of sensor array the Divine Right vessel was using. Tass arched an eyebrow; it was an old model array the Divine Right had phased out of service almost a decade earlier. The HUD updated again to reflect a 99.99 percent chance they would evade detection.

"Advance to the observation post, Zdrev. Slow and easy," Tass instructed, then waited as Zdrev slinked around the corner and confirmed the way forward was clear. The end of the passage was a circular space large enough for two observers to stand in comfortably and observe the smuggler's field through a narrow rectangular opening in the durcrete wall. Zdrev placed his front paws on the edge of the opening and peered through it with his ears forward. Tass patted him on the back of the head, then leaned forward to look through the opening, as well.

Externally, the Divine Right raider occupying most of the smuggler's field appeared to be nearly identical to the standard Septisolaran raider employed by all seven Houses: an overall "squashed" ovoid shape 300 feet long and 150 feet wide, with armored upper and lower hulls separated by an equatorial trench where the weapon turrets, airlocks, sensor arrays, maneuvering pods, and the like were located. The Septisolaran ships were essentially light freighter hulls sandwiched between the thick armor shells of the upper and lower hull and equipped with anti-starship energy weapons and upgraded maneuver pods and main drives. The Divine Right copies, however, were light warships whose outer hulls had merely been constructed to look like the Septisolaran ships; they had more advanced weapons, shields, and sensors, but lacked the heavy armor and overpowered drive systems of the Seven Suns' design. The Divine Right raiders had fared poorly in the early stages of their attempted invasion of the Commonwealth, and the ships were soon pulled from frontline service, with all production ceasing soon thereafter.

"Obviously not a frontline ship, Zdrev, but it also isn't the sort of ship the Divine Right would just allow a rogue crew to run off with so they could play space cattle rustler with the Ain," Tass said as he studied the raider. He hit a chin switch inside his helmet and opened a magnification window on his HUD. The only openings in the armored hulls of the Septisolaran raiders were for the outsized maneuvering pods; the hulls of the Divine Right raiders, on the other hand, were replete with hatches and access panels. The number of open hatches he saw seemed *excessive*; he considered counting them, but decided it would have been a waste of time. "Zdrev, give it a good sniff for me, will you? Maybe we can figure out why all those hatches are open."

Zdrev tilted his head from side to side and tipped his nose up as if he actually were sniffing the air. After a moment, he pulled his ears back and recoiled slightly.

>>ANALYSIS: MULTIPLE NON-CRITICAL FAILURES IN (LIFE SUPPORT) AND (AIR FILTRATION) SYSTEMS

>>ON BOARD AIR QUALITY: ... ... BREATHABLE (TECHNICALLY)

"Technically breathable, eh? So...the ship stinks and they are desperately trying to air it out? Isn't that interesting." Tass deactivated the magnification window, but quickly keyed it back on and focused on the raider's starboard airlock where two individuals had stepped outside for a moment to get some fresh air. He increased the magnification and frowned when he saw the unit patches emblazoned on their shoulder armor. "This isn't a rogue crew, Zdrev. Those are Divine Right Naval Infantry—you remember those guys, right?"

Zdrev emitted an impressively realistic growl and targeting data for the two Naval Infantrymen appeared on Tass's HUD. Tass chuckled and reached over to give Zdrev a pat on the back. "Yeah, *those* guys." The two Naval Infantrymen went back inside the raider, and Tass shut off the magnifier. He stepped away from the observation port and motioned for Zdrev to do so, as well. "We should get over to the rendezvous coordinates before Kaya and the others get impatient and do something rash."

>>ALERT: HOSTAGE SITUATION.

"What?" Tass went back to the observation port as Zdrev dropped his head and leaned to the side to try to get a better view of the raider's port airlock. A window opened in Tass's HUD as Zdrev fed him sensor data and showed him an enhanced view of two more Naval Infantrymen as they half-dragged, half-carried a woman whom they had put in a hood and bound hand and foot. Given the Divine Right's history regarding the treatment of prisoners, Tass decided his rendezvous with the Ain would have to be delayed. Zdrev zoomed in the woman as the Naval Infantrymen brought her on board the raider, and he highlighted her Ain body armor and the clan markings and assignment tabs emblazoned on it. A chill went down Tass's spine. "Can you identify the hostage, Zdrev?"

>>WORKING...

>>ANALYSIS INDICATES TARGET IS (HUMAN, FEMALE), MARGIN OF ERROR IS (ZERO POINT ZERO) PERCENT.

Tass let out a brief sigh when Zdrev looked at him with a decidedly canine grin. "Very funny, but I picked up on that."

Zdrev's ears swiveled back and his tail drooped, but not because he thought Tass was unhappy with him.

\>\>FURTHER ANALYSIS INDICATES TARGET IS (AIN CH'TIMA), MARGIN OF ERROR IS (FIVE POINT ZERO) PERCENT

Tass didn't want to teach Zdrev bad habits, so he cursed silently and said, "That's what I was afraid of. We need to find—"

\>\>INCOMING SECURE TRANSMISSION FROM (SEPT LEADER AIN CH'KAYA)

Tass winced inwardly. Sept Leader Ch'Kaya was not only a member of the Ain aristocracy, but she also belonged to Clan Ain itself, and Ch'Tima was her younger sister. His eyebrows rose in surprise when Zdrev sent him the transmission data; it was being broadcast on a strange frequency with just enough power for Zdrev's "ears" to pick up. He tapped the side of his helmet with two fingers to signal Zdrev to patch her through.

"Hey, Kaya. I hope you're still waiting for me. I had to take Zdrev for a little walk before we headed over to your place," Tass said, with what he hoped sounded like natural good cheer, using her personal name without titles or honorifics. It wasn't likely that the Divine Right would even be able to detect the transmission, let alone intercept it, but he was a firm believer in maintaining communications security.

The Ain, however, had more of a casual on-again, off-again relationship with CommSec.

"Tass, they have Tima."

"I know," he replied in a sympathetic tone. "Zdrev and I just saw her."

"These Divine Right? They are not honorable foes."

"No, they are not," Tass said. Another window in his HUD opened as Zdrev began showing him different routes they could take to board the raider, sorted by chance of detection and probability of success. Tass used his wrist comp to select one, then signaled Zdrev to run a quick self-test. "So...how many guests do you have in town?"

"There are eighteen total around town, but I don't know how many are still on the ship." Kaya paused, as if considering the wisdom of continuing.

He practically felt her defiant shrug over the comm channel. "These Divine Right think they know how to steal cattle. Ha! Pathetic. House Khep? House Mo-Si? They were at least creative when *they* tried to steal cattle. These *azzi* don't even know how to build a proper raider."

Azzi was a Septisolaran term that loosely translated as *uncultured barbarian outsider*; it was not an insult the Ain bestowed lightly. Tass looked out the observation port and noted both airlocks were guarded by a pair of unarmored sentries. Divine Right raiders had a crew of thirty, which left eight unaccounted for somewhere on the ship...but only four of them were Naval Infantrymen. Tass signaled Zdrev forward. "Let your people know these raiders are pros, Kaya. They might be the worst cattle rustlers in history, but they are *not* some ragtag band of deserters playing pirate."

At first, Kaya didn't reply, but then she asked warily, "Noble ke'Dolh? You aren't going to do anything rash, are you? I believe this is something we should all do together."

"I never do anything rash, Ain Ch'Kaya," Tass reassured her as he pulled himself through the observation port. He drew his needler pistol and motioned for Zdrev to proceed. "I will need to take Zdrev for a quick walk before we get together, though; he's putting on a little weight and needs the exercise. Feel free to start your party without me. Don't worry—we'll be along. We'll bring the Noble Ch'Tima along, too."

He heard Kaya start to speak, pause, then say, "Honor to your House, Noble ke'Dolh, and luck in...*on* your walk."

"Honor to House Ain," Tass replied, and then the signal dropped. He glanced at the threat return indicator and saw that he and Zdrev were still well below the Divine Right's detection threshold. Tass gave the raider's gun turrets a wary look, then quickly moved down the slope to the edge of the smuggler's field. The raider sat in an oval depression that was slightly larger than the ship and deep enough that the equatorial trench was even with ground level. Normally, the only access to the ship was via the two boarding ramps running from the edge of the depression to the airlocks.

The catwalks were protected not only by two sentries but also by the armored gun turrets, capable of being remotely controlled by the sentries or by someone on the ship's bridge, on either side of the airlock. He ignored the ramps and followed Zdrev across the field to the rim of the depression near the raider's port side.

Once there, Tass secured his needler pistol and dialed up his armor's leg augmentation. He glanced in the direction of the airlock sentries, then leaped across the fifteen-foot gap between the edge of the ground and the raider's hull. He activated the molecular grippers in his gloves and the soles of his boots just before he landed, then waited for Zdrev to follow. Zdrev landed just beneath him on the downward curve of the ship's hull and locked himself into place with the molecular grippers in his paws just in case Tass needed to slide down the hull and take cover behind him. Tass gave the mech-dog a thumbs up before he proceeded further up the hull to where the slope was gentle enough for him to be able to move easily over it. With Zdrev at his side, he drew his needler pistol and made his way down the length of the ship. When they were even with the port airlock, they slid cautiously down to the edge of the upper hull and paused while Zdrev used his passive sensors to see if the Naval Infantrymen were nearby. He indicated that the two sentries were alone.

"All right, buddy, I'll take care of the one in the airlock and you take care of the one on the boarding ramp. Non-lethal attack modes preferred," Tass said. Zdrev locked his gaze onto the Divine Right crewman standing on the boarding ramp and pinned his ears back when he was ready to pounce. Tass maneuvered onto the upper frame of the airlock, took a breath, then released it as he dropped down to the boarding ramp.

As soon as the sentry in the airlock came into view Tass shot him in the neck with the needler pistol and rendered him unconscious before he had time to react. Tass caught him before he fell to the deck and placed him in a corner of the airlock. There was a dull thud behind him as Zdrev took down the other sentry. Tass holstered his needler pistol and unslung his inertia carbine while Zdrev silently dragged his unconscious target into the airlock. A moment later, Tass and Zdrev crossed the inner threshold of the airlock and made their way cautiously down the short corridor that connected to it.

After fifteen feet, the corridor led them to a four-way intersection. Tass knew the raider's engineering spaces were aft, off to his right, and that the rest of the deck consisted mostly of maintenance spaces, storage, and two of the vessel's four cargo bays; fortunately, he had Zdrev. "All right, Zdrev, time to find your friend Ch'Tima. Where'd they take her?"

In an outdoor setting, the passive sensors of a canine mech-sent were no match for the nose of a biological dog when it came to tracking by scent, but on a starship, the differences between the two were not nearly as extreme. Zdrev pointed his nose at the deck, and after a moment of analysis, highlighted on Tass's HUD the route the Naval Infantrymen had taken Ch'Tima. The scent trail crossed the intersection and stopped at the doors to a personnel lift.

"They probably took her up to the personnel deck so the captain could see her," Tass explained to Zdrev as they passed through the intersection and headed for a ladderwell beside the lift tube. "We'll take a peek at the top of the—"

The doors to the lift nearest to Tass and Zdrev opened, and two Naval Infantrymen preparing to exit the lift car stared at them in surprise.

Zdrev reacted first. He waited a fraction of a millisecond to see which of the Naval Infantrymen had the fastest reflexes, then sprang into action, hitting the man in the center of the chest just as his pistol cleared its holster. The Naval Infantryman fell backwards onto the deck, his pistol clattering across the floor and his helmet automatically deploying under the force of the impact. His personal shield attempted to activate as well, but only managed to short out Zdrev's stealth field. Zdrev clamped down on the helmet's faceplate and tore it off. He clamped his muzzle firmly onto the man's face and injected him with a fast-acting sedative.

The second Naval Infantryman might have been fast enough to squeeze off a wild shot in Tass's direction if he hadn't started to pivot toward Zdrev, who was now in plain sight. The man's brain registered Tass's presence too late for him to stop his turn, so instead he snapped on his shields and deployed his helmet.

Tass swung his inertia carbine around and fired off two shots, each one making the distinctive *thume*-sound of an inertia weapon fired in an atmosphere. The point-blank range meant the energy from his first shot completely overwhelmed his opponent's shields. The second shot struck the naval infantryman in the center of his armored chest, instantly creating a half-inch diameter divot in the armor. The initial impact was enough to force him back a step, but the particle burst lost cohesion and expanded rapidly, causing a fatal shockwave as it passed through him. The Naval Infantryman stood motionless for a moment, then fell dead onto the deck.

"Quick, Zdrev, up the ladder! We have to find Ch'Tima—fast," Tass said, and motioned with one hand toward the steep set of stairs leading up to the crew deck.

Zdrev dashed past him and ran silently up the ladder. When he reached the crew deck, Tass heard someone shout, "Look out! Something followed the girl onto the ship!"

Zdrev yelped to signal he was in trouble, and his shields sparked under a barrage of energy weapons fire. He leaped from the floor to a nearby bulkhead, then pushed himself off toward the overhead. He rolled in midair, activated the molecular grippers on his paws, and began running along the overhead while the Naval Infantrymen continued to fire at him.

Tass went up the ladder in a crouch and used the ladderwell's open hatch for cover. Once at the top, he rolled quickly clear of the hatch in case one of the Naval Infantrymen thought to seal the ship's emergency bulkheads and hatches. The closest of the infantrymen saw him and started to bring the barrel of his energy pistol down when Tass shot him in the chest.

The second infantryman heard the *thume* of Tass's carbine and saw his companion begin to collapse onto the deck. He realized his comms were being jammed and quickly fell back to doorway behind him while firing at Zdrev on the overhead.

When Tass saw him, he was most of the way through the doorway, so Tass temporarily increased the aperture of his inertia carbine and fire at the bulkhead between him and the remaining infantryman. The impact from the particle burst punched a five-inch diameter divot in the front of the bulkhead and caused a much broader area of spalling damage on the opposite side. The spall shrapnel overloaded the naval infantryman's shields and struck him in the shoulder with enough force to spin him around away from the bulkhead. When he staggered into Tass's field of view, Tass fired an anti-personnel burst at him and sprinted toward the doorway.

Zdrev dropped down to the deck beside him and indicated that Ch'Tima had been taken through the doorway and down the corridor beyond it.

"They took her to the bridge. Probably just the captain there by himself now," Tass said, and peered through the sights of his carbine at the bridge door. It was closed, but not locked. Zdrev presented him with a list of options for forcing their way onto the bridge. "We'll go for Plan Delta. He won't expect us to go for his head."

Zdrev leaped through the doorway, easily clearing the body of the second naval infantryman, and bounded down the corridor. He turned sharply to the right before he reached the bridge door and drifted around the corner before heading down a side corridor. Tass shook his head in amusement as he ran after him, and when he rounded the corner, he found Zdrev sitting patiently on the deck across from a maintenance panel.

The Divine Right raiders had been built based on the original Septiso-laran raider blueprints, and there were a number of design flaws long since corrected by the Seven Suns that were still present in Divine Right ships.

Tass drew his Utility Cutting Tool (UCT), energized the blade, and quickly cut through the latches securing the maintenance panel. After quietly lowering the panel to the deck, he used the UCT to make a small puncture in the inner bulkhead and moved aside so Zdrev could place his nose against it. Zdrev did so and mimed the act of sniffing while using his passive sensors to analyze the spaces on the other side of the bulkhead. When he was through, he backed away and sat down again.

Tass shut off the water valves and used his UCT to cut the pipes out of the way while he studied an overlay of Zdrev's scan results on the deck plan. The captain's head was empty and the door leading to it was open. A short distance away, Ch'Tima was lying on the deck of the captain's ready room. The Divine Right captain had been surprisingly easy for Zdrev to locate—he was standing in front of his command chair on the bridge shouting at the main screen; things were not going well for his crew in town. Given the captain was likely only moments away from recalling prisoners could also be used as hostages, Tass quickly used his breaching cord to outline a three-foot by three-foot square on the inner bulkhead. He moved to the side again, armed the breaching cord with his wrist comp, and drew his needler pistol.

Zdrev was already in midair when Tass tapped the detonate button for the breaching cord, and he crashed through the bulkhead before the smoke from the breaching cord had cleared. His paws barely touched the deck when he leaped again and threw himself on top of Ch'Tima to protect her with his shields and his body.

As Tass made his way through the breach, he heard the whine of a needler on rapid fire and went flat against the deck as a barrage of needles sparked and ricocheted off of Zdrev's shields. Zdrev growled menacingly, and Tass lunged through the open doorway. He saw the Divine Right captain running into the ready room and fired a burst from his own needler pistol at the man's chest. The captain let out a strangled cry when the needles hit him. Then his momentum carried him forward to crash on top of his desk before rolling noisily off as he fell unconscious onto the deck. Tass retracted his helmet and winced; the air on the ship was a potent bouquet of machine oil, urine, sewage, and sweat. He shook his head and went to Ch'Tima's side.

"It's okay, Ain Ch'Tima. It's Zdrev and Marshal ke'Dolh," Tass reassured her after Zdrev hopped to the side and began helping him ease Ch'Tima to a sitting position. Tass took the hood off her head as Zdrev ran a quick medical scan of her.

"Noble ke'Dolh!" Ch'Tima exclaimed, her face pale and her eyes still wide with fear. Tass cut the ropes binding her wrists with his UCT, and she threw her arms around him in a fierce hug.

Zdrev relayed his scan results to Tass's ocular HUD; Ch'Tima was recovering from being shot with a stunner, but was otherwise unharmed. Zdrev also informed him that additional friendly forces were *en route* to the bridge. Tass patted Ch'Tima on the back. "It's okay, Ch'Tima. You're safe now."

Ch'Tima suddenly pulled away from him, fresh panic on her face as Tass moved to cut the ropes binding her ankles. "I can explain—this *totally* was *not* my fault!"

"Oooooh, this will be good. A story for the ages, no doubt," the soprano voice of Sept Leader Ch'Kaya said unexpectedly from the doorway leading to the bridge. When Tass turned to look at her, one corner of her mouth quirked up in a smile, and she stepped to one side to allow a pair of Ain men in assault armor past her.

They were large, tough men, even more so than the typical Ain, and they looked like they'd been partially assembled from a bin of antique cybernetics decorated in House Ain colors. The battle flashes on their armor and their cybernetics indicated they were veterans of more House raids than Tass could count easily, as well as the first battle, referred to simply as the Betrayal, when the Septisolarans had fought against the Divine Right. The entire town was full of such veterans; the Divine Right had made a poor choice in the target for a raid. The two Ain gave Ch'Tima and Tass a nod and a casual, "Good day, my Lady, Noble ke'Dolh." Then, with a whirring and clicking of servo motors, they took hold of the unconscious Divine Right captain and carried him out of the ready room.

"Kaya, I was just trying to—" Ch'Tima began after rising to her feet, but stopped when her sister gave her a stern look.

"Now is not the time for your, shall we say, *debriefing*, Ain Ch'Tima. This enemy vessel is not yet fully secured. Your duty now is to get clear of this vessel and report to Medical Officer Songon at the Field Command Post," Kaya told her, perhaps more sternly than she intended, because her expression softened, and she gave Tass a questioning look. He nodded and she said to Ch'Tima, "The Noble Zdrev will serve as your escort and stand watch with you. Is this clear?"

Ch'Tima snapped to attention as Zdrev took up position alongside her. "Yes, Sept Leader."

"You have your orders, then. Carry on," Kaya said, and motioned to the doorway to the bridge with a nod of her head. She put a hand on Ch'Tima's shoulder when her younger sister drew even with her and lowered her voice to just above a whisper. "Zdrev can link to the House comm net. Mom and Dad are worried. It wouldn't hurt to give them a call."

Ch'Tima almost sighed, but thought better of it and simply nodded. "I will."

As soon as Ch'Tima exited the bridge, Kaya turned and wrapped her arms around Tass in a fierce hug. "Thank you for saving Tima!" She loosened her grip on Tass and backed away to look him in the eyes.

Tass rolled his shoulders. "There's no way I would leave anyone in the clutches of these Divine Right *azzi* if Zdrev and I could do anything about it, Kaya."

Kaya laughed brightly. "You have no idea how adorable it is when a Makhtari tries to cuss like a proper Septisolaran."

He arched an eyebrow at her. "Commonwealth Marines are never adorable when cussing."

"Hmmm," Kaya replied noncommittally. She turned to frown at the raider captain's desk and said, "You were right about our would-be cattle rustlers not being Divine Right runaways. They were regulars on a covert supply run that went bad because their ship broke down. They were improvising this cattle raid in an effort to not arrive home emptyhanded."

That time, both of Tass's eyebrows went up. "Oh? They have a home, do they?"

"Only one Jump away if they were planning on hauling cattle in this wretched excuse for a raider," Kaya replied. She looked at him with mischief in her eyes. "Speaking of which, we seem to be in possession of both crew and ship. Care to pay a visit to their home to see if we can collect the rest of them?"

Interstellar Cattle Drive

Cedar Sanderson

There's a reason most genetic enrichment is done via frozen pipes of somatic material. It's the way it was even before humans sprang off the mudball they originated on, and reached for the stars. However, you have to start a herd somewhere. And there are always the purists who insist nothing beats flesh to flesh and beating hearts. Can't decide if they are romantics, or perverts. Some of both, quite likely.

Not my job to figure it out, but there's a lot of time to kill when you're riding herd on the long haul, and you wind up thinking about the strangest things. Like now, while I was walking along the spider's span, over the herd, and both watching them mill about restlessly and pondering the nature of my life's work.

They knew it was time to move. They always did. Dumb balls of hooves and hair and horn they were, maybe. Cattle have a sense for a lot of things, though, and if you spend enough years intimately acquainted, you'll learn to read them. I squinted at the far end of the hold, but the doors were still shut. Down below me, horns rattled, and the noise level picked up. I took the rest of the span at a fast walk. You don't want to run on the slender steel wires. Fall under the herd and you can panic them, and, well, you won't have to worry about what the herd boss'd do to you if you survive.

Getting the herd to the destination without losing too many of them, in good condition, was the ultimate goal. The other facet of my job would kick in when we dropped out of transit space, nearing the planet. Once you got within shooting distance of people, well, it could be hairy. In transit, you only had to worry about the myriad of ways cattle have of dying or killing you. It was enough for the moment.

"John." I toggled the talker embedded in my temple, speaking aloud and receiving on the bone induction speaker. "They're bunching up. When are we opening the doors?"

I couldn't see him, but I knew he was in the same segment of the ship with the herd.

"Soon. I know the beef want through, but the boss says not for another sixteen hours."

I swore under my breath without transmitting. I imagined he could fill in my reaction just fine, anyway.

"I know he has a schedule," I transmitted when I was done venting my spleen. "But the herd is bunching up and impatient."

"On my way," I heard.

I was standing on the walkway looking down at the herd when John showed up. I knew he was coming before I could see him, because the tail-end charlies all turned away from the object of their desire, fringed ears perking up in curiosity. One thing you could count on with cows was their desire to know what was coming. They hadn't known predators in more generations than I could count offhand, but still, instinct is bred into their bones.

Their reaction gave me an idea. John slid over the spider's span with the elegance of a man accustomed to this peculiar mode of transit. I called out to him, rather than use the transmitter, once he was close enough.

"What if we decoyed them back down toward the other end of the arc?"

I was referring to the far side of the hold. The ship was a huge donut. Or, well, a ring, only a fat one. The directional spin went in two directions simultaneously to eliminate the tides that a single-spin rig created. They weren't any too good for a human, but they'd kill a cow in hours. This way, we had something like gravity, if less than most planets, and that was sufficient. The problem on the long hauls wasn't the loss of bone density and muscle wasting. It was grazing and spreading the manure out to a healthy level. Lock a cow in a small space and let her stand in her own waste for very long at all and you have a dead cow. Give her space to wander, green stuff to chew on, and distance from her own droppings, and you have happy cattle. Which was what we wanted.

The drive was simple enough in space. Open part of the ship to the herd at a time, giving the other parts of the ring time to recover. Most of it was a closed, self-sustaining ecology at this point. The boss studied it with an eagle's eye, gauging when the herd could rotate through. Problem was, cows don't do science. They have their own internal timetable, and the herd was a stubborn mob.

"You think we can?"

John knew as well as I did there were ways to move the herd, but generally only in the direction they already wanted to go. Towards water, or food. Away from stinging pests, but those we didn't have shipboard.

"I think it's worth a try," I retorted, pointing at the doors, which were in plain sight. "If they rush those..."

"We'll lose at least a few head in the crush." John was morose. It was a natural state for the lanky man with his close-cropped dark hair, laced with silver. The drooping tip of his nose over his overgrown mustache added to the effect.

"We can take advantage of their nosiness." I pointed, now, at the cows below us, who were craning their necks to see what we were doing. "If I go back, almost past the curve, and catch their attention?"

"Huh." He scratched the back of his neck while staring at nothing in particular. "Reckon it's worth a try. You goin' down to turf?"

We didn't, as a rule, go to the level of the herd. Cows can take a notion and turn you into a smear if you look at them funny, and they get to define "funny" themselves.

"May have to." I shrugged. "Not asking you to."

"I won't. I'll stay up here to explain why you got yourself kilt."

"Suit yourself." I was already moving towards the ladder, the only way to get onto the turf from this height. In the service tunnels, you could just open a door. I was going to climb down a series of bars bolted to the bulkhead of the hold. That in and of itself was going to be odd enough to get the cattle's attention, which meant I wasn't doing it right there by the herd.

I trotted back, headed for a position where I'd have room to maneuver, but wouldn't be out of their sight. John stayed where he was, slouched against the railing, staring down at them rather than watching me. At least, last I saw, since my back was turned to him now and I wasn't going to look back and check on him. The old man could take care of himself.

I also wasn't worried he'd tell the boss on me. The boss wouldn't have an objection, so long as I didn't get myself stomped, or spark a stampede. The latter wasn't much of a problem, but it also wasn't unheard of. Cows are... well, they're not a smart critter.

I got to the ladder I'd decided was optimal and started down, looking towards the herd while I lowered myself over the edge. Some of the tail-end charlies had lost interest and begun to crop at the grass again. Now, though, I had their full attention, and I could see heads popping up all over the herd as I made my way downward. I got to the bottom rung and let go, dropping a couple of feet into the springy turf. The grass was short as a lawn here. It would be knee-deep when we opened the doors to the next arc for them. I enjoyed the feel of it under my flat-heeled boots. Cowboy boots where they were worn in conjunction with stirrups had high heels, but I hadn't so much as seen a horse in years. I walked on expanded metal grating ninety percent of my life aboard ship.

I walked slowly and deliberately out to the middle of the hold, then turned to face the herd. A few were already wandering my way, big ears perked up and wide-eyed as they tried to figure out what a human was doing on their turf.

A herd has a hierarchy more rigid than most human social settings. The boss cow was the one I was looking for. She'd be the one I needed to turn around and head in this direction. The bull was the one I was worried about. He generally didn't give a damn. Until he did. And then, brother, you'd better be running.

Once I had the attention of the outliers, I waved my arms in the air over my head, and jumped up and down a little. I felt ridiculous, and tried not to look up and see what John was doing above me. I figured he'd get his laugh in, but if this worked, it would save us both some trouble. The herd bunching up against the hold doors made life difficult when the time came to open them.

More of the cows were paying attention to me, or just as likely, to the movement of the herd starting to shift. Like humans, they tended to pay most attention to what the guy next to them was doing, and set their pace accordingly. Which makes sense with cows; herd animals are going to herd.

Panicky herd animals. I started to move backwards, intending to draw them with me, down to the grass they'd grazed over a few days before. It wouldn't hold them long, but it might just buy us the time we needed. Cows don't have a migratory instinct, or this would never work. Just that they like to eat, and they won't stay on ground they've grazed if they have a choice. Interesting, that...

My world went topsy-turvy while I was paying attention more to the herd than where I was going. There shouldn't have been a hole in the ground. We don't have burrowing pests on the ship. Unlike the soil microbes, there's no actual use for a prairie dog.

Shouldn't have been a hole, but there it was, and I'd put my boot down in there hard enough to send me over backwards, with a shout and my arms flying around like the clown I'd been imitating. I heard the pop of something letting go in my leg, and only then did I feel it.

Hitting the ground like a dropped sack of feed, I lost my breath in the impact and laid there staring up at the curve of the bulkhead far above me, wondering why they'd bothered to make it blue like the Earth's sky. I could feel the thud of approaching hooves, but for an instant it didn't matter to me. I was just trying to recall what a sky ought to look like.

Then reality smacked me in the face with all the force of a thrown fish. The herd was on the move, and I was in their way. They might not step on me, at first, but if they were all moving, the later ones wouldn't care what was underhoof.

I rolled over and grunted as my foot came out of the hole. A friendly nose came into view. The first of them had reached me, and was regarding me mildly out of big brown eyes, breathing warmly grass-scented air into my ear.

"I'm going to get up now," I informed her politely. "And then I'm going to hobble thataway."

Her ears moved slightly, but otherwise she wasn't inclined to go anywhere at all, having reached the object of her interest. I got on my hands and knees, and could feel her nosing my back. I straightened up, on my knees, and grabbed her right at the withers, where there was a convenient tuft of fur and hide. She did exactly what I was hoping for and backed off a few steps, eyes rolling in mild alarm. The momentum had helped me get all the way up, and the pain caused a wave of red to veil my vision for a moment. I let go of the cow, not wanting to be dragged, and wavered, one foot raised as much as I could manage. Once I could see again, I took stock.

The herd was indeed headed for me. My antics of falling and then rising again probably did it; enough of them had come to see what it was about that the others were tagging along. Which was the idea. Only now

I couldn't really keep moving ahead of them and I needed to get back up the ladder with one good foot. Or reach an access door.

I looked up. John was standing above me, hands on his hips.

"Got yourself in a right pickle." He didn't yell, and I strained to hear him, but at least the cows weren't worried about his voice. "Can you make the door?"

"I guess I have to." I spoke in the same conversational tone. Shouting seemed like a really bad idea about now.

"You start that way. I'm comin' down there."

I started to protest, as this seemed like a way to get two of us in trouble, but he was already over the edge. I hobbled a few steps, feeling the sweat pop out on my forehead from the pain of moving. Gritting my teeth, I kept going. I plotted a diagonal approach. I didn't want to cut straight across the herd's path, but I needed to work with them and also toward the bulkhead.

They split their attention between John coming down the ladder, and me bobbing along slowly in the same general direction. It seemed to take an eternity, but finally I reached out and stabilized myself on the cool wall of the hold. John was already on the turf and working his way towards me. He pushed his shoulder under my arm on the side with my useless leg and grunted.

"That didn't go so well."

"The cows moved," I pointed out. "Without a stampede."

"Right. Now let's get you safe." He opened the door with his free hand, and helped me up and in, slamming it shut in the face of a curious beast. The seal hissed, and I lowered myself into a sitting position, leaning back against it.

They came for me with the utility cart, and it didn't take long, as John had been transmitting since I'd gone down, evidently. Katie was driving, and as soon as she stopped and took a good look at me, the grin about split her face from ear to ear.

"What'd you do there, big boy?" She hopped out, medkit in hand. "Gone and busted something?"

I grunted and eyed her with suspicion. "You're entirely too happy about playing doctor."

"Nah." She crouched next to me and pulled an injector out of the bag. "I could tell from the sour look on your mug it's not too bad."

"Ow." She'd hiked the leg of my jeans above the top of my boot and injected something into the flesh of my calf. "You're not going to take my boot off, are you?"

I knew from painful past experience that things would start to swell as soon as that was done, but more, the action of pulling it off was going to hurt. A lot. Even with the shot she'd given me sending icy tendrils into the heat of the pain.

"Nope. Not here. Back at medbay, yes. By then, you won't be able to feel it." She rocked back on her heels and looked at my face. "Hm. Think you can get on the cart, or do I need to throw you over my shoulder?"

Katie's not a small woman, but I'm taller than she is by more than a head. "I'll manage."

It was more than a little awkward, and John, who had stepped back and silently watched her work, lent me his shoulder again, but we got me loaded. I grabbed the roll bar and braced, because as soon as I was on, she was taking off.

"It's not a race," I growled half under my breath.

I don't know how much of that she heard, but she'd caught the idea of it, because it set her off belly laughing. She was still chortling from time to time when she pulled up at the medbay.

Medbay, bunkrooms, and mess were all on the inner wall of the torus. Since the ship spun in two different axes, placement of the herd was chosen first, then crew quarters. Which meant that walls were, well, let's just say you had to be creative from time to time when the tidal motions meant up was now sideways. It was supposed to be optimal for maintaining bone density. I regarded the concept with a jaundiced eye and decided they didn't care about the humans so long as the cows made it safe. At least we were transporting cows on this run. I didn't want to think about that trip with the camels.

Katie came around, but I declined to let her help me in. The leg was numb, and I could hop. She shrugged, chuckled, and went to open the door for me. The doc looked up from one of the beds and frowned.

"Your timing is inconvenient, Braddock."

"There's a convenient time to get myself busted up?" I scooted my ass onto the table and got my legs up by hooking the good foot under the now-useless one and lifting it. "Mind waving your magic wand over this?"

He had gotten up, but not quickly enough to reach me before I was on the table by myself. "You realize just because you can't feel it right now... Also, it's not magic."

"Don't care what it is." I leaned back, feeling the tired wash over me. "Let's do this."

"You realize..." He started to wheel a tray over, then pulled down a monitoring arm towards my leg. "That you could have been killed out there?"

"Cows were crowding the hold doors. They get dumb when they start to panic."

"Cows don't have a migratory instinct." He was looking at the monitor, his lips pursed in a prissy moue. "They can wait until we're ready."

I grunted as he pulled my boot off in a quick motion, using both hands and not an ounce of gentle. "Tell *them* that. They're trained to go round, and convincing them there's still grass back thataway isn't easy."

"It's not a break." He manipulated my foot and ankle while looking at the monitor. "Sprain, that's all."

He hit me with another injector, not telling me what it was, but I suspected it was something to aid in the healing. We didn't have magic nanobots, but there were other things. I wasn't clear on how they worked, but they did. I used them on the cows, too.

"So now you can go back to your research and I can get back to work."

He sniffed. "I would like to have a paper on the effects of reduced gravity on cattle gestation by the end of this run, yes. You, however, are confined to the bunkroom for a week. Stay off that foot."

He stomped away, and Katie stepped into the place where he'd been, swinging the monitor arm away so I could sit up, and offering me a crutch.

I accepted it. "Who pissed in his breakfast?" I asked her as I slid cautiously off the table.

She winked at me, but didn't answer my question until the door had closed behind us. "Captain might have said something about humans not being large animal livestock, and he should make sure he was up on both kinds of critters."

Having a veterinarian as a doctor wasn't strange. There was no point in having both; we needed both, and the doc might be prickly, but he seemed to know his stuff.

"That'd do it."

"They do needle each other." She didn't interfere with my slow progress, but she also didn't return to her workspace, either. "Captain said he'd be along to check on you, by the way."

"Did I break my transmitter in that fall, or is no one talking to me?" I growled. "I dislike being kept in the dark."

I saw her jaw work, then heard her voice in my head. "Growing mushrooms already?"

"Still works, then." I shrugged. "I can take a hint."

She pulled a face, and I took advantage of the temporary respite from pain to put my feet up on the couch. I had an upper bunk, so by unspoken arrangement, when sick, the uppers crashed on the couches. This was the first time I'd had to take advantage of it.

"Hey, Katie?" She hadn't left, heading for her own bunk to grab something quickly. While I was taking advantages... "Can you toss me my tablet?"

She dropped it on my chest on her way out the door. "I'll make sure someone brings you a tray at dinner."

"Thanks."

I leaned my head back and looked at the ceiling. A week seemed like a long downtime for a sprain. It would also take us into the planet approach, and put me back into the roster just in time for unloading. I could take a hint, just like the cows knowing when it was time to move. I needed to find a new berth. It wasn't the accident. This had been coming for some time. I would be the first to admit I didn't ride well with a team. I signed on for two reasons. One, I needed a job. And two, I needed to be on this particular ship.

I was alone in the bunkroom, which was passing rare, so I logged into the tablet and pulled up messages without worrying who was standing behind me. I'd hear the hiss of the door if someone did come in. I didn't think I'd have anything from my employer, not while we were in transit space. That would come later, when we dropped out. I was hoping to have something indicating why the sudden cold shoulder from the crew, though.

My in-box remained empty. I toggled into the research folder I'd set up months ago, and started to work through the last few weeks' work again, looking for missed connections and subtle cues. Something was going on, something I'd been sent to look for, and to my frustration, I hadn't found it. Being confined to the bunkroom wasn't helping, either. Oh, I could probably challenge the doc's verdict of a week down. I probably would. Sitting on my ass for that long would be a challenge.

The door hissed open and I looked over my shoulder.

"Scuttlebutt says Braddock broke his leg." The scruffy yellow beard framed a snaggle-toothed grin. "I sees it and believes."

"Ayuh." I grunted at Frast. I really didn't want to spend a lot of time with the shirker. He was the most creative avoider of work I'd ever met, and it would have been amusing and educational if he hadn't managed to shove most of it off onto me.

"So whaja'do?" He shuffled fully in the room and stood looking thoughtfully down at my boots. The decision to leave the boot on until the swelling moderated likely meant I'd sleep in it that night.

"There was a hole. Found it the hard way." I was hoping he'd get bored and go away again, but instead he hitched up the heavy duckcloth pants he favored, and took a seat on the low table in front of the sofa, putting his face just a little higher than my own. I was trapped.

"A hole? We don't have prairie dogs." He scratched at his neckbeard, looking at the ceiling instead of me.

I wondered if he was baiting me. Of all of the crew aboard, I was the only one with ground experience. Unless I wasn't the only one holding back. On paper, I was the same as them, just another cattle bum slinging herds on ships.

"No. Didn't stop to investigate."

"Cow could break her leg," he said, and this time he made eye contact.

"You're more than welcome to go look at it yourself. Herd was moving, last I saw, towards center arc." He was right, but volunteering was out of character for him.

"Mebbe." He scratched again, then stood up. "Think I'll talk to John."

I was alone again, with an uneasy feeling that the visit from Frast was some kind of fishing expedition. I'd been keeping my head down, working, listening, and saying little. Maybe someone thought being on my back would loosen my tongue. Problem was, if that was the case, they knew more already than I wanted them to suspect.

It was going to be a long week. I started reading again. Not much else I could do, for a day or two, at least, until the leg started to heal.

Katie got in the habit of bringing my meals to me, until on the fourth day I managed to hobble into the mess on my own power. I had taken off my boot on the morning after my fall, and my ankle had turned into a spongy aching mess. It wasn't much better, but I was sick of the bunkroom and running out of ways to keep my mind off both the pain and the uncertainty. Since I'd been down, the comms had been off to my implant. No one was talking to me. Not even Frast, after that one strange conversation.

Oh, they had a few words when they came into the bunkroom for sleep. But the running poker game had moved elsewhere while I was occupying the sofa. The social time, limited as it had always been, wasn't including me. Something was wrong, but I'd be damned if I was going to ask what.

Katie, though, always had a laugh and a kidding tone when she came in bearing a steaming tray. I'd come to look forward to her visits. She had her own troubles, so I didn't bug her. She could talk to be privately if she wanted, and she evidently didn't.

The mess fell silent when I crutched in for breakfast on the fourth day. I pretended I didn't notice, making my way to get the tray of food that popped up on the server when I walked in.

I sat alone, though. They'd gone back to the usual chatter after a long moment, but I knew where my limits were. My nerves were frayed to raw edges and I'd wind up picking a fight if I tried to push.

There was no way I was going back to work yet. But the ship was dropping out of transit space, so all hands would be on the spans, keeping an eye on the herd. Cows don't understand what's happening, and unlike people, you can't warn them it's coming. Unlike the rest of the crew, I had the feeling that more was coming than just return to realspace.

It was, after all, why I was on board. I resisted the urge to roll my shoulders and work out some of the painful tension in them. Not while I was in public. Instead, I ate my last bite and stood, before picking the tray up to take to the bin. I couldn't stand and hold the tray at the same time and use the crutch.

One-handed meant everything was a little harder. I left the mess behind me, but I didn't head for the bunkroom again. I needed to move, to work out the kinks from sitting too long, and the buzzing of my mind as we neared the drop. I couldn't do anything while we were still in transit. Fortunately, with everyone headed for the cows, I could have the observation room all to myself.

I don't know why they included it. Maybe the ship designers thought wealthy herd owners would travel with their cows. Hell, for all I knew, they had at one point. If so, it had been a long while. The room was dusty, but the view was worth the sneezing. I didn't push my luck by sitting in the upholstered chairs, gone stained and sticky with years of neglect and occasional use by careless crew. No one cleaned in here.

I stood and looked out the clear walls, tipping my head back slightly to take it all in. The walls curved inward, forming a domed room at the hub of the ship, suspended inside the donut hole of the torus formed by the cattle's range. Transit space was weird. You couldn't see the stars, of course. Instead, it was a slowly shifting gradient of colors. I'd been told they weren't real colors, but they looked real enough to me, as the orange shaded to violet and then to an unearthly blue.

It was quiet, and I found that I'd relaxed, being here away from any people. After a minute or two of watching the space around the ship, I slid my tablet out of the cargo pocket, and leaned a hip against one of the bar-height tables, taking the weight off enough to prop the crutch and have both hands free.

I wanted to get the news as soon as we dropped into the real. I had a countdown on the tablet, but I also watched the windows. There's no physical shift, in transition, but your head doesn't know that. I staggered, wincing as I put weight on my ankle, then regained my balance. I should have sat down, but I hadn't been able to bring myself to trust that uphol-stery. I'd rather snuggle up to the cows. They smelled better.

The stars bloomed again, after a split second of utter darkness, and I pulled up the messages on the tablet. It would read from the mail repeater that was moored near the transition ring, and depending on how far we'd emerged from that... It took a couple of moments.

The bulk of them were junk, but there were two I pulled open. It was still silent in the corridor to my hidey-hole. I read them, then looked up again to see the stars.

I hadn't intended for the observation deck to be anything more than a quiet place where I could be private, but I sucked my breath in hard enough to make a noise as I saw what was out there. The messages hadn't been specific, but this... I toggled my implant for the first time in days, and transmitted on a private band.

"Captain Jagion, we have company."

"What do you mean, 'company'?" His tone even though the sub-aural transmission was desert-dry.

"There's a ship close enough I can read her hullplates." I shoved the tablet in my pocket. "And they just launched a shuttle."

The sleek little boat slowly arced towards us, the deceptive speed of long distances tricking the eye into believing it wasn't moving fast at all.

"The *RS Debora Radislava*," I read off the side of the big cargo ship that hung dangerously close to us. "I'm headed for the docking ring."

"Braddock," he barked. "Stand down, you're not fit."

"Fit enough. Everyone else is with the herd. They'll have counted on that."

I was making good time, considering. I was closer to the docking ring than any other crew, to the best of my knowledge. What I wasn't so sure of was if I could be in position before the shuttle docked.

I got lucky.

When the first one came through the hatch, blaster held low in one hand, I pressed the muzzle of my own weapon to his ear.

"Suggest you stop." I heard the rasp in my own voice. He might take it as anger rather than breathlessness from my near-run, on top of days spent off my feet. I'd gotten soft all too quickly.

"Holy..."

Whatever he'd been able to blaspheme was cut off by the growl of the man behind him.

"Clear the hatch, you numbskull."

"Can't." He was rolling his eyes, trying to get a look at me, but I was tucked behind the slender cover of the ring structure and he couldn't even see my hand without moving his head. Which he wisely chose not to do. "They got the drop on us, boss."

"You idiot!" The swearing was uninventive, and I tuned it out as I used my own transmitter to put it on broadcast.

"Damn cow..." The exclamation was strangled off, and the man who I'd ambushed was jerked back abruptly.

I stayed in cover. They could hear their own voices, now, as I replayed from the beginning. I really did sound brutal there, rather than gasping. Good. They hadn't shut the hatch, though.

"*Radislava,*" I called out. "Might as well go home. Don't push your luck."

"Luck?" The loud one, the second one in the stack to come through the hatch, had it gone by their plan, shouted back. "You're the one got lucky."

"'Luck favors the prepared.'" It was trite, but true. "Any part of y'all comes through that hatch, I blow it off."

There was more swearing. Then, I heard the rustle of shipsuit material and the scrape of a boot. They were going to take a potshot at me.

I pressed back into the hull metal, flat as I could go, and closed my eyes as the bolt seared past them. Even through my eyelids, I was a little dazzled, but I kept my word. I fired at the leg that was stepping out in the wake of the shot, and the wearer of what had been a booted foot screamed and fell backwards. He'd been hesitant, and it saved his life.

"Captain Jagion." I was still transmitting on general broadcast, and my voice rang through the entire ship. "The crew should stay away from the docking ring."

It wasn't safe to approach. The corridor from the crew access faced right into the open hatch, and I wasn't going to chance the rustlers wanting a profit more than their lives.

"*Radislava,* you belly-crawling, no-good cattle thieving rustlers, you get off this ship." I didn't broadcast that.

"Says who?" The loud one wasn't the one I'd winged, more's the pity.

I didn't switch back on the broadcast just yet. No point in making a spectacle of myself. "Ranger Braddock, that's who. You have two choices. Launch, and take your wounded back to the *Radislava*... The Rangers will be waiting when you return to base. Or you can surrender, we will care for your man, and you'll be in a cramped custody until we reach planetside."

I didn't really want to arrest them. I didn't know how many were in the shuttle, but that class could hold six comfortable, eight if you didn't mind putting the small ones on laps. We didn't have the crew space for them, nor the facilities to keep them safely separated. That, and I hadn't exactly told the captain who I was and what I was insurance against. There still was the possibility someone in the crew was behind the coincidental placement of the *Radislava* right on top of our transit space.

There was muffled arguing going on in the shuttle. I couldn't make out most of it, beyond the incredulous outburst of "a Ranger?" but I could afford to be patient. I held my weapon at my side, relying on my ears to pick up any approach to the hatch and my cover. The implanted hearing protection I'd gotten years before hadn't been cheap, but it was worth every credit I'd spent. I leaned into the hull, and listened as their bluster ran out of steam.

They didn't even say goodbye. The hatch slammed shut, and I could make out the dogs clicking in, then a faint hiss of compression before the rings by my shoulder rotated. Then, and only then, I moved. I left the crutch leaning against the wall. I had no time for it. The rat-bastards hadn't closed the inner seal—they were going to do an emergency launch, and try to kill me on their way out.

I lunged for the lock button and slammed it shut as the shuttle broke away. There was a whine of escaping air, then the seals closed fully, and I slumped to the floor next to the controls, breathing hard. My ankle announced it didn't like how I was treating it.

"Braddock?"

That wasn't a transmitted voice. I looked up at the ship's captain, edging into sight at the T-junction. "Better get someone tracking that shuttle, make sure it doesn't come back."

"How did you get them to leave?" He relaxed and walked normally towards me.

"Pointed out I had the drop on them." I struggled up to my feet and started to hop over to the crutch. "They saw the math wasn't in their favor."

"You really are injured." His tone was flat, and he'd stopped just inside the dock.

"Ayup." I grabbed the crutch and swung around to look him in the eyes, leaning on it. "Doc said it was a sprain, but I think he may not have looked any too hard."

The captain blinked. "He told me it was malingering."

"Katie was standing right there when he said I should stay off it for a week."

He looked away. "Thought she was sweet on you."

I snorted. "Have you seen me? She's kind. That's enough."

"How did you know they were coming?" He looked back and now his eyes were narrowed in thought.

"You've only seen half my papers." I shifted so I could see past him, but the corridor was still empty. "Where's the crew?"

"I told them to stay back until I knew more about the situation." He leaned in, almost within arms reach. "What do I need to know, Braddock?"

"You needed a hand. The Rangers wanted me to keep an eye on the drive." I shrugged. His eyes were wide, now. "I was ready when we dropped into the real. This is a pattern: piracy right at the most vulnerable point when all hands are with the herd. Only I had a good reason not to be in the hold with them. That worked out, I think you'll agree."

"Yes." He looked down at my booted foot. "I wish you'd told me sooner."

"Captain." I could be patient. He wasn't the problem. "You have a mole."

"The doctor?" He turned, now, and joined me in watching the corridor.

"I don't know what bee got in his bonnet." I shook my head. "But he put me in the right place to do this, and I don't think he would have if he was in on the plot and wanted everyone busy."

"Then who?"

"Talk to Frast. Or I can, if you'd prefer." The scruffy man was off, and had been avoiding me ever since that one conversation.

"You sure?" The captain looked sidelong at me. "He's been aboard for three drives with us."

"No," I admitted. "It's a gut feeling, that's all."

"I'll have a word with him. You should go to medbay."

"I'm fine." I didn't really want to go back to the bunkroom, but I had to admit I wasn't up to minding the herd, either.

"You're not." He grunted. "If that's a broken bone, you need it braced up in case the *Radislava* makes another go at us."

"They won't," I assured him. "I told them they have Rangers waiting on them to come into port."

What I hadn't told them was which port, and I was assuming they would decide they needed to duck into transit space and go elsewhere, anywhere. I'd been bluffing. One man against an entire crew is bad odds. That, and I had a name for my employers now. It was enough to start the tracking.

Which meant my job was mostly done.

"Captain, if you can keep my role in this confidential..." I rolled my shoulders, then started moving. The crutch threw me all off.

"Are you sure, Braddock?" He was walking slow, to keep pace with me.

"Would prefer it." I didn't add, but suspected he'd guess, that I might wind up undercover with any of the crew again on another ship. Hopefully not his.

"I'll try."

It didn't help the crew wanting to hero-worship a bit, though. By the time I walked down the plank onto the spaceport, in the wake of the cattle drive, with my duffel slung over my back and my ankle in a brace that hid the cast over a busted ankle bone, I was thoroughly sick of it. No one was obviously waiting for me, but when I got into one of the robotic jitneys, a man slid in on the other side without speaking to me.

"Message came in this morning. The *Debora Radislava* turned up at Firdaus." He spoke without looking at me.

I grunted in acknowledgement. "That was fast."

"Known port for a suspect ship. We had elements in place."

I turned and looked at him, and he reluctantly made eye contact.

"I don't want to do this again."

"You're blown for a while. Here." He handed something over.

"What's this?" I took the data gem. "Where are you sending me?"

"How does brand inspector sound?" He gave a glimmer of a smile. "Your own ship, solo work, but you're still a Ranger."

"Color me suspicious."

"You need time to recover," he said, then shrugged. "We're not putting you out to pasture, Braddock. Men who understand cows will always be needed. Think of it as a working vacation."

I slipped the data gem in a secure pocket to review later. It was the best I could hope for. Sitting and rotting while my bones healed up would have been a misery. "Thanks."

He didn't wait for the jitney to come to a stop, simply stepped out and walked away.

I scooped up my bag and looked around. The saloon doors caught my eye, and I headed for them. Time for a little R&R now that the job was done, at least for the night.

The cows had come home.

W.A.R.P. In Sector 3!

Jesse Barrett

"Wait," the pilot said, looking up from her controls. "We're carrying what?!"

"Prohibited cargo," Les, the loadmaster, sighed.

The captain's head tracked from the forward display to where Les was standing just inside the bridge bulkhead, deadly as an auto-turret.

"You said it was animal husbandry forms and farm implements," he said. It was not quite stated or asked.

"It is, mostly. The live turkeys are an established bio-line, preferred in many colonies, and the equipment is fairly high-end, but nothing particularly special..." Les trailed off.

"But?" the captain prompted.

"But Cincinnatus is a prohibited colony."

"That doesn't normally impact basic survival supplies," the pilot chimed in.

"Which was my thought when I accepted the cargo," Les agreed. "Then I looked up the restrictions. Unfortunately, the bioengineered birds, embryo tanks, and gene scrubbers move things from simple farm implements over into the Prohibited column. It would seem that they had some problems with 'excessive and exotic use of genengineering techniques.'" Les sighed again. "And since I didn't know there might be problems when we loaded on that last station, the noseys might have noticed the manifests."

"I filed a standard flight plan, Les!" the pilot said, her voice growing louder and sharper with each word.

"And as soon as the Patrol computers put one and one together, there will be an interdictor on our tail," Captain Rogers finished.

"At least it's not bloody cows," the co-pilot and navigator said in his thick Biafran accent. "My family kept bloody cows back on Earth, and still keeps them in the colony now. I hate bloody cows."

The pilot growled and muttered something unintelligible as she tapped the small figurine of Kamdhenu kept in a dead readout. To this day Captain Rogers had no idea how those two stayed married.

"Right. Azikiwe, plot us a new course that avoids anything official that we can. Sarika, I don't know, fly casual until Az gets you the updated courses, then go as low-profile as we can. Les, let's go inspect the cargo you brought on *my* ship," Captain Rogers said, turning sharply and heading through the bulkhead and towards cargo bay one.

The Independent Starship *Dawn Trader* was a former Patrol craft converted into a fast freighter. Quad jump nacelles gave her twice the distance that was standard for her size, and her impulse drives could push almost eight Gs with enough power. Since their Grav systems could only comp six, speed runs quickly got uncomfortable, and maneuvering at speed could be, in the captain's understated idiom, "unpleasant." Most of the time, they cruised at between two and three gravs of acceleration and comfortably had twice that in reserve. That and her ability to skip almost half the standard jump points normally meant fairly quick and easy runs. She had three cargo bays, one large and two smaller, as well as a half-dozen small cabins if they were hauling passengers rather than just cargo. The *Dawn Trader* also mounted two "decommissioned" missile ports, an obvious railgun, and "lookout" turret that *might* have had one of its old ion cannons concealed in its rebuild mechanisms. Captain Rogers believed in the old Terran Scout motto of "Be Prepared," and between his pilot and nav, there wasn't much that couldn't be scavenged eventually and for the right price.

And then there was Les.

He exemplified all of the old clichés about navy quartermasters. He was efficient to a fault, could pack the bays and cabins, if necessary, to the consistency of a rubber brick, and had more larceny in his black heart than any single person should.

He just didn't have quite as much good sense as he should.

"Man at arms, please report to Cargo Bay One," boomed out of the 1MC. Captain Rogers winced slightly as he released the button. It seems that the engineers had finally gotten the volume back to par. Now he'd have to see if they could cut it by half for normal messages.

Les winced also, but not because of the message volume. It would seem that the captain wanted the Gunny with them for this little "chat." He gulped.

All the cargo bays had an airlock between them and the rest of the ship. This made it easier to get in and out if something was being loaded in vacuum, or occasionally rapidly unloaded. Today, it felt like more like a mantrap to Les.

Despite this, both sets of doors opened normally as the captain led Les purposely through them.

The Gunny was, of course already there.

No one on board except maybe Captain Rogers knew his name. He was just "the Gunny." He was hired as primary fire control and ship's security, and he had been born for those roles. He was inspecting a large plasteel animal crate from inside of which came clicking and whispering noises, and what could almost be described as an ominous cooing. He was also looking slightly above his eye level, which was not where one would expect someone to look at a turkey.

The Gunny stepped back from the crate, his hand unconsciously going to the blaster on his hip as a deep, threatening "GOBBLE" echoed though Cargo Bay One.

"Just what, may I ask, the hell is that?" he asked, gesturing with a knife hand at the crate.

Les sighed again. He was doing a lot of that today.

"Hostile Environment Meat Bird; TK500M."

"What?""Deathworld Turkey."

"You have got to be kidding me!" the Gunny exclaimed. The captain just did the turret-tracking thing again, from the crate to the Gunny, and then back to Les.

"Explain," was all Captain Rogers said, but the meaningful look at the external airlock controls drove home the point.

Les began speaking much more quickly. "You know those giant turkey legs all the reenactors like to serve? Where do you think they come from? They were originally created for survival in hostile environments. Worse even than Terra. They started with the North American Turkey, added some fighting cock, and then some emu and cassowary. They wound up with a...larger specimen that was more than capable of taking care of itself in just about any circumstance where humans can live without extraordinary measures." Les cleared his throat audibly. "Females produce several eggs a week, provided they have enough feed, and the males have been trained for both security purposes and even riding on worlds near one G or less. Good meat, too. Juicy and tenderizes easily. Make sure you get the skin off, though. That makes cow leather seem easy to chew.

"Problem is, they were a little *too* successful. Many of the traits they wanted will heterodyne in the profiles they used. As a result, they are kept sterile, and they should be gene-mapped with each generation to ensure that they haven't deviated too far from the template. That's why they need the incubators and the gene scanners. Otherwise, they can go feral and become truly nasty."

"How nasty?" the Gunny asked, in spite of himself.

That sigh again.

"On at least one world, they regularly hunt feral hogs in flocks that can run into the dozens. That one was actually an intentional release. Unfortunately, they didn't scan the templates closely enough, and a few weren't sterile, and the rest, as you say, is history. Auzeeland lost that war and literally abandoned one of their continents to birds, the pigs, and anything smart or sneaky enough to survive with them."

"I'm starting to understand how they wound up on the Prohibited list," Captain Rogers said, quietly.

The Gunnys spun on his heel to face Les, knifehand raising.

One more sigh. "It gets worse," Les interrupted. "They added duck, for some reason. Just a little. When some of the odder survival traits bleed through... Let's just say that if you ever see a feral TK500M with a green emu's head, save your last round for yourself."

The Gunny stopped, just stopped, knifehand raised and his mouth open. He had no idea how to respond to that.

Captain Rogers looked across the cargo bay. There were over four dozen of the heavy-duty animal crates, and nearly half as many standard shippers neatly stacked between them. Apparently keeping some distance between the males was a Good Idea.

This, he thought to himself. *Is the cargo that will bring me down? A shipment of faire food to a backwater colony that has already played a little fast and loose with its genengineering.*

"Not on my Watch," he said quietly but firmly. Les and the Gunny stopped staring at each other and looked at the captain. "Beg pardon, sir?" the Gunny asked.

"Okay, grab the seconds and I want this stuff in place so that the catapults can dump it all on command," Captain Rogers said. "I want someone physically in here on the cat controls until we make landfall on Cincinnatus. I'm serious about that. If it takes suit catheters and the Gunny here securing your people to the console, so be it. The controls will be manned *at all* times, in addition to connected to the bridge and Engineering. I will *not* allow a shipment of killer turkeys to take me out of the sky."

He rounded on Les and stared him down. "Do. You. Understand?" he asked quietly.

"Yessir!" Les walked quickly over to the intercom to wake up the bosun and the loaders. Normally it would be two on and two off, but with them loading themselves, he'd sent all three off to their racks after takeoff.

"Were you serious about securing them to the controls, Captain?" the Gunny asked as they walked away from the oddly disquieting sound of feathers and talons shifting.

"Check in regularly. If that panel doesn't have someone within five feet, break out the ankle chains."

"Aye, sir!"

Their new course was set to take almost twice as long as the old one, but it avoided most "official" entanglements. It also used almost twice as much fuel and ate into their profits on this run, but now Captain Rogers had a better idea of why some "simple farm supplies" had such a high payday.

The problem was that their second-to-last jump point was monitored, and if they had shown up on the Patrol's sensors, it wouldn't be too hard to work out an approximate systems entry vector and have something in their way. Unfortunately, anything else either put them in major traffic lanes where they *would* be noticed, or with jumps that were long enough to not be worth the risk.

Azikiwe was good and their systems were solid, but ships still disappeared every year. This left them hoping that with all the data going into the official systems, the pieces wouldn't be put together until afterwards. At which point, if there is no official evidence of the final hand-off, it never happened.

Captain Rogers, Sarika, and Azikiwe were on the bridge, and the Gunny was monitoring the loaders. Knowing those three, said monitoring probably involved a deck of cards. Les...well, Les was physically chained to the primary controls for Cargo Bay One. It seemed he had to go to the head and didn't believe that the captain was serious enough to follow through with his threat over a "quick pit stop." The Gunny waited for him to finish before he hit him with the hand stunner, and he woke up a few minutes later with a mid-range hangover and his ankles shackled to a padeye normally used for harnesses in zero G. He was NOT pleased, but he had been warned, and the intercoms could be disabled from engineering.

"Jump in thirty seconds, Captain," Sarika reported, her hands on the control yoke rather than monitoring the autopilot. She counted the last ten seconds down, and then there was a brief moment of disorientation and the screen flickered into a new starscape.

"Nothin' on passive, Captain," Azikiwe reported. "Estimated time before full update ta' planet, approximately six minutes. Transit time to planetary orbit, fourteen hours with current vectors." So far, there weren't any sensor systems that were capable of FTL readings, so they had to wait for everything to catch up with their appearance.

It was a tense six minutes, but it didn't appear that anything had been waiting in their path, and they didn't show any unusual traffic, yet. That could change as they made their approach, but everyone took there not being a Patrol interdictor waiting for them to be a good sign.

"Let's give it an hour on this approach and then seconds to duty stations and try to get some rest. I want the best at the controls as we make final approach to the planet," Captain Rogers said. The he leaned over to the intercom. "Gunny."

"Aye, Captain," that worthy responded quickly.

"Give it an hour and then send the bosun in to relieve Les. He can take a meal pack, two water bottles, and a fresh suit honey bag. Les does not leave that point until we make landfall, or the cargo is off my ship."

"Understood, Captain."

Captain Rogers then headed for his own stateroom to try and get some rest.

Ten hours later, they swapped back. Technically, it was early, but no one really wanted the seconds handling this planetary approach. The only thing reported on the changeover was a sensor blip that could have been a warp exit, but it was masked by the mass of one of the planet's three satellites. Both the pilot and the nav reviewed the readings, and neither were willing to say what it was definitively.

They were on final deceleration into orbit when Azikiwe suddenly spoke up from the primary sensors, with unusual formality.

"Sensors to Pilot. Warp exit on our deceleration path!"

Sarika swore loudly in Hindi, and then slapped the main intercom. "Everyone strap in for high-G maneuvering. Ten seconds!" she announced.

"Gunny, get rail and missile solutions on that ship, now," the captain demanded.

"Definite warp entry readings behind satellite two, near where the blip was earlier. Signature appears to match the warp exit now on our path."

Everyone was then slammed sideways as the pilot's countdown reached zero. Several minutes of rapid maneuvers followed and they shot off on a new vector at two G more acceleration than their inertial dampers could handle.

The radio crackled to life.

"IS *Dawn Trader*, reduce acceleration and assume parking orbit at the following coordinates. Prepare to be boarded. You are suspected of carrying Prohibited Cargo." Coordinates and vector information appeared on the incoming data channel. "Damnit, they are maneuvering, adjust..." Then the transmission cut, apparently a bit later than the speaker intended.

Captain Rogers slammed the intercom switch.

"Les, depressurize the cargo bay *now*, and prepare to jettison."

"Nnnnuuurrrrrggggggggg..." They heard a grunt and a *clank*. "Roger, Captain. Deconpress...fuuuuuuu..." Metallic clinking sounds rapidly faded into hissing silence.

Several seconds crawled by.

"Cargo Bay One reporting: we have decompressed to vacuum and are standing by on the catapults," Les gasped over the ship's radio. "Please try to refrain from high-G maneuvering without warning, if at all possible. Out."

Say what you may about Les's judgment sometimes, Captain Rogers thought. *He is more than competent other than that.*

"Gunny, recalculate the missiles for zero-energy drop in two minutes. Activation and intercept about here, if the activation code is received." The captain marked a point on the most likely intercept vector. "Drop a second set here and timed for final atmospheric approach. Get the details on that from Azikiwe. Continue updating the railgun and let me know if it looks like they will get into ion cannon range. That little guy we have concealed doesn't have much, but it may come in handy."

"Roger, Captain," the gunny replied.

The first waypoint came and went, and there was no reason to light off the missiles they had dropped. With nothing more than some compressed air launching them, it was unlikely that they would be detected unless and until they went active. If they didn't, twenty-four hours after a preset deadline they would either head for a hot reentry or detonate.

They were just starting to feel some atmospheric friction when they learned that the Patrol gunners also knew their job. The ship rocked as one of the two impulse drives went offline, along with about half of the ship's power and an unknown number of systems.

"Multiple Ion cannon hits, captain!" Azikiwe cried. "Starboard impulse drive out, starboard warp nacelles out, reactors one and two offline."

"IS *Dawn Trader*, you have been ordered into parking orbit. Comply or be destroyed."

"Gunny, light the candles," Captain Rogers ordered. "Sarika, ass to the planet, I want a best speed to minimum jump distance. Az, gimme something safe near that trajectory and feed the updates to Sarika. I don't want a micro-jump like the Patrol used to drop in ahead of us. Those are too dangerous without way more time or computing power than we have. I want a solid jump, inside of three-quarter range that we can then use to bounce away from.

"Les, dump the birds. Prepare for high-G maneuvering."

There was no answer on the ship's comms.

In Cargo Bay One, Les was just finishing slicing through the padeye with a pocket cutter. He knew the captain meant it about chaining someone to the board; he just hadn't planned on it being him. Next to him, the primary controls for the bay were still sparking as various capacitors discharged while the lights in the bay flickered uncomfortably. Whatever had hit them had made a real mess of the systems. Fortunately, the catapults were intended for use in combat drops, and were both heavily shielded and contained redundant circuits. Unfortunately, the secondary controls were next to the main bay doors, far out of reach of his current position.

Since the chain was stretched tight and in contact with his suit, he heard a faint pinging noise as it broke loose, and he staggered across the hold. He'd partially dislocated a knee on one of the maneuvers, so an irregular stagger was all he could manage. Somehow, he made it to the controls and slapped the emergency launch code. Les just barely managed to secure himself before the next set of maneuvers reminded him that they could pull more Gs than they could compensate for.

"IS *Dawn Trader*, this is your last warning. Assume parking orbit and prepare to be boarded or we will be forced to... What do you mean incoming missiles? From the ship? What vector?!? Evasive—" Again, the transmission cut off suddenly.

The main viewscreens on the bridge of IS *Dawn Trader* tracked from planet back to stars and suddenly everyone was forced into their acceleration chairs.

"The patrol interceptor is veering away from ta' planet. Should throw off the vectoring on ta' missiles and let ta' noseys outmaneuver th' candles or take them out if their PD is any good," Az reported.

"Correcting to jump vector. We will reach it thirty seconds before we reach the calculated jump point," Sarika reported. "Time to jump at max acceleration: twelve minutes, thirty-seven seconds. Minor corrections for the duration."

In Cargo Bay One, Les was strapped to the aux controls and held in place by about 2 Gs of acceleration. He watched the monitors as the cargo boxes tumbled toward the planet, the emergency tracking and stabilization systems on some still functional and transmitting as others tumbled on their almost impossibly accurate trajectory to the Cincinnatus colony. The durable plasteel cases mostly survived reentry to slam into the colony at terminal velocity, destroying anything they hit even close to. The crates with the TK500Ms had more redundant systems and a surprising number actually made the surface, blowing apart as emergency protocols engaged and freeing their violent and agitated cargo to wreak havoc in the burning ruins created by their support equipment. At maximum range on the ship sensors, and far too close on the repeaters still active on a few of the crates, Les watched as their erstwhile cargo created carnage wherever they landed.

Scant seconds before they jumped out, he could remain silent no more.

"As god is my witness..." he breathed, as reality flickered, and the screens went black.

ALSO From RaconTeur Press

Ghosts of Malta

Knights of Malta

Saints of Malta

Falcons of Malta

Space Cowboys

Space Cowboys 2: Electric Rodeo

Space Cowboys 3: Return of the Bookaroo

Space Cowboys 404: Cow Not Found

Space Marines

Space Marines 2

PinUp Noir

PinUp Noir 2

Your Honor, I Can Explain...

You See, What Happened Was...

He Was Dead When I Got There...

All Will Burn

All Will Burn: Fierce Love

Moggies in Space

Moggies Back in Space

Full Steam Ahead

Giant! Freakin'! Robots!

CALL TO ACTION

At Raconteur Press, our motto is Have Fun, Get Paid. Hopefully you enjoyed the stories in this volume. If you did, please take the time to leave a quick review. Our authors love to hear that people enjoyed their stories and it encourages them to write more of them.

And if you liked a story by a particular author, go ahead and find their author page and give them a follow to get notifications about their next release. It might be with Raconteur Press or it might not but it'll probably be another fantastic story.

Enjoy our stories?

Want to see more of them?

Leave a review!

It's like a hug without all that awkward eye contact

Made in United States
Troutdale, OR
11/22/2024

25195131R00126